Tales from the Island of Papa Doc

Tales from the Island of Papa Doc

From The Same Author:

Les Enfants Malades de Papa Doc.

Chronique de la Décadanse du Chef Suprême.

L'Avènement au Pouvoir du Professeur Leslie Manigat.

Caricatures de République Bananière.

Ces Caricatures qui nous Gouvernent.

ISBN: 978-0-578-24231-6

For information, email:
cdesroches2000@aol.com

Populire Editions
301E John Street, #2645
Matthews, NC 28106

To my mother Rolande Bruno who passed away on distant shores.

To my grandson Ezra who spoiled me and helped me recapture my childhood.

With many thanks to my colleague Dr. Ronna Feit who patiently edited the first and last drafts of the manuscript.

"Reading makes immigrants of us all. It takes us away from home, but more important, it finds homes for us everywhere."

Jean Rhys

"He asked him if he knew how to defend himself against sharks, and Euclides told him yes, for he had magic tricks to frighten them away."

Gabriel García Márquez

Shark Season

Before the rise of the men in blue, sharks had the worst reputation on the island of Haiti.

Around that time, every islander, every single soul seemed to have a deep, intimate understanding of sharks.

They were mean, monstrous killing machines; the true overseers of the marine cemetery; a clear and present danger to the society of swimmers and wanderers trying to flee the estate of Papa Doc.

The Patriarch had lost his temper and had become a Führer, a leading cause of death in the West Indies. He had his men; they wore blue. They were known among the scribes as *Homo Papadocus*.

The tale of the shark had a life of its own. It kept hurling and waving in the echo chamber of life.

Have you heard the news lately? Big Tooth Megalodon is back from extinction. It's making a killing in the fishing town of Martissant.

Some took the news with a grain of salt; some found another

reason to be scared to death.

"The fear of sharks is the beginning of wisdom." So spoke Dieuseul, the local incarnation of the ancient philosopher. "They are invisible, they are gray, they are white, they are in the water to take a bloodbath."

Sharks. It was the talk of the town. Especially among kiddies, the confused and fragile little creatures the grownups called "*timoun*".

The whispering ocean near the fish market was a constant reminder of the sharks. They've been enemies, ancestral enemies, since the days of the Trade. Since the time they started to follow the slavers' boat heading west to the Caribbean Archipelago.

"But where in the world is the shark?"

"Look deep little man, it is watching you!"

From the ocean, the fear of sharks traveled to the shallow waters of the river where tadpoles changed into infant piranhas.

To add insult to injury, the most beautiful American car of the hood harbored in its back a solid pair of fins.

Did some renegade tiger sharks with a bad attitude ruin the reputation of an entire species? Were they scapegoats? Were they black sheep? Were they bull sharks? They were blamed for everything that happened at sea.

Around that time, the four million children of Papa Doc lived in a state of terror: a seismic island floating among the Grand Antilles, near Cuba that looks on the map like an alligator taking a sunbath. In their native enchanted tongues, the indigenous Taïnos had called it Ayiti, Kiskeya, and Bohio.

1957. Gone were the days of serenity. The apocalyptic event happened on a Sunday. September 22. The final solution.

Malè pa gen klaxon. Calamity doesn't blow a horn. So said the local wisdom. Yet, they should have seen it coming.

The omen took the shape of a mysterious physician. Papa Doc: the new embodiment of the Reaper.

He was sharply dressed, in the impeccable regalia of a funeral director. More than a fashion statement, it was a program, a manifesto of terror. His dream was to become the most captivating dictator in the world.

As a young man, he wanted to join the military. To wear the khaki outfit. To be an officer and a gentleman. They rejected him. The same way the Fine Art Academy of Berlin had rejected an obscure young man called Hitler.

They said he was shortsighted. They said he was too short. They said his blood pressure was too high. They said he wasn't fit for the artillery. They said. They said.

One day, they were going to swallow their tongue and their words. They were going to pay a heavy price: with pints, with gallons of blood.

He had to settle for something else. A career as a country doctor. That's how he got his notorious moniker: Papa Doc.

Country doctor? General practitioner? It was just a stepping stone. To him, it was something lame and pedestrian, like a health officer, like Doctor Charles Bovary before he met Emma Rouault. He was giving shots, nursing sores of poor peasants stricken with yaw and elephantiasis. He never forgot his true calling: a sweet and tender love for firearms.

At the Military Academy, they had laughed at him. "What a strange fella. He must be out of his mind. He looks sad like a gravedigger." The young Papa never forgot the contempt, the scorn he saw in their eyes. He resented them with a vengeance as though they had left in his mouth a lingering taste of *Camoquin*, the bitter pill for malaria.

On his medical file, they had written: "Unfit. Has a weak constitution." It was the *coup de grâce*, the last nail on the coffin of his dreams.

One day, he was going to show them. He was going to steal the thunder. He was going to wear the helmet and the light-brown uniform. He was going to replace the khakistocracy by the free will of the men in blue.

When he emerged from the abyss as the top predator, life left the town of Papadopolis (formerly known as Port-au-Prince.)

From land to sea, from longitude to latitude, fear turned into panic, panic into paranoia. The night became longer than a week of eight days. It stayed still, moved slowly like a giant turtle of the Galápagos Islands.

The night was speckled with airborne and low-life creatures looking for prey in the hood.

The islanders had reasons to shiver. Going back to the time the Devil was a corporal in the Napoleon army, they had not seen anything so gruesome. They were living on borrowed time. In Papadopolis, the horror film Rex Theater was showing was in fact reality.

Memory is the ability to forget, to select, to free space in the calabash of our head. From the mental ward of Brooklyn Hospital where I am assigned today in solitary confinement, I travel back in time, to regain my faculties. To try to make sense. To exorcise the ghosts of the past. To decrypt the particulars of the long-gone time when I was a boy, when I was swallowed by a marine creature but survived to tell the tale to a captive audience: my fellows, the colorful patients of the cuckoos' nest.

Coney Island. When I was dragged to the beach last summer, a thousand and one images came to me, overflowed my memory. Remembrance of the times I left behind in a bag of bones. Snapshots in black and white. Anonymous tomb-stones of the ocean.

I cannot stay still. Like a fish of the seven seas, I travel from one time zone to the next. I dream of a better yesterday. I was surprised to see last night the nature boy I used to be.

How many of my childhood friends of Martissant actually saw a shark? In a book? A magazine? At Ciné Sénégal?

The aquarium was nowhere to be found.

The museum of horror? It was the Palace. In the half-light of the white bunker, one could see some specimens in their natural habitat. They were dressed in denim blue. Around their neck, a red handkerchief adjusted with an empty box of matches. Their fiery eyes were concealed under dark sunglasses. They were the henchmen, the boogeymen of the Doc.

On the west side of the island, a new species was created. It came from the lab, the Petri dish of Papa Doc. Year after year, *Homo Papadocus* roamed the streets, the open arteries of Papadopolis.

The men in blue had a *"non jwèt"*, a sobriquet. They responded to the moniker of *tonton macoute*. It was meant to be derisive. In their innocence, in their naïveté, they loved it and adopted it as though *tonton* was their first name and *macoute* their last.

Homo Papadocus had his own practical tools: a machete or a fire stick. Born too late in a world too old, he didn't have to reinvent the wheel. He rode a low horsepower vehicle.

This now-defunct Germanic SUV was the Dampf Kraft Wagen, better known at the time as the DKW. Its engine sounded like a giant popcorn maker. The aroma of its muffler brought fear into the lungs and the heart of the islanders.

Under the blue indigo sky of the Caribbean, *Homo Papadocus* thrived. From Moonday to Sunday, every day of the week became the day of the hunter.

Like pirates of the Caribbean, he was a gatherer of riches. Like hurricanes and earthquakes, he created havoc wherever he went. Lately, he has been subject to archeological excavations in the ruins of the Palace.

When Robert Bruno vanished on that night of curfew, some people said he was captured by the men in blue. Some said his rickety boat capsized near the Isle of La Gonâve. Some others said he reached the promised land of Elsewhere.

He is the uncle I hardly knew. I was too young to register a clear image of his face. Through his children and grand-children, I picture him as this tall brown man who was elegant like a hidalgo. His battle against the goons of Papa Doc was a quixotic adventure.

Those who carry his blood in their veins still worship his memory. For many, many years, they waited and waited. The miraculous return only occurred in their dreams.

A quarter of a century later, when the cells of Papa Doc were emptied, a procession of skeletal ghosts, human remains, mummified spirits, relics of former selves got out. Robert Bruno wasn't part of them.

Shark or not, one thing was sure: falling into the hands of the *tontons* was the worst-case scenario. In squalid dungeons, they tortured with a refinement that was way beyond the imagination of the marine creature. In the hit-parade of horror, the shark arrived behind as a distant second.

In her sibylline voice, the black magic woman had said to Robert: "*Pa koute kòlè ou.*" (Do not listen to your anger.) *Pa kite van pote koze ou ale.* (Do not allow the wind to carry away your parley.)

The walls were no longer innocent; they reported what they saw. As though the pandemic had arrived already, social distancing became the norm. Every gathering of two or more was mayhem in the making. Even Boy Scouts in uniforms, armed with flashlights, getting ready for a late hike in the mountains. To whom it may concern, they looked like young infantrymen, beardless rebels, Lilliputian guerilleros.

Robert Bruno was a vocal man. He was wired that way. He had studied engineering in Brazil. A woman, a beautiful Amazon was waiting for him at the mouth of the river. But he wouldn't leave. He was too proud for that. It was personal. He wanted to fight the Doc in a mortal combat, mano a mano. He wouldn't listen to anyone. Even to his own mama, Eugénie Bruno.

On their part, the *tontons* were motherless cowboys, natural born killers. They were called *sans manmans*. They would do anything to please their Papa Doc. He taught them well: "A good *tonton* should be ready to kill his own for the triumph of the Revolution." They were good listeners.

A *tonton* arrested his own son. The young man was involved in subversive readings. He was caught red-handed with a copy of *Anatomy of a Dictatorship*. He was brought to the Doc.

At dawn, the *tontons* reported to the Palace covered with blood, smelling like goats with garlic breath. Papa Doc showered them with praises. For Christmas, he spoiled them with the flashy guns they had seen at the movies.

To the Doc, red blood over blue uniform was a good sign. It meant the *tontons* had worked hard during the night shift. Papa was affectionate with the *tontons* that he regarded as his *enfants terribles*. They might have been psychos, but they were his children. He was a sucker for a good story, a blow by blow rendition of arrests and torture. He gave them the green light and took full responsibility for their deeds.

Like the arithmetic book of Maître Faustin, life in Papado-polis was full of riddles. Page after page: problems. No solution in sight. Same antics, day in and day out.

Nonetheless, at sundown, when the kiddies gathered to have their *tête-à-tête*, to share stories about Bouki and Malis, the sharks remained the dominant characters. They were on everyone's lips. Ready to embark on new adventures in the wild.

Homework was done. It was Bibil's turn to talk that evening: "Krik, krak! The canoe was sailing in the coastal waters of Tiburon when a school of sharks started to follow. What do you think happened?"

19

Like coconut water, the consensus was clear about the temperament of the sharks. They had no sense of civility. They were territorial and hostile to humankind.

At the lighthouse where Bonga saw everything in the horizon (from quick bites to total annihilation), the sharks had numerous mug shots, a long rap sheet of crimes and misdemeanors.

Some folks were snake charmers, some folks were butterfly collectors, some folks were horse whisperers, Bonga was a connoisseur in marine affairs. That's how he got his job in the first place. He knew how to read the commotions of the sea. He had a great sense of anticipation, the ability to hear the Hitchcock soundtrack that says: "Watch out! Something bad is about to happen!"

His most casual fairy tale was enough to panic, to keep at bay the bravest of them all. In cold blood, he would ask the dandiest questions: "Who among you kiddies wants to be a scuba diver? Who wants to explore the remains of the Santa Maria? Who wants to help me retrieve the sunken treasure of the Spanish galleon under the belly of the giant octopus?"

Not in a million years...

Yet, foreigners with masks, oxygen tanks, and swim fins were bold enough to venture into the unknown. How could they be so poised? What was their secret? Did they have a pass, a VIP ticket to the no man's land, the titanic aquarium that we call ocean?

At the age of innocence, around the time I had my first communion at Sainte Bernadette, I learned a lot about the world at large. I got a degree in history and zoology from my comic books: Captain Nemo, Tarzan, Marvel, Daniel Boone, Captain Miki.

Once in a blue moon, when my soul was heavy, I would confess to Father Alexandre some random sins I committed through words, in ignorance, by omission, or by action. In the schoolyard, at lunchtime, I had devoured graphic novels. They portrayed young adults kissing each other with the intense passion of gourami fishes.

The clandestine literature was brought to school by our classmate Sherer Désilus. We were the same age, but he was much older in the affairs of the heart.

I read my romances with premature interest. It was my

guilty pleasure. I did not understand all the French flowery words, but the images spoke to me in a vivid language. I wouldn't quit despite the moral anguish, the terrifying prospect of missing my admission into Heaven.

To further my education, Ma Fifine bought my comics religiously from the *bouquinistes*. They were secondhand booksellers who set up shop near Notre-Dame, the colonial cathedral where was held the funeral of Simalo, the beloved goat of President Antoine Simon.

The historical event took place in 1910, when the 20th century was young and restless, when palace revolutions happened regularly; especially on weekends when the Pretorian Guards were playing dominoes, smoking Lucky Strike cigarettes, and drinking demijohns of spiced rum.

Three days of mourning and national remembrance were declared to honor the departed pet of the President. From dawn to sunset, the flag was flown at half-mast. Ambassadors of friendly and civilized nations came to the Palace to present their heartfelt condolences to the afflicted Head of State.

When the Prez was overthrown and exiled in August 1911, the Archbishop of Port-au-Prince canceled the upcoming mass of requiem for the repose of the soul of Simalo.

A few weeks later, Antoine Simon Junior arrived on the shores of Germany with his luggage full of gold. Once again, a presidential family member had discovered a mine on the walls of the Palace.

My personal treasure trove was my comics. I was deep into images as though they were the fine, enlightening prose of Jean-Jacques Rousseau preaching the return to nature.

Through the comics, I learned that the indigenous populations of this continent knew how to do long-distance communications. They knew how to Tweet with smoke signals. They knew how to settle their differences and bury the hatchet of war with a peace-pipe ceremony.

At the age of 8, when creativity reaches its peak, I wondered. Could we try the same approach with the sharks? Could we sign with them a pact of non-aggression? I was young but busy, desperately searching for solutions to the pressing problems of the world. I didn't want to be a victim.

Can sharks become vegetarians and eat seaweed? Can we bribe them with Cuban cigars?

The dream of my life was to die of old age, in my hammock, with all my blood inside my body.

Nobody dared to initiate the talk. Nobody tried to invite the supreme chief of the sharks, the leader of Sea World to a round of negotiations over lunch, in neutral ground, at a sandbar, under the coconut tree of a deserted island.

It would have been nice and civil to say: "Hello, is it me you're looking for? Can we all get along? Can we make peace and sing along *Frère Jacques*? Won't you be my neighbor?"

To the kiddies that we were, the illusion was perfect. Sharks were floating monsters. They were armed with a sharp hand-saw. The same kind of handsaw our neighbor Boss Phanor was using to fabricate coffins for those who were departing to the land of no return. Those who were ex-isled from life. For better or for worse, to heaven or to hell.

Boss Phanor stopped making the elegant mahogany furniture that built him a reputation as a gifted artisan. Whether he liked it or not, coffins had become the fastest-growing segment of his solitary craft.

It was a time of cataclysmic proportion. Papa Doc, the Supreme Leader of the hilly island, threatened to amass a

Himalaya of cadavers. He was dead serious; he was a man of his word. Many times over, he had proven himself. With his nasal voice and the superb eloquence of a Roman emperor, he had said: "I don't want to see anyone on my way, excepted myself!" The chorus of foes and stoic gladiators responded: "Ave Caesar, those who are going to die salute you."

Papa Doc was a gifted marketeer. He conducted an excellent campaign. He knew how to sell snake oil in rural areas. That's how he obtained 122% of the ballots. On that sunny day of September, thousands of folks (reputed dead for many years) left their graves to fulfill their civic duty and cast their votes for the selected. In fact, only one vote really mattered. The vote of the Army, following the instructions of the Ambassador.

"I am going to make this country great again." Papa said it on the campaign trail. Perhaps he won't be the last to use the magical words.

On the official pictures of the time, he appeared as an original, an eccentric hunter holding a rifle in his limousine. Those who laughed at him ended up crying.

The promises of the electoral campaign were long gone. No

more mister nice guy. He was a doctor. He became a butcher. He was in a frenzy for fresh blood.

He knew how to see the unsaid; how to diagnose internal signs of discontent. He believed in preemptive measures. On the wall of his office, his motto was affixed: "Prevention is better than cure." In the wee hours of the night, while evil spirits were on the loose, he was busy writing death certificates for the upcoming doomsdays.

To leave is to die a little. Or maybe a lot. For many islanders, the only trail to salvation seemed like a song of Bob Marley: *Exodus, Movement of Jah People*. Exodus: by land, by air, by sea. Those who couldn't leave, those who chose to stay, were living on the margin of life, in interior exile.

Nou nan dlo! Loosely translated by a toddler, this Creole expression would sound like: "We are in the waters." Better yet: "We are in deep doo-doo." Pardon my French. Yes, we were in deep trouble. It was the time of the sharks.

According to the testimony of the Cyclopes, those who could see far and beyond, sharks had an appetite of fin gourmet. They had a lust, an irresistible craving for tender, delicious chunks of flesh. On the menu, they often confused human beings with sea lions and filet mignon. They had the best dentists in the universe. They would sink their pearly white into anyone, even Agwe, the Voodoo god of the ocean.

In the wild, with a proper diet, their life could reach half a century. Better than most islanders. Fifty long years. Enough time to do damage and send many to the land of the ancestors. In the cold waters of Greenland, they just forget to die. They live to be half a millennium.

"I am not selfish. I share with you everything I know about the shark." That's what Bonga would say to us with a great white grin that made him look like Louis Armstrong.

He would follow-up with new, amazing discoveries: "Some sharks have a double-edged hammer. They can crush human bones and suck the marrow with a straw."

 Bonga did not study marine biology. He guessed it. We learned so much from him. Among the kiddies of Martissant, his reputation as a reliable source of disturbing information was impeccable.

White shark, silver shark, blue shark, skin-deep they are color blind. They believed in equal opportunity. When it's time to eat, they don't care about skin color.

Without red lights, stop signs, cops, and speed limits, they go fast, they are fierce. They can swallow kilometers in a matter of seconds.

Just like Papa Doc (whose grandpa was born on another island where the natives used to eat their enemies) sharks had complete disregard for Amnesty International and the Universal Declaration of Human Rights. As a matter of fact, they had their own organization: the Society for the Protection of Hostile Animals.

From a distance, they watched closely those islanders who were foolish enough to get their feet wet. Those who were bragging about their ability to swim like a fish. Those who claimed the capacity to stay underwater for days to carry passionate love affairs with mermaids.

Life is better on the other bank of the sea. Some islanders were brave enough to sail through the Bermuda Triangle on their journey to Nordic lands. Lands of honey, lands of milk. Destinations with fancy, exotic names: Key West, Miami, New Haven: El Dorados where the streets are paved with good intentions, and silver, and gold. Bountiful lands where greenback, large bills of fifty or more grow on ordinary trees. Lands where people waste no time picking up from the macadam pocket change like quarters and dimes. Lands where good jobs are a dime a dozen. Lands where Job, the destitute, can change into Croesus or Midas in a matter of months.

On the gigantic screen of the drive-in movie theater, the mirage was perfect. The siren song of elsewhere was getting loud.

It was a time so ancient: television sets were in their infancy. They were small and cranky. Always ready to blow a fuse and make us cry. It was a time of paper trails, time of books, storytelling: *The Odyssey*, *Voyages Extraordinaires*, *Gulliver's Travels*.

Among the best destinations was the Department of Emigration. In the majestic building, one could get the cutest little book: a passport.

It was a key-book that gave access to the Ali Baba Caverns of the world. The password was: "Open Sesame."

It was a time of horror. Nightmare on Main Street. Near the lily-white edifice of the Palace, Paramount Movie Theater was showing *Dracula*, "the terrifying lover who died, yet lived."

Screen legend Christopher Lee was on top of his game as the romantic bloodsucker. For the paltry sum of twenty cents, one could get the best nightmare on earth.

Around that time, kiddies were afraid of sky creatures, intergalactic witches, non-identified flying sorcerers: the *loups-garous*.

When the moon (locally known as the State Company of Electricity) was taking a nap from shining so bright, *loups-garous* traveling at the speed of light leapt from one roof to the next, in search of the young blood and the tender meat of innocent newborns.

On the island, natural death was unheard of. It was just a scam invented by foreigners to hide the fact that evil forces were at stake everywhere around us.

The night was the twilight zone. A narrow corridor in the valley of shadow. Time of curfew. Time of anguish. Time of agonizing fear.

Nonetheless, *loups-garous* and sharks were overrated. Some other beasts were on top of the food chain. They had a human face like you and me. They had the blue uniform and the carnivalesque red bandana around their neck.

Some *tontons* had warlord machineguns; some had pistols. The poorest of the poor, the low caliber exterminators carried their machetes openly in the streets of Papadopolis.

Kiddies were afraid of sharks and *loups-garous*; grownups were afraid of *tontons*. The worst-case scenario was at night when some *tontons* were moonlighting as *loups-garous*.

For many islanders, waking up in the morning was a pleasant surprise. They were dead people on vacation at a resort island; they were zombies walking through life with a coffin under their arm.

Do you like the odor of napalm in the morning? An aroma of gunpowder floats in the air. The *tontons* had a particular taste for the Technicolor movies the critics called "spaghetti westerns". They were fresh products imported from Italy and Hollywood.

At Ciné Sénégal, bullies fought to get their tickets. Fueled with testosterone, they pushed, they shoved. It was just a warm-up before the main event. They wanted to see *Django*. They wanted to see *The Man with the Golden Pistol*. They wanted to see *Kill Them All and Come Back Alone*.

The films' titles sounded like the manifesto of terror the *tontons* were looking for. On the screen, they saw themselves in the mirror. They were sons of a gun. They were Lee Van Cleef. They were Fernando Sancho.

In the heat of the action, inside the theater, it was not unusual to hear live gunshots from trigger-happy *tontons* reaching their climax in the orgy of violence. Licensed to kill, they were in their element; transported into a world where cruelty is king.

The henchmen of the Doc controlled the land, the *loups-garous* the sky, while the sharks, with their high-tech radars, controlled the sea.

Sometimes, sailors and boat people, on the way to Florida, were captured by the Bahamian marine. They would throw themselves to the sharks rather than return to the death lab of Papa Doc.

Beyond the borders of the island, any other land would do. Any other rock, any atoll of the ocean seemed to be more appealing, more enticing than the estate of Papa Doc. Even places with threatening names like Caiman Islands, Cayo Lobos, and Devil's Island.

The jaws of the sharks were more clement than the dungeon of Fort Dimanche.

At the Sunday school animated by Sister Norbeck, a tall American evangelist with a pointy nose, Brother Serge, a one-arm preacher, shared his testimony with the terrified kiddies.

With a luxury of details, he recounted that Wednesday of June, when he was attacked by a hungry metallic shark who converted his left arm into lunch.

In horror, he saw a river of his blood merging with the blue of the ocean. Until that day, he had not realized how much of a fighter he was. With his right arm intact, he swam like a champ, got out of danger, and was rescued by the terrified onlookers.

The close encounter with the jaws of the ocean was a turning point in Serge's life. He abandoned Agwe to join the sect of Miss Norbeck, with the promise of an afterlife in Heaven where only beautiful little fish are allowed. A place where sharks, *loups-garous*, *tontons macoutes* and other scary beasts are tamed, banned, or extinct.

In the meantime, the hope of getting a visa was a good

incentive to convert and engage in the ways of the Lord. It was a win-win situation.

Brother Serge was a living proof of Megalodon's return. The scar tissues of his missing limb carried the signature of Big Tooth.

Fear was a constant companion. After Brother Serge's testimony, it felt like the Lock Ness monster had moved into my neighborhood. I stayed away from the shallow waters of the river which was infested.

Not by the legendary shark.

Not by the toothy crocodile.

Not by the yawning hippopotamus.

Infested with tadpoles.

In a game of hide-and-seek, I was afraid of tadpoles and tadpoles were afraid of me.

"Where I grew up people were happy just to wake up alive every day. And every day they had to fight to stay this way."

James MacManus

"The past is a foreign country; they do things differently there."

Leslie Poles Hartley

A Quiet Man Called Sandino

Grandma Eugénie Bruno was the embodiment of that school of thought that says: "*Se pitit mwen.*" This is my child. Now, forever my baby.

Her son was 35 years old, but it did not matter. Until the end. The umbilical cord was never cut.

Uncle Sandino spent a lifetime with his mama in a one-room apartment. At night, he curled up in bed like a fetus and slept with his socks on. He would wear her old, raggedy dress as a pajama. Especially when his Long John was not yet washed at the local laundromat: the river.

The water that came from the mountains of Odan was fresh and sparkling like in the first morning of the world. It was before the tree population of indigenous mahoganies was wiped out by arson and the malady of charcoal.

Whether he needed it or not, Grandma Eugénie would wake Uncle up at 2 AM to make him pee in the white enameled pot. She would make a hissing sound to encourage his sleepy, reluctant bladder to release the golden warm fluid. If he had trouble falling asleep, she would sing him a lullaby:

"Sleep my baby, sleep

If you do not sleep, the crab will swallow you

The crab in the okra…"

When grandma passed away, Uncle followed her immediately to the grave. He died of a broken heart. He was the perfect son and would not dare outlive his mama for too long. He had no reason whatsoever to stick around and wanted to join her in Heaven.

When she was alive and kicking, Grandma Eugénie didn't play games with Uncle. She warned him several times, in no uncertain terms, with a lash, about coming home late. "I am not going to cry for you; I exhausted all my tears when Bob was snatched by the men in blue. I have no water behind my pupils for someone like you who is clearly suicidal."

In Martissant, when the sun went to bed and was sound asleep, Bwapiro, a giant of Rabelaisian proportion, tall like an electric pole, roamed the hood. He was in a feeding frenzy. Some called him Midnight Master. According to reliable sources and true to life testimonies, Bwapiro had the appetite of an ogre and was far from being vegetarian. He didn't care much about the coconuts and delicious papayas of Martissant. He wanted meat.

Uncle Sandino took punishment from his mama in stoic fashion: for breaking curfew, for heavy drinking, for losing his mind at the time of carnival.

The festivities would start on the first Sunday of January to end in February or March with a climax: a grand finale followed by the morning blues of Ash Wednesday.

Nine months later, the maternity ward of General Hospital would be crowded with a flock of brand-new kiddies shouting desperately: "Where in the world is my daddy?"

This is how Weber Sicot, the iconic saxophonist, was conceived. In the midst of action, in the carnivalesque cortege of a pedestrian band called Otofonik. At least, that's what was reported by his main competitor: Nemours Jean-Baptiste. The bad blood between the two maestros was resolved with a soccer match at the Sylvio Cator Stadium. It ended with a draw: 0-0. Both teams won one point.

Like the rain after a sunny day, Uncle Sandino accepted punishment from his mama with philosophy. It was a time when crying was a sign of protest, another form of misconduct that led to additional penalties.

Uncle would come back home from Mardi Gras in the little hours of the night when the cats were gray, and the dogs were dreaming about tasty bones. On that night, he was drunk like a *pipirite*. He had lost a shoe from the single pair that Grandma bought for him with his money.

Having a second pair of shoes was a luxury few people could afford. Unless you were Imelda Marcos, the dragon lady of the Philippines who managed to amass 3000. They were stunning like Cinderella's glass slippers. Unfortunately, Imelda was not a centipede, not even a spider. She only had two feet.

Like a vigilant soldier, Grandma Eugénie would not sleep until Uncle had returned home. In the middle of the night, she would ambush him at the door to inflict the usual, predictable punishment. He could not scream; fearing to awake the neighbors who always slept with one eye open.

Until the end, Uncle remained a good, obedient boy. At the tender age of forty-three, he said to me with candor: "She is my mama; she can punish me whenever she wants."

While youngsters had a spreadsheet of grievances against their parents, while some were talking about incompatibility of temperament, Uncle never mumbled a word of protest. You'd never see a whisper of resentment in his eyes. You'd never catch a shadow of anger on his face. He would be sweet to his mama seconds after punishment was inflicted on him. He was sorry for the pain he caused her. Sometimes, they would cry together.

Between the two, there was a great love story. Something similar to the passion between Còcòtte and Figaro. They would live happily ever after until Uncle came home late again.

Even though Grandma had a black belt in punishment, no ill was ever intended. It seemed to be part of a script, a role-playing of intimidation. He had to listen if he wanted to survive. Predators like moving prey. The danger outside was grand. Grandma had to remind him constantly that life under the Doc has no happy ending.

It was a time of dangerous crossings when crocodiles in the water disguised like floating trees. They concealed their nature under a wooden mask.

When clouds of mosquitoes are flying, you don't know which ones are males which ones are females. Robert Bruno was betrayed by a frenemy, a chameleon. In his early forties,

Uncle Sandino was too young to see these things. He was possessed by the music of Nemours Jean-Baptiste.

Even though he got his name from a Latin American guerillero, he was not much of a fighter. He was a thirsty man. He would not leave for tomorrow the grog he could drink today. You'd never catch him with a bottle of Merlot, Shiraz, or Cabernet Sauvignon. It would be a disgrace.

A good shot of rum had a tonic effect on him. It was his mouthwash in the morning, his cup of coffee, and also his breakfast. He sipped throughout the day like a baby his bottle.

Uncle Sandino was immune from human emotions of anger and resentment. He had no time for that. It was as though all negative emotions were distilled by alcohol. If Pope Francis didn't live too far away, I would ask him to add Uncle to the pantheon of Catholic saints.

Rum was a good medicine against fear. Uncle would not tell you the opposite. Under the spell of rum, the timid becomes bold.

During a night of curfew, when the time came for my mother to give birth to her 4th child, my dad panicked. He didn't know what to do. Before the rise of Papa Doc, he had been in the military as the chauffeur of General President Paul Magloire. His Excellency had the reputation of an iron man with velvet gloves. He was the life of the parties at Djoumbala Night Club where he danced like Fred Astaire. Some saw in him a pleasant autocrat, a sympathetic conservative with a *laisser-faire* attitude.

Just like Uncle, my dad liked his liquor. He mostly sipped when he was playing dominoes with the dream team of Martissant. Players would come from other hoods to challenge them. When they lost, they would nurse their wounds with more alcohol.

On that Saturday night, Dad was sober. He had a high tolerance for spirits. He knew how to exorcise them with a good cup of coffee. When the signs of labor showed up, he was clearheaded, entangled in a Shakespearean dilemma: to go or not to go?

It was dark out there. Dark like on the eve of the world's creation. Always on time at sunset, like a widow, the night was wearing its funeral evening gown. Everything was invisible, except the translucent fireflies.

Delivery time was looming with clear signs of water break. The maternity of Chancerelles was a bridge too far, 6 miles away, on the other side of Papadopolis. The hospital was across Pont Rouge, near the red spot where the founding father Jean-Jacques Dessalines was assassinated.

It was an original sin, just like the time Cain killed Abel. Cain was the only person on earth with a sibling. Yet, he did what he did. What was he thinking? He wasn't raised like that. It was a bad precedent for humanity.

It was dangerously late. At the little house of Martissant, they had to make a critical decision. To go or not to go? In the lingering atmosphere of witch-hunt and women profiling, Titine, the midwife was no longer around.

As though it were a horror story of the Middle Ages, Titine had been labeled, "positively identified" as a *loup-garou*. She was accused of being a predator who selected this noble profession (midwife, not witch) in order to prey on the babies she would bring into the world for a short period of time. Enough time to visit the planet and gain some baby fat, but not enough time for the kiddies to get a sense of their own existence and recognize themselves in the mirror.

For her, any little hole in the roof was a window of opportunity to insinuate herself into a house, to suck blood, and have supper.

Anyway, it was the narrative that was flying around, from mouth to ear, about Titine.

Quite often, babies would pass away mysteriously. Even before they got the chance to be baptized. You would think they were children of a lesser god. You would think they were "*pitimi san gadò*". A garden of millet without a guardian.

In a memorable homily in Latin that everyone understood miraculously, Father Alexandre revealed to the horrified parishioners that the lack of a baptism certificate could leave babies in limbo and complicate their admission into Heaven.

Everybody, faithful Christians, devoted worshipers, impenitent procrastinators, even those who were not in odor of sanctity with the Church because they were absent regularly, were summoned to fulfill their religious duties towards their newborns without further delay. In a firm unusual tone, Father Alexandre threatened to excommunicate those who refused to comply.

Although the Prez for life was a medical doctor, infant mortality was going through the roof, floating haughtily in the sky like a multicolor kite. Papa Doc was himself quite sick, troubled by early dementia and impotence. By the time he was inaugurated, he already had a foot in the coffin. But when everyone thought he was done, he rallied with a spectacular comeback.

While he was deep into the maze of a coma, he got a sense of his own mortality. He became more deadly. As the Supreme Leader, he wanted his subjects to join him in the afterlife, the same way in ancient India women were buried with their deceased husband.

Like fresh milk exposed to the sun, babies of Papadopolis had a short expiration date. They had an aversion to life as though it were a painful disease. Puppies and cats seemed to be more resilient. For the adults themselves, life under the Doc appeared to be a burden, like a stubborn smallpox, a persistent mumps, a pain in the butt, a nasty case of hemorrhoids.

This situation did not sit well with the dwellers of Martissant. They were confused, suspicious, paranoid. Babies were hidden in a red cocoon; heavily guarded with an arsenal of amulets and magical bric-à-brac. Childless, virgin priests tried in vain to console and raise people's spirits: "God works in mysterious ways." It wasn't enough to dry the tears. Some fellas had two candles lit up: one for the Catholic saints, one for the divinities of Voodoo.

Life in Papadopolis was a bonfire at the beach; widely exposed to the soaring winds of the Caribbean.

It was a good time to be a fortune teller. Women and shamans who were born with a crystal ball in their hands were making a good living. To parents in distress, they provided a vital service.

"Just say no! Don't eat, don't drink from anybody. Do not accept a glass of milk from a laughing cow or a bearded goat. It's a formula for disaster."

In the curriculum of each family, survival skills were the most important subject. Kiddies were advised to spit on their piss to protect themselves against evildoers.

It was a bad time to be a baby. A strange, mysterious time like the 19th Century when Gustave Flaubert, the renowned novelist from a bourgeois family was losing his four siblings at a very young age.

Flaubert, the award-winning author of *Madame Bovary*, the surviving son of Doctor Achille-Cléophas, was himself so crippled, so zombified by childhood illnesses that he was known at one point as the "idiot of the family".

It was a time of quarantine. Well-wisher's visits to newborns were barely welcomed. Every embrace was a virtual kiss of death. Even close family members brought with them, inside the house, innocently, the *movezè*, the bad spirits of the outside world.

The inhabitants of Martissant had to find a scapegoat. A sacrificial lamb. Titine, the midwife, was not a local. She came from the countryside. She was not a natural-born citizen of the hamlet of Martissant. Not even an anchor baby. She was an outsider. She had settled there illegally, in a wooden abandoned house, a former possession of General Saint-Surin François Manigat who died in exile, in Paris, seven months after the birth of the 20th century.

"L'enfer, c'est les autres" aptly said French philosopher Jean-Paul Sartre at a café near La Seine, the river that cuts Paris in a long, Caesarean section. In broken English, Sartre's quote would sound like: "Hell, it's the others." Titine was "the other", an alien, an intruder, an immigrant. She had to go. "Take a

hike, take a broom, fly away." For humanitarian reasons, her life was spared, fortunately.

Titine returned to her village in Saltrou, a smoky savanna that belonged to an American company. Her native town had the undeserved reputation as the Salem of the Caribbean.

It was a time when stepping outside at night was to flirt with disaster. A trip in the twilight zone. The *macoutes* had received the go-ahead from Papa Doc: "Shoot first, verify after if you have time."

According to a communiqué published in *Le Nouvelliste*, the Prez decided that starting at 8 PM, all lights, including candles and matches, should be off on all houses. Now, the curfew was perfect: inside and out.

For some curious reasons, the word "danger" did not figure in Uncle Sandino's dictionary. To his credit, he was brave like his name commanded. Maybe he was immune to that form of weakness that people call "survival instinct". Perhaps he was living in a bubble, floating in the blissful, ethylic atmosphere of spirits.

He spontaneously volunteered to escort his sister to the

hospital. To him, it was the most natural thing to do. The night of Papadopolis was crowded with restless and somnambulic henchmen. Uncle Sandino didn't give a fig about that.

Brother and pregnant sister ventured out. As expected, it did not take long for whom it may concern to show up.

The *macoutes* had a high sense of smell, an array of odorant receptors in the gray cavities of their nose. Something you would expect to find in some other species like the Labrador Retriever, the German Shepherd, the English Springer, or the Belgian Malinois.

When the moon was gloomy and showing its dark side, they had the ability to see in low light. At a distance, they could tell with laser-light precision: "This mosquito is a female and that one is a male; they'll be both dead in a minute."

A mile away, they could feel that something was wrong. Somewhere, not too far, a woman and a man were out in the streets at night.

Like sharks in the ocean, they smelled blood, water break, the distinctive fragrance of amniotic fluid.

Who were they, this woman and this man? Was it a covert

operation? Was she carrying a bomb or something even more dangerous in her belly? Was it another one of these desperate attempts to undermine the government?

Uncle and her sister were quickly surrounded by the authorities. The men in blue didn't know what to do. To kill or not to kill? For some unknown, irrational reasons, they decided to make an exception to the rule.

Maybe they were in a festive mood that Saturday night. Perhaps they were bored of killing. Maybe they had already reached their quota of blood for that particular night. Perhaps they were low on ammunition and wanted to save the bullets for somebody else.

The day after, on May 11th, upon return to Martissant, Uncle Sandino became an unlikely folk hero, a shining star, an alpha male.

After a successful delivery, mom was safe at the Chancerelles maternity. Everybody in the hood was praising Uncle with the most flattering terms. Misses Jones, the Jamaican storekeeper gave him access to her tumescent cinnamon buns. At least two other attractive Creoles who were known to be prude offered him coconut cookies, finger-licking conch, and lubricated oysters.

In their book, a bold man was undeniably sexy and good daddy material. Somehow, Uncle, the reluctant lover who had an intimate relationship with his bottle, managed to have a daughter with Jezebel, a woman who had dismissed him before as a mama's boy.

The neighbors looked up to him like an alien. Was he a lunatic? Was he the reincarnation of Augusto César Sandino, the guerillero of Nicaragua? They did look alike. They were both short; they had the same West-Indian features, the mixed blood of many colors.

Stranger things had happened in Martissant, but the neighbors could not come to terms with the previous night's event.

A cigarette tucked behind his left ear, Yoyo the toothless, iconoclast drunkard of the village who, in a previous life, had been a French professor at a well-known college on Long Island, found the right words to express the sentiments of the community: "In a million years, I would never think that such a tiny man could carry in his pants such a big, watermelon pair of balls. Let us drink in his honor!"

Everybody exploded in joy and laughter.

Because of these extraordinary circumstances, my uncle and I developed a very close bond. He spoiled me rotten like the son he never had.

He was my sole uncle. The other one, Robert Bruno, had been stolen from our affection by the men in blue.

"Anyone who neglects a godchild is damned to hell, she used to say. It's worse than abandoning your own child. It's my obligation to raise you to be good and clean and hardworking, because I will have to answer for you on Judgement Day."

Isabel Allende

"The sun was gone, but he had left his footprints in the sky. It was the time for sitting on porches beside the road. It was the time to hear things and talk."

Zora Neale Hurston

A Bloody Day in Texas

My earliest memory of Ma Fifine goes back to a certain Friday of November. It was a typical Caribbean evening when the sun was sinking into the ocean to allow the marine breeze to take over the thrill of the night.

I was 5 years old. She must have been in the glory of her early forties. I am far from being sure. It was a time so ancient that birthdates were vague, enrobed in mystery, buried in dust in the antiquities of the National Archives. The two-story colonial building was invaded by a variety of worms and academic insects who made their living on dry, starchy paper.

From lily-white, the record books would turn into an oatmeal color, as though a brown little lizard, from the cute iguana family, had peed on them on purpose, to insult our majesty and ruffle our feathers in the wrong direction.

"I was born under President Antoine Simon." It was at the time an appropriate answer to the age-old question of privacy. In the Blue Mountains, country-dwellers were even more germinal and creative about their DOB: "I have been through 39 harvests of coffee." In other regions, people stopped counting after 40. They were on a winning streak and did not want to attract bad luck. Any year after the 40th birthday was a bonus.

Her name was Josephine; just like the French Empress who was born on the sister island of Martinique. Some called her Mrs. Benoît, but for the intimates, she was just Fifine. When I listen to the Frenglish song of Charles Aznavour "You are the one for me, formi, formidable", she is the one who comes to my mind.

She was a plump, honey-colored Creole with a heart of gold. The kind of Madonna you'd see in portraits of the Renaissance. Anyway, that's the distant and fond images of her that I capture these days when I go back in time in the treasure hunt for memories.

It was love at first sight when we met at the maternity ward of Chancerelles. I was five hours old. She took me into her arms like a bouquet of chocolate sunflowers. My mother said that I cried when Ma Fifine left the room to go fetch some water. I thought she had vanished into thin air and I would never see her again. I had the shock of my life when she magically reappeared and held me again.

This place is strange. How in the world is this possible? Do people still exist when we don't see them? It was my first internal monologue. My eyes were googling wide, looking for a logical explanation.

From day one my destiny was sealed. I loved the idea of having these two women in my life. Long before I was born, Ma Fifine was chosen as my *marraine*, my godmother. "My next baby is going to be your son", she was told by her best friend and neighbor, my mom, Rolande Bruno. It was a choice made in heaven.

Marraine. In the French parlance, the word sounds sweet like "*ma reine*" (my queen). Yet, I never called her *marraine*. Not even once. It would have put too much distance between us. To the others, she was Fifine. To me, she was Ma.

At a time when danger was hiding in plain sight, she was my shell, my angel, my guidance counselor at the school of life where bullies wore a blue uniform.

"What's today's date, Tato?"

"It's November 22, Ma."

"How did you know that?"

"I am a big boy, Ma. I am going to be 6 next year."

Our gingerbread house was located in the garden city of Martissant. We were sitting under the almond tree in the front yard. It was our private time to bond after her long day at work in the grocery store where she sold all sorts of stuff: baguette, butter, sugar, salt, rice, beans, cigarettes, smoked herring, and rum. All the nutrients that keep people standing one day at a time, happy, and upbeat like a true islander.

"*Sak vid pa kanpe.*" An empty sack cannot stand up. The only thing that's really yours is what you have in your belly. So spoke the local wisdom, through the watering mouth of the troubadour.

It was a time when sugarcane was king. Some young fellows were brave enough to do their shopping from the screaming and frightening train that carries in its tummy a big load of juicy sticks en route to the Barbancourt rum factory.

They were children of a Voodoo god, roaming the savanna like wild foals. They were young characters in a tragic play: the never-ending story of *Les Misérables*.

In train language, the wheels on the rails were singing: *Ban m janm pran kann*. Take the cane, give me a limb, take the cane give me a foot.

Those who have the memory of an elephant still remember that morning of November 1917 when the train killed 50 in the neighborhood of Thor.

The soul train was possessed. It was swinging left and right like another disaster waiting to happen. Exhausted and hungry, like a giant snake on the rails, it was looking for meat. The train of the sugarcane company had a bad reputation. It was a repeat offender, a man-eater.

On that Friday, as usual, Ma Fifine and I were chatting like two old friends and accomplices. She would lecture me about the ways of the world. Newcomer to this planet, I was curious and had all kinds of existential and colorful questions about the mysteries of the land. "Why do dogs bite? Do cats have nine lives for real? So, the chameleon has a palette under its skin? Is it okay to wear sunglasses at night? Why are the men in blue so mean? Were they raised without a mom? Is Papa Doc their real dad?"

I was a late bloomer in kindergarten. The almond tree that provided shelter and snacks for our conversations was my tree of knowledge of good and evil.

Papa Déus, my godfather, was traveling to the south, carrying back and forth random traders to the coastal city of Petit-Goâve. They were mostly *madan sara*, female merchants who borrowed their nickname from a restless tropical bird. Above all, Petit-Goâve was the hometown of *dous makòs*, a local delicacy made with coconut milk, brown sugar, and a decadent flavor of vanilla. The aroma of *dous makòs* was good enough to make a Pope lose his Latin.

At this epoch, Petit-Goâve was a charming hamlet anchored in the southwest of the island, a hundred miles from the epicenter of Papadopolis. There were no welcome signs at the town's entrance. Just the fragrance of *dous makòs*. When you arrived in Petit-Goâve, you just knew it. Like an excited teenager, your nose told you: "We are so there!"

In Petit-Goâve lived a *timoun*, a boy wonder who had a promising handwriting. He was a free-spirited child who drank his milk straight from the cow. He played soccer in the barnyard with a rag ball. Barefooted, he had his little winky hanging under the amused eyes of a well-endowed onlooker:

the donkey.

In Papa Déus' frequent absences, I would be the man of the house. It felt good to be the protégé and the protector at the same time. For some irrational reasons, Ma Fifine felt safe with my presence. I was her shield against the ills of loneliness.

When I wander in the labyrinths of the past, I regain the vivid memory of a watermelon-red bibelot I was playing with that evening of November 22, 1963. It was such a cute gadget; it secured the event in the temporal lobe of my skull.

Far away from home, something gruesome and outlandish had happened. On the small transistor radio, which was one of our most sophisticated appliances, Joe Solon, the show host with the Stentor voice and the perfect pitch in French announced the dramatic news: "Le Président Kennedy a été assassiné!"

I barely knew my ABC, but instinctively I was able to read the sorrow in Ma Fifine's face. I panicked. I was confused.

I was completely taken aback. How on earth is this possible? How could that be? A stream of strange ideas was floating in my mind like seaweed on the floor of the ocean. I was deep into the abyss of that era of darkness and confusion that Swiss psychologist Jean Piaget called "childhood."

It was a time so ancient. Most products had a unique American name. It was a time so far away when islanders didn't care much about particular brands. Who cares about Polaroid? All cameras were called Kodak. Who cares about French toothpaste Fluocaril? It was called Colgate. Who cares if it was Westinghouse or General Electric? All refrigerators were called Frigidaire.

It was a time when dressmakers and tailors were going out of fashion. Near the dock of Columbus Kay where the French used to sell African slaves, the Croix des Bossales market was invaded by the Salvation Army with truckloads of salvaged wardrobes from Miami.

On the island, the pre-owned, certified clothes that made some dudes so handsome (gave them a sense of Camelot) were called "Kennedy."

"Le Président Kennedy a succombé à ses blessures..." President Kennedy succumbed to his wounds at the Parkland Memorial Hospital.

How could that be?

Ma Fifine had to explain to me that the radio host was not talking about used, recycled clothes. Obviously, she was hesitating as though she were about to give me a bitter pill. She didn't want to shock me; she had to break the bad news with diplomacy.

"What is it Ma?"

"The most powerful man on earth, someone white, mightier than Papa Doc, was gunned down today in a distant and troubled place called Texas."

It was indeed shocking news. Another crucifixion on Friday. This was real. Not like at Ciné Sénégal where actors died in a movie this Friday and reappeared the following week in better fighting shape.

Some actors were predictable. They would die regularly. Such was the case with Fernando Sancho and Lee Van Cleef.

Sancho was the eternal villain. 1963 was his best year. He acted in 13 movies. He died in 12 of them.

I could not believe my eyes when I saw him in a convertible in my hood of Martissant. He'd been invited by a powerful local *macoute*, Antoine Khouri. When the announcement was made in *Papa News*, I was skeptical.

Sancho received a spectacular welcome from kiddies and movie aficionados. Yes, it was Fernando with his signature bushy mustache. He was the living proof that actors are not cartoon characters. They are real. Oh my gosh!

On the big screen, Fernando was the embodiment of the Papa Doc doctrine: "It is good, it is legitimate to be bad." This is how the "legal bandit" philosophy was born on the island. It became a blueprint for future practitioners.

I had no idea who JFK was. I was just in synch with my mama. When she sang, I sang; when she smiled, I smiled; when she sobbed, I sobbed.

Her sadness was contagious. JFK was murdered. Ma Fifine had lost a loved one. Someone she barely knew. But it did not matter. It was someone she worshipped like a movie star. The kind of guy who gets the girl and all the Marilyn Monroes of the world. The happy ending was ruined. She felt diminished.

The five-year-old that I was had already accepted the fact that we were living in a Wild Wild World. It was an age when news bulletins were soaked in blood. Violent death was a fact of life.

1963. The year of living dangerously. The end of all illusions. According to the Constitution, Papa Doc's non-renewable six-year term was coming to an end. But paper is paper, and bayonet is iron. At the Military Academy, he had been diagnosed with a "weak constitution." He was going to show them what that meant in reality. The *Manual of the Perfect Dictator* said it loud and clear on page 57: "Annoying articles about term limits are breakable like dry banana leaves."

Nonetheless, some fellas were hopeful. The nightmare, the noise, the fury were about to end. They stayed still to listen to the steps of Papa Doc leaving the Palace. They were sure Kennedy was going to show him the door to Switzerland. The expiration date went by. Papa Doc stayed. Until death do us part.

November 22, 1963: another date "which will live in infamy." A few months earlier, an entire family, the Benoîts, had been assassinated in Papadopolis. A gentleman whose first name happened to be Benoît was also murdered. Since my godfather and adoptive dad Papa Déus carried this last name, it was obvious, even to me, that our family was at risk.

To many, JFK's assassination was a disaster. The *tontons* were happy. They celebrated that night with a concert of gunshots. They acted like outlaws at a bar of the Wild West after a bank robbery.

To the men in blue, Kennedy was international public enemy number one. They also had Dominican President Juan Bosch on the hit list. Of course, they wouldn't be able to locate the Dominican Republic on a map, but it did not matter; they wanted to shoot someone. Preferably, a foreigner for a change.

The fact that Kennedy was shot on the 22 (the magic number of Papa Doc) added to the legend that no matter where they live, the enemies of the Doc were condemned to early death.

To reinforce his aura of mysticism, Papa appeared in public like Baron Samedi, the god of cemeteries. He was a genius at this game. Like the Joker in Gotham City, he knew how to fool everyone, including JFK.

According to the history books, Papa Doc died in his bed in 1971. Did he? Not long ago, in 2010, when the earthquake Goudougoudou made half a million victims, I really thought that the Doc had returned.

Those who went to the cemetery to bury their loved ones were surprised to read the fresh-new epitaph on Papa Doc's tombstone: "The reports of my death were greatly exaggerated."

"In America only the successful writer is important, in France all writers are important, in England no writer is important, in Australia you have to explain what a writer is."

Geoffrey Cotterell

"Shortly after Mira came Lucien Evariste, commonly known as the Writer, although he had never written a word, and Emile Etienne, commonly known as the Historian, although he had only published one pamphlet that nobody ever read..."

Maryse Condé

The Totalitarian Temptation to Write

In the Americas, the island of Haiti has the highest concentration of writers per square mile. This is quite a paradox in a country with a shortage of schools, libraries, electricity, paper, and ink.

For some magical reasons, the land is fertile in writers, the way the State of Idaho produces tons of potatoes, the island of La Navase yields mountains of bird droppings, and the Republic of Colombia harvests (among other sweet things) a great deal of marvelous coffee.

On the island of Haiti, writers emerge from the soil like Chanterelle mushrooms. They burgeon and flourish in the most unlikely place.

One day or the other, in the middle of the night, one comes to terms with the frightening reality: "Oh, no, I am a writer."

It is quite difficult to escape the curse of the rainy season. The itching. The longing. The irresistible temptation to write.

Some areas of the island have their own creative groove. Jérémie, in the south peninsula, is the city of poets. There is something mysterious, *un je ne sais quoi* in the south seas that inspires tender, melancholic meditations about love and loss.

Jérémie. What a coincidence? What's in a name? In the French dialect, the word "jérémiade" means lamentation and moaning.

It would be heartbreaking to be born in Jérémie and not hear the lyric invitation of the Muse. It sounds like the mermaid's song from the depth of the ocean.

As far as I remember I was born in Papadopolis, the tormented capital of the underworld. It was an apocalyptic night of curfew. A night *à la* Mussolini. Avanti! Avanti! Maybe *à la* Alfred Hitchcock. The Birds. Carnivorous guinea fowls were flying everywhere. They were agitated; they were in a frenzy as if a plague, an earthquake, a rain of tears, and blood were about to fall over the island.

I was a few seconds old when I found myself in a state of terror. "Welcome to the era of Papa Doc", said the nurse with a smile. I screamed.

It did not take me long to realize that my gut feeling, my first impression of the world had been accurate.

Time-traveling at night is not always easy. Visibility is close to zero. Especially in the womb. One may end up in a beautiful country in the wrong epoch. That's how I landed at the maternity of Chancerelles circa the sixties.

I cannot complain too much; I have had some good moments in my random journeys around the world.

I have lived on the sister island of Tahiti on the flip side of Planet Blue. It was in the 19th century. During my mysterious excursions, I have encountered and spoken to the most unlikely characters. I once met Flaubert at a café in Paris. Even though it was a long time ago, I still remember what he said to me: "The only way to endure existence is to throw oneself into literature like in a perpetual orgy."

He was the one who introduced me to Emma Bovary who had a great passion for theater and romance novels. Emma, hum, what a woman! If she were still alive, she would have loved to read *Lady Chatterley's Lover*.

In the 18th century, right before the French Revolution, I met the aristocratic François-René de Chateaubriand who lost four of his siblings before he was born. He was to become the famous author of *Memoirs from Beyond the Grave.*

In my teenage years of madness at the Price-Mars Institution, I was fortunate to have three distinguished citizens of Jérémie as literature teachers.

Teachers? Are you kidding me? They were *maîtres*, *professeurs de belles lettres* (masters, professors of fine arts.)

They were three musketeers who taught literature with a passion. You would think our life depended on it. They came from Jérémie, the city that gave birth to the dad of Alexandre Dumas.

They were bright scholars with a sensitive soul. Maître René Philoctète was a nervous wreck when his team was playing at the Sylvio Cator Stadium. Maybe it was just a coincidence, but his soccer club had a poetic name: Violette.

The green lawn was balding and dusty like the butterfly's wing, but to him, Violette was poetry in motion.

He was thin and fragile like a child. The kind of man you would never hire as a bodyguard. The kind of man who would not last two weeks at Shawshank, Alcatraz, La Bastille, or in the dungeons of Papa Doc.

He attempted and failed miserably to settle in Montreal, among the Almost Dead Poets Society. Before he knew it, he was feeling the icy breath of autumn, coughing and puffing gray smoke and ashes. He was a shadow of his shadow and felt already like a departed.

His hair was gone to the unknown cemetery where follicles rest in peace, leaving behind the shiny skull of a calabash. On the radio, Nat King Cole was singing the *Falling Leaves* of Jacques Prévert. Maître Philo was swallowed, eaten alive by nostalgia. He missed the fiery blue of the sky, the warmth of the ocean, the lagoon where, as a boy with short pants, he fished for crabs and oyster shells.

Now, he was a miserable child in a new weaning period; he missed the milk and the honey of his motherland.

Under his cap, under his heavy coat (carnivalesque attires), he had nothing left aside from his bones, his skin, and his genius.

He did something so suicidal that he survived to tell the tale. Under the dark sunglasses of the astonished *tontons macoutes*, he defied the odds, returned to his native land, and published a memoir of his time in ex-isle under the title *These Walking Islands*.

It was Maître Philo's renaissance. He received from Legba, the Voodoo god of the gates, a new lease on life. A lease that lasted a quarter of a century.

The motorway between Papadopolis and Jérémie was like the road of Golgotha. Capital punishment. A torture to go from A to B. It made more sense to take a chance and cross the path on a frail boat. Indeed, when you look at it from the lighthouse's perspective, when you look at it through the lenses of the geometry professor: the shortest distance between A and B is the sea.

Maître Jean-Claude Fignolé was an aquatic creature. He studied agronomy because marine biology was not on the menu at the State University. He was a proud Jérémian and often felt out of place like an immigrant in the capital city of Papadopolis. His voice was coarse like someone who had sung too loud with a choir of sirens.

On weekends, he suffered from land sickness. So, he bought his own caravel, *Agwe,* and proclaimed himself Admiral with the right to select his successor.

His life was a long journey of discovery among the natives of Papadopolis.

On his captain logbook, he wrote many novels. His penmanship was remarkable until the last drop of ink. His *Toussaint Louverture* was the saga of the former slave who became an intrepid general and the most powerful man of the Americas. They called him the "Centaur of the Savanna." He was deceitfully captured and put on a boat heading to France for a voyage of no return. By a strange and poetic coincidence, the name of that ship was: *The Hero*.

At the Price-Mars Institution, Maître Fignolé taught writing with the composure of a Shaolin master. He was relentless in the mortal combat against bad sentences.

It was a time when speaking was underrated. Writing was everything. Some students lost their grip on the walls of the school. They were dyslexic Einsteins who were good with numbers and bad with letters. They had trouble with the never-ending 4-page essays, the infamous "dissertations". Some left the island to continue their studies in cooler climates where teachers are more clement.

One student of the Institution, Pierre Clitandre, became a novelist and a gifted painter. Another one, Amos Coulanges, morphed into a guitar in Paris. He remains a towering figure with his bodacious creations that are rooted in the island's folklore.

Maître Fignolé was a man of altitude. Always above sea level. Maybe he was from another era: the end of the 19th, the end of illusions. He was the kind of guy who could have written *The Flowers of Evil*. He was more aloof, less adjusted than Maître Philo. He was detached from the ground as if, in a previous life, he had been a bird.

I was drowning in deep reveries when I woke up in the middle of the class. The girl sitting next to me was the subject of my wandering. She was giving me the foxy look. She was smiling the kind of smile that says: "Get me if you can." I did not know what she meant. She told me light-years later when it was too late. When we were too far. When I was on Mars and she was on Venus.

My teachers were crazy about literature. They would spend weeks talking about Etzer Vilaire, the Jérémian bard who wrote a dark and decadent novel in verse called *The Ten Black Men*. He was the "witness of our demise", the most gifted poet of his generation.

Personally, what I truly wanted at that age was another type of literature: *How to Attract Women without Even Trying*, or something practical like *Seduction for Dummies*.

It would have saved me a lot of heartaches. I was too young to crack the code: the enigma of the Sphinx, the hieroglyphs of the Giza pyramid. I was clueless in the foreign language women speak with their smiles. That's how bad I was, that's how bad I have remained. I guess it's safer this way.

We were both 17, but mentally she was 27. What if I had kissed her and changed our destiny? What if she had kissed me in the name of the women's lib movement?

My Adam's apple was going up, was going down, swallowing words that sounded like heart-seeking arrows. I was ready to succumb to her charms. I was ready to give her my most precious possession: my virginity.

On that day, Maître Fignolé was about to teach an important lesson about writers in general, the *Confessions* of Jean-Jacques Rousseau in particular: "Whatever we say about ourselves is pure poetry."

That's the only sentence I remember from two semesters of literature with Maître Fignolé. It was more than enough. With such a revelation, I could have had a successful career in law enforcement.

I, also, have the right to remain silent. Nobody asked me to write these pages. Nobody asked me to put words on paper. I should have listened to Charles Bukowski: "Don't do it!"

I close my eyes and I write. I don't want to see what I have written. Writing is too intimate, too revealing. That's why I waited so long to declare my flame.

I love her. Tell her if you see her.

Fignolé. What's in a name? Can a name, a single word be a manifesto? Something subversive, hazardous to the health of Papa Doc?

It was a time when many names were blacklisted: Alexis, Benoît, Fignolé, Magloire, Manigat, Jumelle. It was a time when the wrong name was a life hazard, a magnet for tragedies.

Many teachers were encouraged to flee. They went as far as they could on the map. Papa Doc was a member of the school of thought that says in scarlet letters: To spread instruction is to spread the insurrection.

My amphibian teacher, Maître Jean-Claude Fignolé, shared his last name with a former Head of State who lasted 19 days in power. In the local Guinness Book, he remains the most ephemeral in the long list of residents of the Palace: generals, adventurers, filibusters, pirates of the Caribbean, carnival kings, and fools.

The President's name was Daniel Fignolé. Before he ventured into politics, he was a brilliant math teacher. Unfortunately, he was a poor chess player; he lacked the poker face and the evil genius of Papa Doc.

Daniel. With such a first name, he should have known he needed higher protection against the fauves. Before he knew it, he was being cast out by the felon officers. They put him on a plane heading north to the States.

His supporters realized that the *coup* was successful when they smelled a strong odor of khaki. It was late, too late. In the hood of Belair, they were hacked by the dozens with machine-guns.

It was subversive to carry the patronym of an exiled

President. Fignolé. It was a beautiful name. In French, it means refined, polished, well-crafted. The kind of name that should be reserved for wordsmiths.

What's in a name? It's a shame we don't get to choose our own. A radio-jockey of Papadopolis fell in love with the name of the famous Austrian actress Romy Schneider. He started to call himself Schneider. The name was like Swiss chocolate melting in his mouth. He was enamored with his new identity: Schneider! He was losing his mind over it. But who am I to judge? Especially, when I am restrained in a straitjacket at the mental institution.

Daniel Fignolé had committed a capital sin: he had made fun of his rival. While he was taking a shower, it occurred to him that the Doc was pathetic. Daniel was a loudmouth and a witty man. He went on the radio and shared his eureka moment with the public. A burst of laughter was heard beyond the borders of the island, all the way in South America.

Daniel Fignolé spent a lifetime in exile on Rogers Ave, Brooklyn. He returned home three decades later to bury his ashes.

Towards the end of his journey, long after the fall of the

Dynasty, Maître Jean-Claude Fignolé became Mayor of the coastal city of Abricots.

According to the legend of the first inhabitants of the island, the departed went to heaven in Abricots. That's where they spent eternal life enjoying the tastiest fruit on earth: the mamey.

Maître Raymond Philoctète, another citizen of Jérémie, was the funniest chronicler in town. As a topic, politics was off-limits, but he was great at making clever social commentaries. He wrote for *Le Nouvelliste*, the newspaper that survived a hundred years of choleric dictators.

Maître Raymond was the gentlest of them all. He did not have the altitude of Fignolé, nor the flamboyant confidence of his baby brother René Philoctète. But, his wit was sharp like a sword, versatile like a Swiss army knife. His best short story was perhaps the mock obituary he wrote about his upcoming funeral, his triumphant assumption to Heaven among the likes of Louis Armstrong and trumpet-playing angels giving a perfect rendition of *La Vie en Rose*.

In the intellectual community, it was a well-established fact that alcohol and tobacco have a positive effect on creativity and eloquence. They were two important ingredients for *la dolce vita*.

That was then. The magic is gone. Tobacco's reputation was killed by medicine and cold science.

When Maître Jacquelin Dolcé was under the spell of rum and other spirits, he got into a trance. His lecture took the tone of a post-doctoral literature conference at Utopia University.

Mister Dolcé was among the finest literary critics. He was kind enough to let me borrow his fresh copy of *The Autumn of the Patriarch* by Gabriel García Márquez. He had purchased the masterpiece at the bookstore La Pléiade, the headquarters of leftist scholars and living room guerilleros. They saw books as weapons in the war against the forces of darkness.

At La Pléiade, they did not accept credit cards. Nonetheless, pipe-smoking intellectuals with aromatic tobacco had *carte blanche*. They were greeted on the red carpet. They were free to grab from the shelves whatever they wanted to read and pay at the end of the month or whenever they got a hold on some liquid. At La Pléiade, they practiced capitalism with a human face.

It took me many years to understand that Papa Doc was our own version of Marquez' Patriarch. It was the main lesson

Professor Dolcé wanted to teach the unsuspecting teenager that I was.

It was a time so ancient that many High School teachers were acclaimed authors and journalists, la *crème de la crème* of the intelligentsia. A dream team of bohemians, freethinkers, poets, and lunatics. Some teachers had their pipe *à la* Sartre. The Cuban cigar, the olive-green uniform, and the long beard would have looked too obvious.

Jacques Prévert said once: "Intellectuals should not be allowed to play with matches." Yes, they would have burned down the palace of Papa Doc.

Some instructors seemed to be more pacific. They wore their sandals like Gandhi. They did not know the full spectrum of the guru's legacy.

In any case, teaching was a good alternative to daydreaming and total unemployment. Social studies and literature were risky topics. Teachers were brave, they were bold. They knew how to walk over the landmines, how to dance over the volcano. They outlived the Doc dynasty.

Most instructors were not paid during the summer.

Vacation was in fact a season in hell. From the end of June, it extended to the dawn of October. Among teachers, the mortality rate was high during that period. The last day of class was a dramatic moment. When we said goodbye to them, we were not sure we were going to see them again in October.

Why would they choose such a profession if they were not candidates to the book of martyrs?

But in fact, they were toughies. By the end of November, they had regained the weight they had lost during the dog days of summer. To many teachers, writing was a way of life. A remedy against the Doc and the ills of existence.

"Human beings are not born once and for all...life obliges them over and over again to give birth to themselves."

Gabriel García Márquez

"My mother was my first country, the first place I ever lived."

Nayyirah Waheed

Children and other Wild Creatures

When I grow up, I want to be King of the Hill, just like his majesty Henri Christophe who built a Citadel in the clouds, on top of the mountains of Milot.

When I was a babe in Papadopolis, it was quite a challenge to be small. The minors, the *timouns*, were reduced to the rank of proletarians, members of the Third Estate, below the middle class (the women), and the aristocracy (the men).

Call me a lunatic, call me an original; from the window of my room, I had my views, my own reading of modern society.

Through my telescope, men appeared to have more money because they were taller in general. They belonged to a caste of giants. They had the despotic right to buy or not buy toys for the *timouns* whose pockets were always empty.

To be a kid was to be a survivor. It was assumed that a tough upbringing was the best way out. It's easier to climb the social ladder on an empty stomach, without the inconvenience of shoes.

In Papadopolis, children had to go on a hunger strike to

protest against the predictable dish of maize flour. It was locally known under the vilified name of *"mayi moulen"*. Kiddies fought hard to change their condition as bottom feeders.

Unfortunately, you will not see the account of these epic battles in books written by grownups. Until this very day, *timouns* have remained unsung heroes of the victory of rice on the national diet.

According to Adoudou, a ten-year-old pundit in the field of social sciences: dogs and cats were actually the lowest class, the lumpen-proletariat of Papadopolis. They had no unions, no shelters, no hospitals, and no vets to speak of.

Some dogs were fierce. They chased suspicious individuals; they did background checks on unknown license plates; they ran after cars as though they wanted to eat their tires alive. In return, unkind fellas acted towards them in a dog-eat-dog fashion. Some canines were treated with hostility as though they were the incarnation of a Papa Dog.

At a dangerous crossroad, when carnivorous guinea fowls were roaming the island, the dogs worked 24 hours a day as non-uniformed security officers. They never saw a check; they never saw the slip of a direct deposit. Not a token of appreciation for their service. Not a saucer of fine Caribbean cuisine. They were not rewarded with a bottle of wine or a shot of whiskey for a job well done.

On behalf of those I love, I have to share this incident that altered the course of my life. When *One Hundred and One Dalmatians* was released for the first time, our dog Django was not invited to join us at the drive-in movie theater. He was left behind with his friend Harlequin, the female Chi-Chi of our neighbor. She was a beautify speciwomen, a cross between a giant Chihuahua and a Chinese Crested.

There was a hot, steamy affair going on between Django and Harlequin. They had the deep connection of avid lovers. Sometimes, they were literally inseparable.

At Drive-in Ciné, the grand premiere of the *Dalmatians* was magnificent. We totally enjoyed the soirée and were welcomed back home by you know who. There were some dreaminess and languor in his eyes, like someone who had engaged in some long, exhausting activity. Django was yawning, sleeping on his four feet, but he would not go to bed before we settled in.

Somehow, things changed the day after when *Le Matin* (the

now-defunct publication; peace to its soul) was delivered. A creature of habit, Django went to pick up the paper without any prompt at the wooden gate of the front yard. This is when he saw a picture illustrated article about *One Hundred and One Dalmatians*. His mood changed instantly.

Until that moment, he had not realized that in faraway, remote countries, some canines were so fancy, they dressed like pimps. They wore a Holstein cow black and white velvet coat.

Until that morning, he had not realized that dogs could become movie stars, glamorous individuals posing for the camera on the red carpet in Hollywood.

He finally understood that because he didn't have a passport, he was missing a lot of opportunities. He couldn't go on a journey of discovery to see what the world had to offer. His native land was surrounded by water.

Until that moment, he had not realized that he was a huge underdog in the uphill battle for life, liberty, and the pursuit of happiness.

It occurred to him that before he went to sleep outside, nobody ever read him a bedtime story like *The Dogs of Camelot: Stories of the Kennedy Canines*, or even *Top Dogs: True Stories of*

Canines That Made History.

That wasn't cool. Now, he could see clearly what the fuss was all about. Why everybody was all dressed up and excited last evening. They were going to see a blockbuster without him. He felt neglected. He could have had a date, a movie night out with Harlequin for a change. She was complaining about the heated rush, the lack of romance, as though she had just listened to Barbra Streisand singing on the radio *"You Don't Bring Me Flowers Anymore"*.

Django went into a philosophic phase of withdrawal, soul searching, and profound ambiguity. Something similar to the "Introspection" of Michel de Montaigne at the time of the Renaissance.

His eyes started to tell a different story. He was sad and depressed as though he had seen the name of someone he knew in the obituary section of *Le Matin*.

He started to pay more attention to the newspaper. Django was far from being superstitious, but he got really scared when he stumbled upon the ad for an upcoming Western: *Django, Prepare a Coffin*.

It took him time to accept the fact it was just a coincidence; it was just a movie. He finally recovered after many weeks of affection and intense therapy. Harlequin played a big part in the healing process.

Amid neglect and adversity, the puppies of Papadopolis remained cheerful. They rarely escaped to the savanna where stray dogs evolved backward to become wolves and werewolves.

They continued to have for their owners the adoring eyes and swaying tails of loving fellows. They deserve a monument in lieu and place of the equestrian statue of Papa Doc that was adopted by subversive pigeons as a poop facility.

When I go back to Martissant, I miss Django very dearly. We had some good moments growing up together. He matured much faster than I did. Half a century later, I am still on my way.

Whether I like it or not, I am rooted in the past. From time to time, my mind wanders among memories like a fish near the reefs of the island.

Sometimes, I emerge refreshed; sometimes, I sink to the floor of the ocean.

It felt good when I found myself at the theater of Kings Plaza (Brooklyn) watching with my boy Ezra the remake of *All Dogs Go to Heaven.*

It was in 2019 BC. A few months Before COVID.

"All men are children. They never grow up, they grow old."

James MacManus

"By the time we learn how to live, it's already too late."

Louis Aragon

The Jungle Book

I am a proud citizen of Martissant, the Latin Quarter of Magloire Saint-Aude: surrealist poet and author of *Dialogue of my Lamps*.

By the time I was grown enough to read his works, he was gone; exiled to the afterlife. It is a place the elders call "*pays sans chapeau*", the country where no one is allowed to wear a hat.

I wonder why.

The first time I heard about him, it was on the day of his funeral. My friend Ito, the boy-scout, said to me: "Mister Saint-Aude was a good friend of my dad."

I felt the pain.

The mysterious and avant-garde poet is worshipped by a small sorority of writers. He belongs to Martissant. Just like Nemours Jean-Baptiste. Just like Konpè Filo. Just like Magny Manigat.

Anyway, I don't want to get distracted. I hear the sound of the Reo outside. My papa is back! You're probably too young to picture my daddy's truck. It looks awesome, like a dinosaur.

The truck's logo was a crown. So, my dad called his machine: *Roi des Routes*, King of the Roads. King like T-Rex.

Among the distinguished passengers from Petit-Goâve, Papa Déus, my godfather, often brought to Martissant a herd of goats and restless turkeys. They spoke foreign languages without any accent. You would think they had studied at the best community college on Long Island.

The bewildered animals were not excited about leaving their hamlet for an unknown destination. That sentiment was voiced in the most eloquent way.

To the child that I was, the cry of distress of these creatures was heartbreaking. That did not prevent me from enjoying (shamelessly, I have to confess) the fine dishes of organic meat of Ma Fifine. It was an out of this world experience compared to the hairy bird I ate today at Kung Fu Chicken.

Ma Fifine was an expert in red snappers and *piskèt*, a dried miniature fish. They were mixed with black mushrooms and white rice. To top it all, she would treat us to a glass of ice infused papaya juice with Carnation milk.

I still salivate and wet my pillow when I visit the island at night. When I realize I was only dreaming, I wake up in a crabby mood.

In the fertile landscape of Martissant, there was a rainforest the size of a soccer field. It had a rainbow of fruits and starchy tubers. It was a time when land was dirt cheap. With a few hundred dollars, one could make a Louisiana Purchase.

No liquid? No problem, man! One was qualified for a verbal mortgage; a handshake agreement signed and sealed under a palm tree, or at the bank of the river.

A word of honor was as good as cash.

Papa Déus made his land acquisition from the estate of Magny Manigat, a biblical patriarch with the predictable long beard that was in fashion in the early days of humanity. He was a living incarnation of the times we left behind.

Mister Manigat was born in Kingston at the end of the 19th century while his parents were living in exile.

The sister island of Jamaica had become a shelter, a *pied-à-terre*, for overthrown presidents, eternal candidates, die-hard conspirators, and the ragtag army of revolutionists. They were banned, persona non grata in their own country, condemned to death in absentia. They were stripped of their most precious trophy: their *haïtianité*, their citizenship. They found refuge in Jamaica, less than a hundred leagues in the open sea.

In Jamaica, former rivals, mortal enemies finally reached a neutral ground, another isle under the oppressive sun. Another place where they could start a bloodless war of arm wrestling. They played epic games of dominoes. They built fortresses in the sand. At night, in their hammock, they had wild, agitated dreams about the day of triumphal return.

In 1912, the Palace exploded, killing instantly President Cincinnatus Leconte. He'd been in power for less than a year. Some felt he had overstayed.

The wooden, prehistoric building was replaced by a state-of-the-art White House. A revolving door was installed to facilitate quick entry and exit of the presidents. The dome of the Palace had the shape of a flying saucer.

Right before Papa Doc, Professor Daniel Fignolé managed to stay in power for 19 days. To his restless enemies, it seemed like an eternity.

Many moons later, Doctor Lafontant stayed inside the White House for 2 hours and 57 minutes. His tenure was so short, he did not enter the History books as a true president. He was dislodged the night of the *coup*, right after a speech of inauguration in which he promised something attractive: authoritarian democracy. The day after, when he woke up, he realized he had changed into a jailbird.

Despite his new, birdie condition, he received from the warden the bowing and reverences that are due to a Head of State.

When Papa Doc arrived, the revolving door was removed. It was placed in the Mausoleum. The time when King Henry was building his Palace with 365 doors was over. A new era had begun. The era of Papadocracy.

Magny Manigat was a good neighbor. He would say to my dad: "Come on Benoît, take that other piece of land; you'll pay me when you can." Papa Déus would refuse. He already had two properties in Cité Manigat. He was content. It was a time when naked greed was still an infant.

It was the strangest time when chickpeas and eggplants grew alone, instinctively. They didn't ask for chemicals; they didn't ask for tap water.

The joyous trees elected the clouds, Stratus, Cirrus, and Cumulus, to irrigate their roots. They grew in harmony with the moon. It was quite a marvel to see the rain, going back up, fighting gravity to become sweet water, and white meat in the altitude of the coconut tree.

We were in 1965 B.C. On the radio, Nat King Cole was singing *Nature Boy*. I was all ears. I didn't see further than the enchanted world of Martissant. I was living in a cocoon, a pink bubble Ma Fifine built for me.

I had some white friends I met in comic books. They were in top fighting shape. They had odd, eccentric names: Tarzan, Sheena, Akim, Zembla. They lived in a Jungle Book among the cousins: the chimps and the bonobos. I followed them very closely. That's how I learned to ride elephants, to run with the wolves, to fly first-class from liana to liana. When I became a teenager, I learned how to tame my dragon when it was on fire.

Joumou pa donnen kalbas. The pumpkin tree does not produce calabash. So said the local wisdom. The plants of our garden had their own children. They grew around their moms and their dads and were generous with their fruits and their leaves. One would think they were following the instructions of an invisible agronomist, the supreme naturalist who famously said:

106

"Grow, multiply, and replenish the earth."

To keep me grounded and sharpen my calculus, Papa Déus assigned me a summer job. He wanted me to count the fruit-bearing trees of our garden according to their species.

He said to me: "Son, you can eat any fruit you want, except the zombie cucumber." I responded: "I know, Papa, I am a big boy now."

It was my signature answer, whenever I wanted to assert my intellectual authority as a child. I had just read *The Little Prince* of Saint-Exupéry. I kind of agree with him when he said: "Grown-ups never understand anything by themselves, and it is exhausting for children to have to provide explanations over and over again."

I was a big boy indeed. I had been under the almond tree of knowledge with Ma Fifine for many years. We would study and memorize together as though she were my classmate: "It is in Genoa in Italy that Columbus was born; his dad was a poor weaver. Since the time he was an infant, Chris always loved the sea…"

It took me a long time to realize that things were not so rosy.

Children's books are written in pink, History is written in red. The blood is often erased with bleach.

Many years later, when I left the folds of Ma Fifine's skirt, I started to read on my own. Weird things like *Pariah*, *The Drunken Boat*, *In Praise of Madness*.

"Come on Tato, I want you to count the trees". I don't know what got into me. I wanted to impress my Papa. For some strange, silly reasons, I consulted the dictionary and decided to use the scientific names of the plants on the list. They often had Latin roots.

On my ledger, the unassuming orange tree became "citrus sinensis", the tomato morphed into "solanum lycopersicum", the modest watermelon took the allure of "citronnus lanatus", the familiar olive tree became the distant "olea europaea".

I guess the teaching of Maître Sauvignon was paying off. He was a great Latinist. His school was the geometric center of the Roman Empire.

Because I was a kiddie, it was quite a challenge to sum up all the trees. It would have been easier to climb the tallest of them all. I was counting stars in the firmament, phosphorescent sand grains at the beach of Mariani. I got lost several times in the web of accounting.

I was on a daze. I probably got too close to the hallucinogenic flower of Datura Stramonium. I almost lost my mind. Maybe I did. That's why I am this way, estranged from myself.

Nowadays, I live in parentheses. I read books on my Apple watch. I Kindle. I WordPerfect. I post my grocery lists as postmodern poetry on the Web. I Photoshop. I cut and paste memories to escape the present.

I look in the mirror and I see my zombie. I cry werewolf in my sleep. Once in a blue moon, I wake up from the somnambulic daze. I become a rational being. I count my blessings as a survivor. And I get lost again in the spiral of life.

My alarm clock crows like a rooster at 4:59 in the morning. I make grandiose projects. I sell the skin of the bear before I catch it in my backyard. I count eggs in the belly of my dreams. I climb the coconut tree in the water aisle of Stop and Shop.

In the ethnic food section of the supermarket, I harvest cassava, avocados, green plantains, sweet potatoes, yams, and jerk seasoning. While I was on a lucky break, I made a miraculous catch of dried salty fish.

At Walmart, a coquette wearing dark sunglasses smiled at me. She scanned me up and down. I got scared. I suspect she was a *femme fatale*, an undercover of the Department of Deportation.

I am afraid of people with dark sunglasses. I've never owned sunglasses. Once, I received a pair from my Valentine. I gave them away. My romantic interest didn't know I had a problematic relationship with dark sunglasses.

I finally completed my assignment. Papa Déus was proud of me. The census bureau I established under a pomegranate tree reached the conclusion that the papaya with its orange flesh and dark shiny seeds was the most prolific dad. It had produced more offspring in our garden. To my surprise, the passion fruit tree was supplanted. It did not come close.

It was a time when the trees had distinct personalities. The *flèdizè*, a local variety of touch-me-not plant, was reserved and sensitive. After taking her shower from the dew, she would cross her arms to cover her chest and keep voyeurs at bay. She was introverted and timid like a beauty of the Virgin Islands.

Among botanists and plants' psychologists, the *sablier* tree was known for its ability to erase memory. Those who were leaving the island, those who were heading north to the gold mines of New York, had to avoid the *sablier*. Otherwise, they would forget to share their bounty with the people they left behind: distant relatives, friends, neighbors, domino partners, former classmates, all the branches of their family tree.

It was a time when "New York" was a generic term for most US destinations. Whether you were moving to the slums of Chicago or the projects of Philadelphia, it was easier to say the magical word with the enthusiasm of Franck Sinatra singing *New York, New York*.

It opened the door to a New World of low-wages and salaried slavery.

Miami? Not a chance. New York sounded better, more prestigious than that attractive other city whose name was being mistreated by the islandic tongue. Miami seemed too close. Walking distance through the Red Sea.

The émigrés were very nostalgic. They carried the island on their sleeves like the pirogue carries the tree of which it was made.

Against all odds, winds, and storms, the islanders remained true to their roots. Centuries ago, the African ancestor had said: "No matter how long a log stays in the water, it doesn't become a crocodile."

Even though they were settled in New York, they dreamed of a return to the native land. A country cured of the virus of Papa Doc.

Despite their reserved nature, the exiles were warm-blooded, sophisticated individuals who knew all too well what they wanted. The prospect of arctic snow falling on their graves seemed to be hell on earth.

They dreamed of a gingerbread house. A garden of organic fruits. A place in the sun where the right to die of natural causes is guaranteed by law. A place where they could be buried in their own backyard. A place where they would reincarnate as a sunflower, a palm tree, or a sacred *mapou*.

"New York was too cold for my taste; that's why in 1969, I moved to Miami Bitch." So spoke the French teacher with the innocence of a choir boy.

I've learned my lesson. I avoid certain words like the plague. Even the elementary word "get" is problematic. It's a profanity in Creole, my mother tongue.

I speak English with the same caution I exercise when I eat broken glass, when I spit fire near the Shell gas station. I swallow my pride and accept the fact I'll always be an immigrant.

Like the French teacher who headed south, I love the warmth of Florida. It's my banana republic, my almost island, my Caribbean peninsula.

To reach Key West, I went through the string of seaside resorts. This is where (for the first time) I saw the sea on both sides of the road.

My linguistic metamorphosis is yet to come. I still have a problem pronouncing "Miami Beach."

As a last resort, I put it in the red-light district of Merriam, the dictionary, the Muse I keep warm in my bed.

"Anyone who has lived to the age of eighteen has enough stories to last a lifetime."

Flannery O'Connor

"I was born with this story. It ran in my blood. I belonged to it."

Gaël Faye

The Mirror Image of Elegance

Show me your closet and I'll tell you who you are.

On the island of Haiti, the dress code was fluid like a jellyfish. It varied with the latitude: from freshwater to seawater.

At the river, in broad daylight, it was not unusual to see the nymphs in nightgowns and transparent attires. They were doing the laundry in shallow waters the color of indigo.

As though they were part of the scenery, they could not care less about the onlookers with their bulging eyes. Like a starfish who'd seen herself in the mirror, they were comfortable in their skin.

Some other time, it was a mermaid in her birthday suit taking a bath in the serpentine river, before the sunset.

They called her *la maîtresse de l'eau*, the mistress of the water. In other circles, she was known as *la sirène*, the siren, which, in the local tongue, sounds as nice as "such a queen"

I never got the chance to meet her. I heard she was full of charms, quite a sensation in the bed of the river.

She was the kind of girl who could have been the centerfold in *Glamour Magazine*; if and only if she were born on the other side of the ocean, in a foreign exotic land.

She was known to be shy, to vanish into thin air when she felt unfamiliar human presence. Even though she carried a mirror, even though she groomed her hair with a golden comb, she was far from being self-absorbed.

More than a woman, she was Erzulie, the goddess of love.

At the beach, the dress code was stricter for the southern belles. They wore vintage swimsuits, as though they were nuns from Sainte Bernadette.

Like Stella in Montego Bay, tourists and visitors could get their groove as they wished. They belonged to planet Venus. Local cougars, late bloomers, and ovulating seniors were discouraged from wearing micro thong bikinis.

The usual suspects, the alpha males, were free to show their fur and their belly full of beer. It did not occur to anyone that it was more obscene.

It was a time so old that slacks were forbidden to *timouns*. The boys wore short pants. Something stylish and well-cut.

Tailors were no jokes. They knew how to make designer's short pants.

With lanky, bony legs exposed, tall adolescents looked like brown flamingos.

"Short pants? We have no problem with that!" So spoke the mosquitoes (musicians who graduated summa cum laude at the Swamp Academy of Fine Arts). They were starving artists in skinny jeans, flying leeches, daredevil aviators who made a living in the bloody, eternal war against humankind.

The problem with tropical paradises is the fact they are not perfect. Here and there, while reading at the beach, you meet some unsavory characters who jump out of nowhere to suck your blood and eat your flesh. Such was the case with Moskito.

You probably heard about him before in Florida, Louisiana, and even up North. He's been featured many times on the cover of *Health Magazine*. His name is Moskito. Yes, that's how the clerk wrote his name on the birth certificate. His brothers and sisters call him Toto.

With their rich repertoire of songs, mosquitoes were the true inventors of YouTube and Bluetooth technology. Versatile soloists, they sounded sometimes like Mozart's Symphony 35, sometimes like Franck Sinatra ("If you can make it there, you'll make it anywhere.") They played *Unchained Melody* ("Oh my love, my darling, I've hungered for your blood.") They banded together to play orchestra and claim their reward in the arms and the feet of their captive audience.

Armed with needles and jackhammers, they dig, they dug, searching for food in a river of blood. They worked their heart out, singing, swinging, sweet and sour songs, elegiac cantatas. They sweat in their brows for every drop they sipped.

"When I grow up, I want to shop at the store where they sell elephant pants."

The store on Caesars Street was called *El Gallo*, the rooster. No less than that. Actually, it could have been *El Pavo Real*, the peacock. The tailors were that good. This is where Joubert Alexis, the original Scissorhands and a friend of the family, displayed his talent as a fine couturier. When he was visiting us, in Martissant, he was escorted by his sidekick, Jupiter, who got free rides in the public transportation because, at 25, he could still pass for a child.

The duo knew how to make miracles with *"retay"*, leftovers, tiny pieces of textiles. This is how, as a man in miniature and Ma Fifine's baby doll, I was able to wear the rich fabrics of Joubert's well-to-do customers.

Allowing a youngster to wear long pants was improper, a violation of the code of conduct, an insult to the aristocratic caste of *granmouns*, the grown ones. When it happened, it was seen as something cute and playful, a waste of fabrics, a child masquerading as an adult, something exceptional that shouldn't be abused.

It was before the War of the Buttons. Around that time, kiddies were part of the Third Estate.

To assert their supremacy, affluent gentlemen wore thick gabardine suits under the smiling sun. It was quite heroic. Those who were too skinny padded their shirts with newspapers.

It looked proletarian to wear a belt. Distinguished gentlemen showcased their suspenders as though their status depended on it. Without them, it was a fashion *faux pas*. They had bow ties, velvet waistcoats. Without them, they would have felt naked. It was for a good cause. Etiquette. Islandic pride.

Patriotism.

Even though the island has one season (12 months of eternal summer), the well-bred fellas always wore their vests. It took time for the Guayabera and the Safari to emerge as serious contenders.

It was a time so ancient; silicone injections were not yet invented. Perhaps they were in their infancy. To enhance their assets, some inventive divas padded their derrière with layers of garments.

It was safe, attractive, approved by the fashion police and the local FDA. Around that time, Franky Limon was making a killing with the hit song *Why Do Fools Fall in Love?*

A matron named Choucoune pushed the *gwo dada* (big butt) phenomenon to a carnivalesque proportion. She became a public figure, received friendship requests, marriage, and other indecent proposals by the ton.

She had thousands of followers in the streets of Papadopolis. Her popularity reached new heights when she started to dance on top of a carnival float until the wee hours of Mardi Gras.

To see the world in vivid colors, a monocle was enough. It

went well with a pipe. It made one look brilliant like Simone de Beauvoir strolling by the Seine River with Jean-Paul Sartre.

Sunglasses were regarded as a vulgar gadget. Something tasteless, reserved for foreigners and local henchmen with scary eyeballs.

Ladies and gentlemen had to show their naked eyes.

In the atmosphere of paranoia, cautious individuals carried in their pocket the most important attire: the talisman, the red handkerchief, the *mouchoir rouge*.

They wanted to protect themselves against the malefactors who are legions in this world. The *mouchoir rouge* was a shield against bad omen, head-seeking bullets, police brutality, jealous and selfish husbands.

Around that time, *Le Matin* newspaper reported the emergence of the charming vagabond persona, the rise of the "*brodè-razè*" culture. It was associated with the emblematic habits of penniless but well-groomed individuals who walked on eggshells, promenading their majesty in slow motion in the rocky streets of Papadopolis.

Their destination was unimportant. What matters the most was the choreographed and aerial manner in which they crossed the bridge to nowhere.

They were thin, undernourished, and elegant islanders. On top of their pedestals and their mountains of illusions, they regarded American and Canadian tourists as blown-up, unrefined members of the British tribe.

To them the visitors were rich but poorly dressed individuals; people they left behind on the sea of civilization.

"A beautiful bunch o' ripe banana

Daylight come and me wan' go home

Hide the deadly black tarantula

Daylight come and me wan' go home"

Harry Belafonte.

"The entire region became a blessed garden called Gros-Morne, where one had only to think of a fruit to see it happen upon a bough."

Patrick Chamoiseau

Hanging Gardens of Papadopolis

What was he thinking my Papa?

Papa Déus wanted me to be somebody. Not Prez for life necessarily. Something more modest. Maybe a Doc of agronomy. I would open my clinic near the garden and take care of the plants. I would become *Governor of the Dew*.

Finally, I ended up in a paradise of concrete and asphalt. To be an immigrant is to play a new character in a foreign movie. To memorize a new script. To wear a mask in a Greek tragedy under the tutelage of Hellenic dictator Georgios Papadopoulos.

I forgot how to say *bonjour voisine*. "Good morning neighbor. How was your night? Your coffee smells good."

I am afraid to stick my nose out. Before the plague, I was already living in seclusion. I was invisible. Like a fish in a tank, I adjusted well to the new normal. It is written in my passport and my résumé: I have experience in calamities, mass casualties, drownings, campaigns of terror, volcanic eruptions, and earthquakes.

I went to the nursery of Home Depot; it brought back memories of my infancy: the friendship I had with the plants as a nature boy.

I was surprised when the cardiologist said to me: "We are all related." She showed me the picture. Like the mango tree, my DNA has the shape of a twisted ladder.

I miss the perfume of Jasmine, Rosemary, Camellia, and Marguerite. Where are they, my Caribbean queens? I carry the same songs of yesteryears. I ask the same essential question: "What do roses dream at night?"

The papaya was awesome. Some trees did not produce the juicy fruits they use to make the chewing gum. They were just like humans: the good, the bad, and a lot in between.

Like pirates of the Caribbean, some trees hid their treasures underground. Some, like seaweed, took refuge in the mangrove. They kept a low profile in the sandy bed of the sea. They'd rather feed crabby animals like lobsters and crayfish.

Some practiced self-defense. The cassava root was lethal when eaten raw. It did a genocide in the piglets' population.

Little piggies were young and stubborn. They would not

listen to their mama. Their mouth was growing long. They were fed up with the baby formula from the titties. They wanted to fend for themselves and eat mouthwatering roots. They would not pay attention to the pontifical lectures of old-fashioned pigs with gray hair. The words of wisdom went straight out, from left ear to right ear, gone with the wind.

The calabash was in a class by itself. It had a horrible taste. Its milky flesh was stinky like spoiled cabbage and decomposed broccoli. The dry, egg-shaped, gigantic fruits were converted into containers for sugarcane syrup and Palma Christi oil. The lubricant made miracles against muscle pains, short hair condition, and baldness among women and men. Palma Christi oil dropped in the stock market when wigs and hair extensions invaded the island.

Cut in half, emptied of the nasty flesh, the calabash became a magnet for money. It was popular among beggars who made a living near Notre-Dame of Perpetual Sorrow.

Smaller calabashes were decorated with flamboyant colors and used as a musical instrument: the *cha-cha*. At the time, a lead singer who respected himself had to be an expert in *cha-cha*, harmonica, or accordion. In the worst-case scenario, he had to have a degree in whistling from the Dupervil Music Academy.

Around that time, cocoa oil had a solid reputation as a male enhancer. Grown men with small hands, VIP members of the Microscopic Club were avid consumers of the lubricant.

According to the peacocks who kissed and told, it worked like a charm. They had performances of stormy proportions.

Some of the handlers and consumers of cocoa grease ended up in Hollywood in the Mandingo big scream industry. Others embraced politics because it's the best aphrodisiac. They were hoping to become the next "dicktator". One of them was erected president under the moniker of Gwo Bozo. He often wore a long red tie as a phallic symbol.

The trees were good allies in the mortal combat against aging, muscle weakness, and premature evacuation. Soaked in agricultural rum, the barks of *bwa bande* was strong enough to awaken a dead man. It allowed some elders to have a new lease on life and stay stiff like the yucca. As though he was a patriarch of the Bible, Papi Lou was still fertile at the age of ninety-six. He was a force of nature.

Around that time, Creole beauties used to love antique

models. They didn't feel much passion for young studs below sixty. Beyond that threshold meant that the man had proven himself. He had passed the test of time. He had good, desirable genes. The older, the better.

I don't know if it was true, false, or all the above. Maybe it was part of the urban legend. Maybe it was just propaganda from decadent seniors who confused their cane with their mojo.

I was too young to be certain of anything. I was living upside down, in the fog of confusion. I tended to believe whatever I heard in the newspapers or read on the radio.

Even though it was forbidden for children to listen to grown-ups' conversation, I did hear that southern belles from Port-Salut used plant concoctions to enhance their garden of Venus. So doing, they gained an unfair advantage over the prudish beauties of the capital. If my memory is faithful, the plant they used was *ti bom* (the little balm).

Mother Nature in her infinite generosity gave us a black coat and palm trees as parasols against skin cancer. The trees provided the shade for sitcom conversations and oral telenovelas. Their branches were 5-star hotels for our chickens to spend the night after a delicious supper of earthworms.

They went to bed early, before Ma Fifine would say: "Go pee before you fall asleep!" Of course, she was talking to me, not to the chickens.

They were early birds and had no problem waking up first thing in the morning to resume their activities and pick up where they left off the day before.

The chicks would wander in the bushes for hours in search of a special treat. But they knew their address by heart and their internal clock worked like a Swiss watch. They would be home before their curfew of 6 PM. Otherwise, they would be reprimanded by Ma Fifine and had to make amend honorable in the cage.

I don't know if they understood French, but I often read them stories: *The Chicken with the Golden Eggs* or *The Misadventure of Mister Seguin's Goat*.

They would follow me in the courtyard, expecting me to feed their belly and their mind. Maybe they thought I was a giant papa chicken. I developed a particular affection for them, especially when I learned in the Encyclopedia that they had kings and queens in their bloodline. They were great-grandchildren of the dinosaurs.

I am not sure I would get along well with T-Rex. Even the most adventurous dentist would be frightened by these gigantic jawbones. I felt privileged to live in the era of chickens.

They had no natural predators in the hood of Martissant, except for sneaky mongooses, dirty rats, human and inhuman meat-eaters.

My kid brother Papo Loco didn't like fish, but he would eat anything once he was told: "It's chicken!" He still doesn't eat onions and vegetables. He continues to call them flowers. To justify his peculiar taste, he often quotes the Chinese philosopher who said: "A tiger cannot become vegetarian."

Around that time, chicken was the ultimate reference in *haute cuisine*. "Hum, this beer tastes like chicken." That's what Yoyo, the toothless clown of the village, would say while he was salivating for his third bottle of Heineken.

The first time I saw Yoyo, I thought he had a big calabash hanging inside his pants. From one neighborhood to the next, he carried his bulging testicular hernia (tenderly called "*maklouklou*") with the dignity of a Senator.

Compared to the ostriches we call chickens today, the local birds were quite petite. Nonetheless, they were omnivorous creatures who had no remorse about eating giant cockroaches. These critters were well-dressed with their dark brown tuxedos. You would think they were on their way to a party at the Playboy Mansion with the rich and famous.

Whether or not we indulged in the guilty pleasure of eating chicken, we were honorable people, molded in a steely material.

Most of the time, we were in good spirits, resilient under fire. We were strong like a bull and rarely caught a cold.

We never had the need for chicken soup.

"Above all, read these stories at night. Remember, I wrote them with the moon as my sole companion."

Patrick Chamoiseau

"I know the sorts of doctors they have in Trinidad. They think nothing of killing two, three people before breakfast."

V. S. Naipaul

The Most Interesting Zombie in the World

We rarely went to the doctor, except for life-threatening circumstances, as a last resort, when the damage was done, when it was too late for a natural or supernatural cure to occur, when we needed a death certificate.

Around that time there was no need for an appointment. Alive or dead, you could walk into a clinic and ask for treatment.

Doctor Wallon was a chain-smoker. He lived in the clouds. His office was packed with dead people's charts. Letting go is hard to do. He kept handy the files of the deceased. In case they decided to return.

It was ashy in there: the foul smell of tobacco in a grave atmosphere of magic. Near the Pétion-Ville cemetery, Doctor Wallon was second to none.

On Halloween 1964, a gentleman called Bonhomme Narcisse who was reputed dead and buried since May 2, 1962, came all the way to Martissant to visit Dr. Bartoli. His death certificate had been signed by two American physicians from the Albert Schweitzer Hospital, near the Artibonite River.

These 5-star MDs were well-respected in the community for their ability to work the night shift. They were compassionate professionals. However, when they say you are dead, you are very dead, even if you were to protest with eloquence at the funeral parlor. The undertaker would put you in your place as a rebellious and arrogant zombie: "The white man has spoken; his verdict is final; you better behave accordingly!"

Some funeral homes were known at the time as a point of no return. In fact, it should have been the opposite when you take into consideration the widespread cases of sudden reawakening.

Mr. Narcisse did not like it too much underground. He was complaining about insomnia. He had a scar on his face and was saying to anyone willing to listen: "Any day above ground is a good day."

With a luxury of details, he revealed to the astonished physician that he'd been downcast by a witch doctor who put his soul in an empty bottle of rum.

Dr. Bartoli was an excellent practitioner. He saved my life several times in the epic battles against diarrhea, chickenpox, rubella, and mumps. He also had a remedy for boredom. He was the proud owner of the first black and white TV in the hood.

It was a time when doctors were blunt, unfiltered like a cheap cigarette: "You have three months to live, max." Just enough time to put things in perspective, to sell a cow, a piece of land, to take measurements and make funeral preparations. Some people slept in their newly acquired mahogany coffin. To get used to it. To make sure it was comfortable.

It was no big deal. At the time of Papa Doc, death was very familiar, an ordinary event like the common cold or the storm after the sunlight.

Kiddies were not involved in politics, but they often got into accidents in the playground and bled. Their wounds were treated with spider web.

As a toddler, you'd go to the doctor untroubled, hoping to watch cartoons before he draws your blood. He would break the magic by saying to your mama: "Your child has an electrical abnormality in his heart. He might not make it to his first communion."

Electrical abnormality? You seemed to be in good running

condition. You seemed to be a bright kid. Was the problem related to the constant blackout?

The growing pains were unbearable: the bitter pills, the cod liver syrup, the harsh laxatives before going back to school. The enema pump hanging on the wall was a good reminder that life is not a garden of roses.

Sometimes I feel like a survivor, a comeback kid. I look at myself in the eyes to confirm it's really me; not another soul who took over my body.

I was afraid to go to bed at night. I had delirium of persecution. The *loups-garous*, whether they were alive and well and living in Martissant or just unsavory characters invented to frighten unruly kids, played a big role in my agony.

I am not sure I have recovered from the trauma of childhood: the blue vultures, the fear factor when the sun goes to sleep. According to my psychiatrist, I should summon the courage to add the Dracula Channel to my cable package, watch some horror movies, and see what comes up in the second-floor apartment where I live with my shadow.

As an experiment, that sounds interesting, but why take chances?

Doctor Bartoli was a miracle maker. His new patient, Bonhomme Narcisse the zombie, was cured of death. He ended up leading a normal life for 32 additional years.

He had numerous fans in the US who greeted him like a rock star at JFK which was known at the time as Idlewild Airport.

To his credit, he was a cool country dweller with a signature grin, quite the opposite of Narcissus, the mythic character. He never carried a mirror or a comb in his pocket. We were in 1964, when Muhammad Ali, the new incarnation of Cassius Clay was shouting: "I am pretty as a girl!"

Narcisse was enchanted to be alive. He didn't allow fame and fortune to get into his head. If in 1964, Papa Doc had not proclaimed himself President for life, Bonhomme Narcisse could have won the elections in a landslide; without the support of the Army, without the support of the Embassy, which at the time represented 99% of the votes.

The zombie Narcisse became so popular that he began to fear for his life. His trip to California was a pretext for a disguised exile. He was too precious to the scientific community to allow Papa Doc to see him as a rival; with the dire consequences that would certainly follow.

His voice was muffled. He carried a saltshaker in his pocket. Otherwise, he was fine. He lectured at Santa Monica University where he was invited as a guest of honor and received the degree of Doctor *Honoris Causa* for his lifetime achievement.

Using a translator and a ghostwriter, he published peer-reviewed articles in the *Journal of Academic Research*. He was praised and decorated for his resilience and fighting spirit by the NAAUP (National Association for the Advancement of Undead People), an institution that catered to survivors of malefic, torture, racism, police brutality, and totalitarian dictatorships.

Mr. Narcisse became a tabloid sensation. He appeared often in vivid colors on the cover of the *National Enquirer* which was selling at the time for three nickels. It's an interesting publication that I consult regularly when I am bored with the reruns of the *Jerry Springer Show*.

With my annual subscription to the *Enquirer*, I get free shipping and digital access to the archives going back to the

Great Depression of 1929. I have no idea why the weekly magazine that is going to be a hundred years old in 2026, was trashed recently as a "scandal-hungry publication." As an avid reader of the genre, I felt personally offended. In this day and age, there is no respect for the elders anymore.

Mr. Narcisse was constantly ambushed by paparazzi who could not get enough of him. They wanted to have his opinion about random topics, world events, and his whereabouts: "Are you familiar with the Voodoo practices of Louisiana? Did you visit the mummies of Egypt? What do you think of the reincarnation of Papa Doc as Baby Doc?"

Somehow, the ingenious Mr. Narcisse who was an underground Casanova managed to find some time for intimacy. With his new flame Angelica, he fathered a couple of children who still live in the upscale section of Miami that is known as Little Haiti.

The Narcisse saga was the inspiration for a movie: *The Serpent and the Rainbow*. In 2010, when Arnold Antonin released another film entitled *Les Amours d'un Zombie*, I felt that Narcisse was very much relevant. He rose from the dead to leave his mark on the screen.

When he passed away from natural causes, in 1994, at the time of the military coup that killed four thousand folks in three years, nobody wanted to believe it. In certain circles, he is still revered and worshipped as an icon. On his tombstone, a diehard fan wrote the following epitaph in Creole: "Sa k bon pa dire" (The good ones don't last.)

Nonetheless, in a recent and memorable issue, the *National Enquirer* reported that Mister Narcisse was seen in full regalia at a resort in the Bahamas, singing in duo with Elvis Presley such classics like: *Are You Lonesome Tonight? Love me Tender,* and *Always on my Mind.*

Of course, the eternal contrarians will clamor they were just lookalikes of Elvis and Narcisse, grotesque caricatures of the originals, a shameful attempt to make a buck on the corpse of long-gone celebrities. *Vive la différence!* Here is the cardinal rule I live by: I don't pay attention to the opinion of the naysayers. They were not there when the event took place. They were not there when the pictures were taken in High Definition. I don't want to hear it. As a matter of fact, I wouldn't be surprised if Mr. Narcisse were to make a third coming to save our souls from the boring diary we call life.

Dr. Bartoli highly benefited from his encounter with

Bonhomme Narcisse. As though he were a human chimney, his revenues were going through the roof.

From chain-smoking cheap packs of Marlboro, he graduated to the thick, flavorful Havanas that say: "I have arrived! I am on top of the world!"

Not every MD had the chance of a lifetime to have such a publicity-driven patient. The wooden gate of the Bartoli's residence in Martissant became a revolving door for reporters (disguised as new patients) who wanted to find out what it felt like to be in Narcisse's presence at the beginning of his second journey on earth.

While taking their vitals, checking their blood sugar, and collecting his consultation fees, he would respond to their nosy questions that challenged the sacredness of professional confidentiality: "As far as I am aware, Mr. Narcisse was my first zombie-patient. However, I cannot exclude the possibility of having had similar cases in the past. Now that I think about it, I have a mental picture of several other patients who could have qualified as such. At the end of the day, aren't we all useful zombies, automates who have been programmed to act and think a certain way? Zombie: isn't it the new normal in this country?"

It was the kind of discourse that could easily make you vanish in Papadopolis. One was under the impression that the good doctor was possessed and was being ultra-vocal.

In the past, he had never missed a patient the way he was missing Narcisse, the most interesting zombie in the world.

"Legally, I am a spirit, I have no age."

Trevor Berbick

"The household cat is really a tiger that has underwent three counselling programs."

Valeriu Butulescu

Urban Cowboy

Outside the borders of the capital lays another country. *Le pays en dehors*. The country outside. The population of the island was divided in two large castes: the peasants and the "capitalists."

Papa Déus used to bring home to Martissant all sorts of birds from the mountains. It was a time so ancient, ducks used to lay giant dinosaurs' eggs. But nobody was having them for breakfast. Why? It took me an eternity to learn the reason. I got the answer when I read the *New York Times* bestseller *The Pros and Cons of Eating Duck Eggs*.

Even though they were lame, baby ducks showed a lot of discipline for their age. They were so cute in their yellow-black uniform, you would say they were girl scouts going to camp. Like children in kindergarten, they followed a straight path on the ground before they learned how to fly.

The ducks became quite famous when French philosopher Jean-Paul Sartre mentioned them in one of his axioms: "One should not take God's children for wild ducks." The quote became a meme among the scribes as though it were the 11th commandment.

On the island, duck tales were quite popular among kiddies. They would narrate stories about Ti Malis, Uncle Bouki, Léo the lion, and all specimens of the animal kingdom. Especially those who spoke the native tongue with a zest of humor.

My baby cousin Ralph could never get enough. He would insist: "Please, tell me another story." He was ticklish. He would giggle endlessly until he got bushed and fell asleep.

Before the advent of television, before the ascension of satellites to the heavens, storytellers were the real stars. The dusk was prime time for the imagination. It was so dark out there, only voices were visible. It was time for stories, time for supper in the front yard: a stick of pineapple-sugarcane, cassava bread with peanut butter, fried pork, crispy plantains, sweet potatoes, and the 5-cent bottle of Coke.

Regardless of the amount of food readily available, our ears hungered for more stories.

Krik! Krak! On a sunny day like today, two gray ticks were chatting on the sidewalk. When Puppy, the vagabond dog stopped by, one of the ticks said: "See you later pal, my bus has arrived." It took seconds for Gracula the tick to find a spot under the fur of Puppy.

In regard to public transportation, the cows of Les Cayes were not as lucky. They had to travel hundreds of miles to the capital on their weary feet. They were escorted by a poor peasant, the well-known *Maroulé*; a pedestrian cowboy who could not afford to ride even a donkey.

The journey towards Papadopolis would last a couple of days under the sun, under the moonlight. The cows were heading to their final destination: the slaughterhouse of Croix-des-Bossales.

Some strange stories were running around town regarding a weeping goat and the cow with the golden tooth. One would think they were humans upgraded into animals. In their teary eyes glared something awkward: a silent condemnation of the world.

At night, in the quarter of Sans-Fil, unsuspecting fellows, drunkards, and fools were ambushed and captured with a rope. Somewhere, somehow, some Frankenstein witch doctor was busy in his lab converting somnambulists and moonlighters into ham, sausages, hot dogs, and tasty animals with horns.

It rubbed salt into the wound. The campaign of terror found a partner in the law of supply and demand of the meat market.

It was a time of high gullibility. Like candies to a child, a part of the human spirit had a lust for legends. In the marketplace, scary stories were accepted at face value. They became bestsellers in the oral literature of folktales.

Then again, when you look at it closely, it makes a lot of sense. Why waste time raising calves when you can change jerks into cows? Especially the haters, your sworn enemies. People who badmouth you for no rhyme or reason. Critics who make you look bad in public. People who pretend not to see you are awesome. People who make you lose sleep and appetite.

It was frightening. Too much to take, too much to swallow. Some grownups made faces while chomping meat. It felt bizarre and unusual like a broccoli sandwich with ketchup.

A strange aftertaste lingered in the mouth. A gut feeling that something was wrong. A taste of blood that was too close, too familiar. The residents of Papadopolis started to question the appearance of every creature. Is a cat a real cat? Is a cow a cow? Are they sincerely who they pretend to be? Is there an afterlife for animals? Will we, someday, reunite with our pets?

It appeared safer to snack on hummingbirds. They were not easy to catch. Some settled for chickens and turkeys they raised themselves. Some did the sign of the cross before eating red meat.

Vegetarian? The word did not exist in the local tongue.

His mission accomplished at the slaughterhouse, the pedestrian cowboy would return home to his village, his own country, the countryside. He had no business hanging out in Papadopolis where he felt like an alien. He was an outsider, a hillbilly, a stranger in his own country. On his birth certificate (when he was lucky to have one), he was classified as "peasant" as opposed to the "citadin", the city dweller who was born with a bottle of sweet, condensed Carnation milk in his mouth.

On his way back to his hamlet, the *Maroulé* would go through Martissant, near the Bata shoe factory, where the smell of rotting leather would remind him of the fate of his unfortunate companions. Alone, he was heading south to his home in Les Cayes.

Diable du sud! Devil of the south. This is how Papa Déus' competitors at domino games used to call him. He got this name from a popular action movie of the early 60s. It was a common practice at the time to assign scary names to the people we respected. Grandma Eugénie who was fierce like a cowboy because she had lost two children to the blue *tontons* received secretly the name of a male actor: Lee Van Cleef. A neighbor who was a great domino player became the terrifying character of Nikolai Gogol: Taras Bulba! His real name was no less than Solomon.

Diable du sud! Yes, Papa Déus was fearless while he crossed the mountains and the hanging gardens of the provinces in his antiquated truck: the Diamond-Reo, factory-made in Ohio, USA.

Papa was a smart cookie. He found a way to attract passengers and keep at bay the evil spirits that caused breakdowns and accidents. The Reo was placed under the protection of the neighborhood patron Saint, the sweet and angelic Bernadette.

On a shiny Sunday morning, before the 10 o'clock mass, the truck was baptized, sprinkled with holy water by the local priest, Père Alexandre. In preparation for the memorable event, it had been thoroughly cleaned and perfumed with basil leaves. The truck was delighted to enter religion, to be admitted among the children of our Savior.

It was a day of joy and celebration in the family. A prelude to my first communion.

Even though it had six legs and a funny nose, the Reo truck was a work of art. It was painted with a garden variety of flowers. You would think the artist was a gifted child. In the naïve tableaux, exotic animals roamed freely, in perfect harmony between prey and predators.

My daddy's truck was agile like a mountain goat. Around that time, being a daredevil, being a skilled truck driver was far from being enough. One had to be a space pilot to defy gravity, to survive the rough surface of nature's skyscrapers.

Every trip was a trek in a no man's land, an adventure in the Grand Canyon. Papa Déus' triumphal return to Martissant was often delayed. I was anxious, scratching my head, chewing what was left of my nails. Did something bad happen like the time when the truck caught fire in the middle of the night?

Papa Déus was the responsible type. He took matters into

his own hands. Our house in Martissant was transformed into a hospital for the victims of the blaze.

By the grace of Sainte Bernadette, nobody died. Serrano, the truck keeper, took things with philosophy. With a smile, he whispered to a plaintive sufferer "If we can survive Papa Doc, we can survive anything, including Hell."

Some passengers were burned beyond recognition. Some developed an allergy to smoking. Some changed race while they healed. To my surprise, they turned out to be whites trying to pass as blacks.

At the age of 6, I learned to accept bad news as a fact of life. Papa Déus was a survivor; the man I looked up to when I raised my eyes. He had seen it all. He shall always overcome.

After each expedition, a visit to the chiropractor would have been a good move. Unfortunately, they were not invented yet. A day at the beach of Mariani, a good massage with Bay Rum, Palma Christi, or castor oil would chase away the muscle memory of pain.

In the narrow roads that lead to the tropical vegetation of the provinces, some trucks were known to be erratic and rebellious. They burned plenty of fuel and broke down at the worst possible time. It was their way to protest against the overload of passengers, the excess of merchandise and screaming animals.

Around that time, traveling at night was highly dangerous, even suicidal. Some counties near the peaks of La Selle and the flatlands of Artibonite were known to be inhabited by secret societies of *loups-garous*. They were territorial and had a huge appetite for fools.

Did they prefer skinny humans to meatier animals? The debate is wide open. In the nightmare republic created by Papa Doc, it was difficult to see the border between facts and fiction. It was a thin and broken line covered with blood and ashes.

It was part of the culture to spread rumors, to tell horrific stories of bizarre encounters with skinless, flying sorcerers on broomsticks. To frighten. To entertain. For the pleasure. To amuse foreigners who had a strong taste for the esoteric. To ensure that children and adults would be on their best behavior.

Contrary to our dog Django who would start to bark aggressively, for no apparent reason, I never had the third eye:

the ability to see the invisible. I never saw anything abnormal, except at night, when the shadows would nag me in my crib.

Then again, who knows what's on the other side of midnight? Why take chances?

As a child of the South Seas, I lived inside a conch shell, far from the world and its turbulence.

I was safe under the shield of Ma Fifine. That's how she raised me, in the incubator. I now live in quarantine as though the virus of Papa Doc is still lurking. I breathe carefully; I wash my mouth and my nose with overproof rum; I touch reality with a pair of gloves.

Recently, I started to hear noises in my apartment of Amity Ville. Am I alone? To my surprise, the dishes had been done during the night. The floor was spotless. A soothing scent of Pine-Sol was floating in the air. A morsel of cassava bread was sitting on the table. It was chatting in Creole with a tasse of coffee.

Was my mama trying to say something to me?

What should I do to escape the past?

"However vivid be one's recollection of the past, any attempt to recall the features of a beloved being shows them to one's vision as through a mist of tears-dim and blurred. Those tears are the tears of the imagination."

Leon Tolstoy

"Happiness is not a big deal; it's just sorrow taking a rest."

Léo Ferré

The Fable of Maître Sauvignon

General Saint-Surin François Manigat was quite a colorful character. Even though he died in exile in Paris at the tender age of 53, his presence was always felt in our neighborhood. The main entrance of the hamlet of Martissant was known as Cité Manigat.

Like a totem pole in a Tahitian village, his sumptuous, abandoned residence remained a monument, a reminder of the times we left behind.

By the time I started to recognize myself in the mirror and learned to say "Ma", another celebrity was emerging in Martissant. He was a musician, the king of the carnival, the creator of *Konpa Dirèk*, a beat that was so infectious, it took over the other isles of the Caribbean.

The name of the musical genius was Nemours Jean-Baptiste.

It felt good to have such an iconic personality in our hood. Imagine John Lennon; imagine the *Soul Makossa* of Manu Dibango; imagine Edith Piaf as your next-door neighbor. You'd be near *La Vie en Rose*.

From a distance, we saw him, like an apparition on his second-floor balcony. He was up there, way above sea-level. You could not pass his house without raising your eyes. For a glimpse. A chance encounter of the second kind.

Nemours didn't have a yacht. He didn't have a car. As a guru, he was way beyond that.

It would have been too mundane for such a mad genius to be seen at the wheels of a Thunderbird or driving a Mustang. He rarely came out of his seigneurial residence. Mostly after the sunset, when he had to perform his latest hits at Djoumbala or Cabane Choucoune, the two nightclubs *par excellence*.

Once in a blue moon, it was a treat to see him walk by, on the rocky street, nonchalant like a commoner, while his song was playing in hi-fi on the radio.

As a child, I had a love affair with Martissant. This is where my umbilical cord was buried. When I had to leave, I put my hood in my luggage.

At JFK, the customs agent was puzzled.

"Do you have anything to declare?"

"I brought Martissant with me. Some coconuts, some

papayas, and a rooster, as souvenirs. That's all."

"Welcome to America!"

Was it the language barrier? I was confused. I thought I was born in America. It took me some time to figure things out. First things first: I needed to climb that damned escalator.

On the island, beyond the mountains are other mountains. From our house on the slope, one could spot on the blue horizon frail wind boats steered by intrepid fishermen. From the distance, they appeared to be tinier than the paper boats we manufactured in class to kill time while Maître Sauvignon was finishing his lesson about the intricacies of the past tense in French. Daydreaming, we were playing hooky inside the classroom.

The conjugation of the verb "être" was going to decide if we were going to be or not to be in the future.

I speak French, therefore I am. It was a gross misdemeanor to speak the wrong language inside the classroom. It was demeaning. Maître Sauvignon would take it personally, as an attack against culture and civilization. "How dare you little rascal? How dare you Dennis the Menace?"

At the little school on the prairie, there was no guillotine; no torture chambers like in the palace of Papa Doc. However, belting was a public affair. To maintain law and order. To repress language code violations.

"Express yourself! Keep a close eye on your tongue! I don't want to hear Creole in my class!"

To speak Creole was to be a second-class citizen. To embrace the language of the former slave. To stick the tongue out. To show poor taste. To spit on the language of the master. Schoolmasters didn't play games with that. They were vigilant like overseers on high heels at a sugarcane plantation.

Within the walls of the school, it was colonial time all over again. The tyranny of the ruling language.

When I discovered *Prayer of a Black Boy*, a poem of Guadeloupean islander Guy Tirolien in which he wrote: "Lord, I don't want to go to their school", I felt vindicated. I was not alone.

Fortunately, things have changed. Have they? I've been too far from my center of gravity to know the truth.

In a candid conversation, Konpè Filo said to me on the

phone: "Here, the more things change, the worst they get." I did not need a degree in catastrophe management to see that by myself.

Maître Sauvignon was a stylish giant. He had a luxuriant mustache between salt and pepper; something decorative and inspiring you could possibly see on vintage pictures of Hugo.

There was something sophisticated and aristocratic about his entire demeanor. The way he walked, the way he spoke, the way he looked at the world from the tower of his head. The floor was his stage and he moved like Paul Robeson in *The Tragedy of King Christophe*. Wherever he went, from one classroom to the next, he left behind a fragrance of *Old Spice*.

He was the kind of guy who could have been in the *Dos Equis* beer commercial as the most interesting man in the world.

His political stance was quite mysterious. At his school, students were required to wear a sky-blue uniform with a Mandarin collar neck. The same style that was in fashion in Popular China under Mao Zedong.

Maître Sauvignon was obsessed with the detail, the particular. He wanted his pupils to look different, to take pride in their alma mater.

Was it just a fashion statement, a quest for the exotic? Students who did not conform to the dress code were sent home to their mama. Tailors and seamstresses of the hood had to redo their homework. They had to fix the collar.

They did that with a sense of urgency. In their book, the word "alteration" meant money in their pocket.

Maître Sauvignon's profile was custom-made for the goons of Papadopolis. He belonged to that class of scholars, agitators of ideas, who used to vanish at night. "The school is closed. Maître Sauvignon is gone for an unknown destination."

That was the fear.

But it did not happen that way. He defied the odds. He played possum. Aside from parents and neighbors, no suspicious visitors.

It took me a while to understand why Papa Déus never allowed me to join the Boy Scouts. Papa Doc wouldn't have any problem describing them as a branch of the Black Panthers or a ramification of the Italian Red Brigades.

Was Maître Sauvignon an underground rebel? Was he on

the hit list? Did he commit in the distant past an original sin, a crime of *lèse-majesté* against Doc almighty? Was he just a paranoid chicken?

He rarely ventured out, even with a mask. He lived in the school in seclusion, as though he were under house arrest, as though the air outside were saturated with a virus. It was a historical event when I saw him once walking down the street with his signature footsteps on the road of incertitude.

Maître Sauvignon was a man of medieval roots. He was well-versed in Latin poetry. It is with delectation that we learned that his patronym was a brand in France. Sauvignon. It came from a vine, the *Vitis vinifera*, an offspring of the Cabernet family.

"*Tu quoque mi fili?*" You too, my son?

I didn't quite understand when he spoke this sentence. I was accused of disturbance in the civic instruction class. Something inside of me said: "If Maître Sauvignon addresses you in Latin, you are in big trouble."

I felt like a tiny cub versus a gladiator in a Roman Colosseum.

I had a reputation for being quiet; except when I was chatting endlessly about the adventures of the lunatics.

Around that time, the American cosmonauts were heading north in the Milky Way. When they arrived at their destination on that moonless night, they got the surprise of their life. Proudly erected in the lunar soil was the Bicolor: the red and black flag of Papa Doc.

It is a state secret that has been heavily guarded. At least, that was the narrative in certain circles of Papadopolis.

Maître Sauvignon was a worshipper of the Greek god Socrates. His elementary school was called: The Pedagogue Institute. No less. Even though he knew the best words, he was very humble. Sometimes, he would turn philosophical with a fancy quotation of the ultimate master: "The only thing I know is I know nothing."

He was a blend of devotion and old-fashioned toughness. Students who put in the effort were handsomely rewarded with generous praises. "A round of applause for Elsie Charpentier who has a bright future ahead of her!"

Elsie always knew the answers. She spoke French like a book. It was frightening. I never figured out her secret. I guess she was studying. Girls are so smart. I felt intimidated. One day, she'll become a shining star.

Aside from her striking mind, she was just beautiful. I still have goosebumps from the time I sat next to her. They have remained on my skin like tattoos. Sometimes I see her silhouette. I swallow her words. They sing to my soul. In my dreams, she appears like the first edition of Rihanna.

Some girls were brave enough to sing in public. They were young actresses in a musical called: Life. They carried a notebook of lyrics and responded to the boys with verses. They recognized themselves in Mireille Mathieu's *Ciao Bambino Sorry*.

The other students who were too shy to talk, the introverted, those who were tongue-tied by the nature of the beast called French, those who had attention deficit disorder, those who were cursed with poor memory knew all too well what to expect from Maître Sauvignon. The belt was their bread and butter.

Their future was bleak, even scary. One day, they'll end up on the isle of Manhattan as human dishwashers. They'll be climbing mountains of plates or burning their manicured nails in the blazes of Burger King. Maître Sauvignon knew all too well how to inspire. He was a distinguished member of the aristocracy of knowledge.

It was a time so ancient that educated islanders, *la crème de la crème* of the intellectual bourgeoisie, truly believed that heaven was near la Seine and hell near the Hudson.

At least one student was immune to pain and verbal whipping. His name was Daniel Mardi. He was quite muscular for his age. I do believe in reincarnation; I am speaking from personal experience. In my flashbacks, I tend to see Daniel as a teenage replica of Mike Tyson. When I saw the boxer on pay-per-view for the first time, I had a strange sensation of *déjà vu*.

Daniel was genetically engineered by his weightlifting dad to be a resilient soul. His flesh was made of steel.

He had complete disregard for the belt. Was it an early sign of Latin machismo? He was the kind of kid García Márquez would have called: *cuerpo de piedra*. Body of stone. In the face of adversity, he stood tall and stoic like an Easter Island statue.

Daniel was a force of nature. He appeared to us like these folks who could walk barefoot on fire, sip Red Devil hot sauce without shedding a tear.

On the other side of the spectrum, Donald Rivière was a hysterical screamer. He would reach high notes of desperation even before the belt connected to his precious skin. "I want to go to my mama!"

What was that? What was he thinking? Was he a bleeder, a hemophiliac? A little bit of bravery young man!

Even though at the time this line of work was reserved for older women, Donald could have made a fortune as a *pleureuse*, a professional screamer at funerals. He was that good. I cannot confirm the news, but I heard he is having a successful career as an opera singer in Italy. A query about Donald in two search engines (Mozilla Firefox and Dogpile) did not bring any results.

It was not unusual around that time to encounter in elementary school students who were older than their teachers. They would come from far away, distant places where schools were still an afterthought. Regardless of their age, Maître Sauvignon would place them where they belonged: in kindergarten.

Around 1:00 in the afternoon, after lunch, they had to take their nap on the mat, like certified kiddies. It was quite a spectacle. Especially when they smiled in their sleep when they snored loud and clear like an asthmatic Reo truck climbing Goat Mountain.

Alex Jean-Philippe was among the giants, the late bloomers. Yet, he was completely comfortable in his skin. The first time he came to class, he gave us a surprised look as though we were a local variety of pygmies, some sort of minuscule actors who just escaped *Honey, I Shrunk the Kids*.

He appeared to us as a questionable character. It took us a few days to break the ice and realize he was indeed a pupil, a man-child, not an inspector of the Board of Ed, not a spy of the Department of Criminal Research.

He was generous towards the miniatures that we were, especially at the end of the semester when he needed help to pass his exams. His wallet was always garnished with crisp currencies of one *piastre* (20 cents) with the effigy of Papa Doc.

They were hard to count, thin, and sharp like razor blades. Alex took pride in the quality of his dough. He said with a straight face that he had a money tree in his backyard. It was the kind of revelation that could have inspired me to become an agronomist.

To ensure his assignments were completed with good faith, Alex the Tall secured for us a line of credit at the nearby bakery and pastry store. We would feast on biscuits, jelly, and zesty lemonade. All we can eat and then some more. We also satisfied our sweet tooth on *tito*, a multicolored candy. Alex would pay the tab without scratching his head. It was money well spent. He moved up in grade every year. At the graduation ceremony for primary school, Alex nailed it with just a few words: "If you think education is expensive, try ignorance."

We never applied for a patent, but we were the true inventors of the ATM. We made constant withdrawals from the pocket of our benefactor. Even though we were often mean to him, he always treated us like a debonair papa.

His mere presence at the school was cinematic. Because he was 24, Alex had among us the status of a senior citizen. Because he came from another hood, two miles away from Martissant, he had diplomatic immunity.

It was a time on the island when all crimes were excused, except bad diction and spelling mistakes. Yet, Alex had no problem writing "L'Afrance" instead of "La France." The "e" in "Alex" was often facing the wrong direction. He was a rebel with a cause: he was fighting the dictatorship of the French dictionary.

Alex was freely allowed to have senior moments. He would forget the two main characters in La Fontaine's classic *The Wolf and the Lamb*. He never paid his dues to the belt.

Mr. Alex Jean-Philippe was the elite member of a small caste: the untouchables. He was free to smoke in the school-yard. It was his only vice. Except for the occasional Heineken, we never saw him drinking on the break.

We resented his privileges. We were relentless in creating new, silly nicknames for him. Alex was the bigger man. He always took the higher road. He would laugh at us and at himself too. He never challenged any of us to a fistfight. He never challenged any of us to a duel with a sword or a pistol. We got away with everything: the not so good, the bad, the ugly, the chewing gum, and the Crazy Glue we put on his seat.

Despite the autocratic régime of the schoolmasters, going to a private institution in our hood was fun. Especially with the presence of Elsie the genius, Donald the whiner, Daniel the martyr, and Alex our horn of plenty.

Tuition was dirt cheap. However, Maître Sauvignon never

174

saw the color of our money. My godfather Papa Déus, an entrepreneur at heart, would pay him with construction materials: concrete blocks, cement, and broken rocks.

Money is overrated and sometimes dirty. Islanders would freely trade services. Just like the Taïnos of pre-colonial times; the times of Cacique Caonabo and Queen Anacaona.

Like a teenage boy on testosterone, our school was growing. It was expanding with the reputation of Maître Sauvignon as a good pedagogue and my daddy's construction supplies. To me, the school's new walls looked familiar. I had seen them before in a more primitive form.

When we stopped peeing in bed, something else started to flow: a competitive juice. We made fun of students who went to Maître Baroulette's institution. "Maître Sauvignon is the man. Why would your parents put you in that smelly school near the fish market?"

We were reckless, unfiltered kids. To us, the real abusers were the parents who could not see that Maître Sauvignon's school was the smart, logical choice.

Before the new constructions emerged from the ground,

some classes were conducted in the Methodist church across the street. This was done with the approval of Pastor Emmanuel Jeanty who famously said to Maître Sauvignon: "Let the little children come unto me."

As a child, my views of the school would vary according to the last time I was punished. School was strict and Darwinian. Survival of the brainiac. Ma Fifine had to feed me a great deal of cow's brain to increase my IQ to a reasonable scale.

It was a world where two tribes were engaged in a fierce battle: the *timouns* (the little ones) and the *granmouns* (the parents and their allies, the teachers). They were armed with their words and their whips. It was not okay for *timouns* to look *granmouns* in the eyes. A child should not play with his shadow. It was not okay to stick around when *granmouns* were talking among themselves. Each child had an invisible tablet in which was written the second commandment: "Honour thy mommy and thy daddy."

In their infinite wisdom, the *granmouns* saw the whip as a good therapy. For cases of bad behavior, small children were treated with the *martinet*, made with soft, tender leather. Later in life, they would graduate to the *rigoise*, made with rough cow's skin.

176

Things were not as bad as it sounds. Parents would reassure us with the most affectionate words: "I am going to punish you because I have your well-being at heart."

I suppose that Ma Fifine and Papa Déus were too soft on me. I never reached the mountaintop of success where my classmates are sitting today. I wouldn't be surprised if one of them were to win the next elections or to launch a *coup d'état*. Whichever comes first, I'll be willing to accept any job. Even a diplomatic position in the city of Whynot (North Carolina) or the town of Needmore (in Texas.)

We didn't go to school for the teachers; we went for our classmates. We built alliances and complicity with them. Everything was a reason for laughter, even our sorrow. That's how we coped with the trials and tribulations of being a *timoun*. We were minuscule characters among the giants who ruled "the earth that is blue like an orange."

In the soft, primitive drive of our brain, we had to save gigabits of information about the world: kings and queens, Beauty and the Beast, Cinderella and the four knights, Ali Baba and the forty thieves. We never talked about T-Rex. He wasn't born yet in the national consciousness. In fact, we had our own version. He lived in the Palace.

We were more familiar with T-Rex's little cousins: the flamboyant chameleon and the silver-gray *mabouya* who walked with the allure and self-confidence of a diva.

I'll always remember that lazy afternoon when a green anole looked at me with a strange attitude. She shook her head as though she was feeling sorry for me. What was wrong with me? I felt inadequate. I turned green with envy. Was I, in her eyes, a freak of nature?

Based on their ancestry, I wonder if these fellas don't harbor in their hearts a complex of superiority.

As students in primary school, we became miniature experts in history and geography. The caves of Lascaux, the mountains of Kilimanjaro, the rivers of France revealed to us their deepest secrets. We suffered with Joan of Arc when she was burned by the British on May 30th, 1431.

Fortunately, we had short memory. The day after we found solace on a virtual trip to South America.

"What's the capital of Colombia?"

"Bogota!"

The class erupted in laughter because in the local tongue "bogota" means bad car.

French was a challenge because at the end of the day we are Creoles. In a surge of patriotism, Maître Sauvignon expected us to write better than the natives of France. To him, French was a trophy we had won on the battlefield; we had to display it everywhere to teach a lesson to the colonizers.

We, the People of the Children's Republic of Zamunda, couldn't care less about language status and rivalry. We knew the best-kept secret. French itself is creolized Latin.

Our classmate Elsie who spent the summer with her parents in Florida introduced us to the joys and simplicity of the English language.

She came back in September with her luggage full of new, multicolored words.

She was the one, the first, who taught us how to say "black" and "white."

"I did not think about the color of my skin. Not any more than I would have bothered to wonder why the sand was white or the sky was blue."

Sydney Poitier

"I've had the misfortune of beginning a book with the word "I" and immediately it was thought that instead of attempting to discover general laws, I was analyzing myself in the individual and detestable sense of the word."

Marcel Proust

The Ocean Next Door

Around that time Martissant had not yet become the notorious shantytown that it is today. It was a rustic fishing village where one could hear with delight the hilarious moans of Brutus, the unshaven goat of Mister Massou; without forgetting the triumphant hee-haw of Aliboron, the donkey of Madame Chéry.

When they were in the zone, in a state of grace, in perfect harmony, they would deliver an award-winning performance.

Because of the singularity of their alto voices, these quadrupeds were part of a caste system, a nobility. They were well integrated into the community as two iconic characters.

It was a time of horse-drawn hearse. A time when donkeys were still used as utility vehicles. They were green, efficient, four-wheel-drive pickup trucks that carried heavy loads of plantains, coconuts, and charcoal to the marketplace. Most of the time, they were on autopilot. They had a built-in GPS. Their feet knew by heart the direction they were heading to.

With his aristocratic demeanor, Aliboron, the donkey of Madame Chéry, never suffered the indignity of heavy lifting.

Yet, he was not a freeloader. He worked as a consultant for personal tragedies and weather forecasts. He had the mysterious ability to predict floods, thunderstorms, and hurricanes. He agreed with Albert Camus when he said: "Disasters always come out of the blue."

The sea was calm. The sky a shade of baby blue. It was a beautiful day, just like in Mister Rogers' Neighborhood. But Aliboron knew for a fact that later the angry clouds were going to swell. A perfect storm was brewing behind the scenes. It was going to rain cats and dogs.

Once again, Aliboron had proven himself. He was known to be more accurate than Captain Meteo, the weatherman of Télé Doc.

Madame Chéry, the Voodoo priestess, was very devoted to her donkey. To her, he was a guru, a god figure. She, herself was a mysterious mulatta; the kind of *femme fatale* you'd encounter any day at the Blue Bayou in Louisiana.

She became lyrical whenever Aliboron's name was mentioned. My donkey this, my donkey that. Oh my gosh! One would say that she was possessed, intoxicated by the aura of the animal. Her zeal was bordering a cult of personality.

On the other side of the spectrum, Brutus, the bearded goat, was a poster boy for the hippie generation of the '60s. He took part in the sexual revolution with his discovery of the horny goat weed, a garden variety of the blue candy. Brutus would roam the neighborhood in search of the best quality grass. When he was in the mood, he would spend his leisure time watching the patriarch Magny Manigat smoking his pipe. The smile upon his face, the glimmer in his eyes clearly indicated that he would ask for his share if he had the gift of speech.

On behalf of all the goats of Martissant, Brutus received the honorific title of Doctor of Pharmacy. The ceremony took place on a Friday morning at the vocational school Saint-Surin François Manigat. The degree was awarded in recognition of the fact that Brutus' distinguished feces looked like medicinal pills.

In the Jungle Book of the island, the cows were mostly known as *pâtissiers* (pastry cooks) because their stools took the shape of artistically decorated chocolate cakes. It was pure delight for the battalions of flees and critters constantly engaged in deadly battles like the acrobatic aircraft of World War II.

It was a bad time to be a dog. In the animal kingdom, dogs

didn't receive much reverence. They were bottom feeders. Of course, they were baptized with fancy, heroic names: Cybele, Hercules, Apollo, Diane, Django. That was it. According to popular wisdom: *Se gwo non ki tye ti chen* (It's the big name that kills the little dog).

A friend of mine who is really smart said in a book that the problematic relationship started centuries ago, in colonial times when dogs were used to chase the maroons, the runaway slaves fleeing the inferno of the plantation.

In 1974, when heavyweight champion George Foreman exited the plane in Zaïre, Africa, with his two German shepherds, it was a big *faux pas*. He made a big doo-doo. He had traveled thousands of miles on a private jet to fight Muhammad Ali. It was supposed to be easy as a walk in the aisle. But he appeared instantly to the locals as a villain because of his two menacing dogs. The proud Zaïrois were pissed at him. Foreman lost the fight in the court of public opinion before he went down and out in the 8th round. He was so devastated, he started to knock on open doors and to fight the Devil as a street preacher.

The world is indeed a strange place where cultural sensitivity doesn't always flourish. Too often, collective memory dictates the present.

In Papadopolis, at Anson Electronics Store, a cute Chihuahua played the role of an alarm system. Big dogs were used as round-the-clock security guards. They never got a vacation. Most of the time, they received poor quality food.

It was conveniently assumed that dogs' palates were not sophisticated enough to appreciate the nuances of Creole cuisine. They were thought to prefer raw bones and fatty tissues to exquisite, caramelized meat. On their menu was the predictable milled corn mixed with tiny bits of smoked herring or fish heads with glaring eyes.

Dogs' life on the island was far from being a gala dinner.

They were not invited to attend the Mardi Gras or the dog race competition at the Champ de Mars. They did not go to the park or the beach. They never went to see a pediatrician, a gynecologist, a urologist, or a massage therapist. They were not allowed to ride a horse or to stick their nose out of the family car. They were not allowed inside the house to sleep in a cushy bed or to watch a favorite TV show. They had to fend for themselves. The dogs who lived near a restaurant often did the sign of the cross. They were blessed.

Because one cannot eat fabrics, the dogs that belong to tailors had a reputation for being blue collars; in other words: starving proletarians. In the French society of the 18th century, they would have been classified as *sans-culottes*, members of the Third Estate.

The dogs that belong to butchers and bakers were members of the upper-class, the cream of the crop of the dog bourgeoisie. They were dandies and *flâneurs* living the high life in a nirvana of croissant, butter, and meat.

Bon chen pa janm jwenn bon zo. Good dogs never find good bones. The philanthropic idea of feeding a grown dog was alien to many islanders. They expected their dogs to be self-sufficient, responsible adults like everybody else. Since they have four feet, they could go in four different directions to find their food.

The idea of buying rat flavored cat food never occurred to anyone. Cats were used as pest control to keep at bay unwelcomed rats. Actually, some big rats came from the sea. They abandoned the sinking boats and swam to the mainland. More than ordinary rodents, they were bullies; they frightened the local cats and ran after them.

Despite the neglect towards canines and felines, the islanders were deep down compassionate people. They carried their heart in the palm of their hands. Generosity and selflessness were served daily on a silver platter. Neighbors were extended family. No sacrifice was too great to serve and protect.

It was a time so ancient that windows and doors were kept open all day long. When my family moved to a new house in Pétion-Ville, the doors were not installed yet. Burglars were low-key. They had good manners. They were so nice and civilized, they only came at night. They tried their best not to step on and disturb anybody sleeping on the floor.

When our grocery store was attacked in the middle of the night, our neighbor Vierge did not hesitate a moment. When she heard Milord desperately calling (*anmwe!*) for help, she thought at first she was having a nightmare. When she rubbed her eyes and realized that someone was in danger, she turned into Superwoman.

While her husband Boss Antoine, the shoemaker, was debating, agonizing over the danger of getting off on the wrong foot, she got out of the house, armed with a broomstick.

It was dark out there, but the two scoundrels clearly understood that Voisine Vierge did not play games with burglars. They ran away like rabbits who had seen the double-barreled shotgun of a sharpshooter.

After that incident, we decided to acquire the service of our dog Django. After the sunset, he had zero tolerance for strangers. It did not matter to him if they were pedestrians or airborne creatures.

During the day, he would chase the rare passing cars with a vengeance. Aside from minor psychological disorders, Django was sweet like a sentimental tiger. He was agreeable, certainly more humane than the men in blue.

On the native island, a very long time ago, when I was a boy and liked to play with matches, cats were treated like poor relatives. They were the usual suspects if anything important (like a piece of meat or a can of milk) had vanished from the kitchen.

They earned a living by going on the hunt for lizards and rodents in the dense foliage and the wilderness that surrounded the house. They put their feet on mute and camouflaged perfectly to beat the gecko at its own game.

Without consideration for the dignity of the animal, corrupt politicians, kleptomaniac public servants have been called "cats" in this country. Even recently, a Head of State mostly known for his sticky fingers and retractable claws received the nickname of Sweet Mimi. This was denounced vigorously as character assassination by the Society for the Protection of Animal Rights. In effect, until then, "mimi" was a term of endearment reserved to cats.

On the island, rumor has it that domino players and heavy rum drinkers had a craving for the tasty flesh of cats. Despite the long and arduous research in the field, no one was able to establish that fact beyond a reasonable doubt.

It was probably part of the urban legend. A campaign of denigration against these valuable players who won, in 1968, the Domino World Cup in Venezuela.

As a teenager, I was madly in love with Martissant. This is where I had my first date in the courtyard of Sainte Bernadette. This is where Yolande kissed me as though she were tired of the waiting game. She was the one who opened for me the gates of heaven. We had good chemistry. The rest was biology.

I never thought I'd be leaving one day. When I traveled to the States, I went to Brooklyn College to please my dad. He said: "Son, I want to have your graduation pictures on the walls of the living-room." He was serious about that.

I did it for my Papa. I was forced to take zoology (among other random courses like astrology, alchemy, and computer programming.) It was do or die with the core classes.

Zoology 101 brought back nostalgic memories of Django. I was surprised to learn that humans and dogs share 84% of their DNA. Doctor Gaspard, our beloved professor, revealed that we are closer to the cats: 90% of shared heritage. Meow, meow, meow.

The zoology class allowed me to have a better understanding of myself. I learned how to read my own emotions and body language.

Now I know why I am mercurial like an Egyptian cat. Now I know why, after all these years, I greet my Muse with the same excitement.

Happy like a dog with a wagging tail.

"If you think dogs can't count, try putting three dog biscuits in your pocket and then give him two of them."

Phil Pastoret

"One of the saddest sentences I know is "I wish I had asked my mother."

William Zinsser

Martissant of my Dreams

No man forgets where his treasure is buried. I shall return one day to kiss the ground that witnessed my childhood.

Around that time, Martissant was a poor man's Côte d'Azur. A vague, fuzzy picture of the past. After the Belle Époque of the late 40s, it was going down the drain; washed away to the ocean with the soil of the mountains. Aliboron, the donkey, was not yet born to predict the thunderstorm.

Yet, I loved Martissant like a baby loves his Ma. It is my motherland. I desperately search for her warmth in my dreams.

Looking for love? Welcome to the southwest of Martissant. No yacht? No problem. With paper and cardboard, I will build you a boat and call you captain. Feel free to adopt Martissant as your port of call.

No private jet? No problem. For one penny you will buy a balloon at Ma Fifine's grocery store.

With a few more cents, you'll be good to go. Good to fly your own kite.

Because men don't live on bread alone, the main boulevard

was peppered with eateries, nightclubs, and bordellos prudishly called *cafés*. Martissant 7 was the beginning of the red-light district that extended to the beaches of Mariani until you reach the estate of a chubby madam who wore her headdress like a queen.

She was a legendary maritime beauty. You would not dare to take her for someone else. Her majesty was none other than Charité Désir: the notorious Gwo Manman.

She ruled over an open-air brothel comparable to the size of a drive-in movie theater. For the grand sum of a dollar, naturists, voyeurs, and exhibitionists were allowed to fulfill their fantasies in the privacy of the mangrove. Because of the wild nature of the vegetation and the battalions of adventurers who were attracted to it, the place received the surname of Vietnam.

Gwo Manman was a *cordon bleu*, the best cook of Mariani 69. Aside from the luscious salty fish, the oily oyster, and the conch on fire, her specialty was *Bega*, a juicy stew of bull's testicles.

Naturally loaded with testosterone, the sought-after mishmash did wonders for dead men walking; those who were past their prime, those who were paralyzed by performance anxiety, those who were cursed with a soft joystick, those who were afflicted with premature evacuation.

It was a time when the local studs had a big craving for Dominican señoritas. The honey-colored Barbies who graduated summa cum laude in the streets of Boca Chica and Santo Domingo were now coming to Papadopolis to sell their virtue for a few more dollars.

Most of the clubs of the south beaches had Hispanic names: Miramar, Brisa del Mar, Casa Blanca, la Ganga. For the price of a pass, one could attend a college-level Spanish class by the bay, at the bar, in the comfort of a squeaky bed with sweaty sheets, or dried semen.

These clubs were cheap paradises of carnal pleasure; creative G-spots where venerable poets wrote their seminal works on olive skin tissues.

It was a neutral playground; one of the rare places where *tontons macoutes* and leftist intellectuals could engage in the Cold War. A war of low intensity in the fraternal quest for exotic adventures. To be at Casa Blanca was to be at a foreign embassy with the diplomatic immunity that comes with it.

The *cafés* were educational institutions where eligible bachelors, very married men, 40-year-old virgins, and medical students could study among other things the anatomy of the female species, the Kama Sutra, Salsa, Lambada, and Spanish for Playboys.

It was a stiff competition for the *bon chic bon genre* atmosphere of the Lope de Vega Institute where standard Spanish was taught by Doctor Lamothe, the former ambassador of El Salvador.

Despite the climate of decadence in the nearby nightclubs, the kiddies of Martissant were able to maintain their innocence in the cocoon of their family. Every Sunday, they received Holy Communion at the 4 o'clock mass.

Nonetheless, it was not unusual to see a heated soccer match going on at the same time in the yard of Sainte Bernadette. Feeling guilty, I'd go inside to put spare change in the offering basket. I was relieved. I had paid my way out. I was a good Catholic boy.

Every little shack in Martissant was a castle of pride. Every little child carried the banner of his family name. It had to stay pristine, unblemished until they grew a bone or a flower.

At Ciné Sénégal, pubescent girls and boys, Lolitas, teenage Romeos, and Juliettes, were free to watch adult movies. For commercial purposes, discrimination against children was strictly prohibited. The theater was not too far from the church of Sainte Bernadette. The proximity between the two reflected sometimes in the movies' titles: *The Devil in Miss Jones*, *Sister Emmanuelle*, *Semen Demon*.

For the business owners, one thing was clear: money has no smell.

On the edge of the street, at the store of Mrs. Gambetta, kiddies were allowed to buy matches, combustible kerosene, 100 proof liquors, and cigarettes for parents and neighbors. It was a time when kiddies were presumed innocent. Like the Greek philosophers, they had strong ethical values.

When kiddies were looking for bargains, they would go further down the street, by the railroad track, to the Bazaar of a fierce old lady. She was known under the moniker of Tigranmoun.

It is safe to assume she was a good grandma to her family.

In public, she harbored a mask of severity. Her mouth was sharp like a double-edged dagger. She was the kind of strange character that children, rumormongers, and haters easily called *loup-garou*. Perhaps it was her way to keep in check annoying solicitors and beggars who navigated near the church.

It was a time when twins were seen as evil. The fact that Tigranmoun's daughter had triplets with a henchman of Papa Doc made the situation even more dramatic. They inspired fear in the soul of the customers.

From the ashes of the past, a new generation has emerged. They are children of Father Time. Nowadays, the grandson of Tigranmoun is a close acolyte of the grandson of Papa Doc. They get along well when they are not fighting.

While sipping a Bloody Mary, they talk about the need to restore law and order in Papadopolis.

In the nostalgic time machine, they often travel back to Martissant circa 63.

In literary circles, they are known as the *enfants malades* of Papa Doc.

"There was so much sentimental restructuring in the neighborhood that we were in a daze, people kept falling in and out of love, and when they left the Saturday night parties the couple weren't always the same as when they came in."

Mario Vargas Llosa

"It is not by food that we survive but by the gaze of others."

Maud Ellmann

The Original Sin

At the Basilica of Sainte Bernadette, Father Alexandre has a grin on his face. His sermon for the Sunday mass is ready. He has a hot topic: Adulthood and Adultery.

You can't go wrong with that.

In the parish of the poor, the good Pastor heard so many wild stories. You would think you were in the heart of the Middle Ages when Chaucer was writing *The Canterbury Tales.*

Despite the sacrifices, the burnings, the Inquisition, it doesn't seem that humanity has progressed very much in the path of sanctity. *Au contraire.*

If he were alive today, Père Alexandre would get bored reading *50 Shades of Gray*. He would think it was written by a choir girl.

With pen and paper, with a magnetic tape recorder, Père Alexandre could have won the Nobel Prize in Erotica.

Some fellas went to church as a cover-up. Some saw Sainte Bernadette as a service station. They went in there for a tune-up of the soul. To wash away the sins they enjoy committing.

The usual suspects adored Father Alexandre. He had a reset button. He was so understanding of romantic infractions, you would think he'd been himself a Casanova in his previous life.

It's Saturday morning. Almost 10. Time for the Reverend to baptize the illegitimates. Those papaless infants born outside of marriage. In the future, they will not be able to become priests. From the magic moment of conception, they were disqualified.

Saturday morning. It's a discreet ceremony. A furtive entrance in the back door. Sunday is reserved for the legitimates. Those lucky sons of a gun who are born according to the Scriptures, in the sweet and sacred bonds of holy matrimony.

Saturday morning. Time for confessions. Time to purge the parishioners of all their deeds.

It was so convenient to sin and ask for forgiveness. It sounded like an ad for a bordello: Sin now, pray later.

Despite the bad rap, some sins are good, pleasurable stuff. Especially at night, in our dreams. When there are no limits to our heart desires. When there is no risk. When the bugs are asleep.

Last night I sinned with Rose, a beauty I knew a long time ago. We had a close encounter at the fountain of youth of Martissant. I saw myself kissing her hand, bowing to her charms, looking at her the wrong way, with concupiscence.

Back then, in the cell of the confessional, I didn't have much to disclose to Père Alexandre, except for some cute peccadillos.

"Father, I kissed a girl and I liked it."

"No, you did not! You're too shy to do such a thing."

"Lying to you would be another sin, Father."

"Son, I forgive you, just in case."

The great sinners were obviously the adults, the *granmouns*. They were pretty good at it. Some even knew which numbers to play when they had adventures in their dreams. It was a win-win situation.

Some would push things too far. They would request forgiveness in advance for the sins they intended to commit in the upcoming days. Especially on Saturday nights when they were more likely to succumb to the devil within.

Some were shameless in the confessional. They would spill

their guts. They took pleasure in bashing themselves. They would say the craziest things. The kind of stuff you would wrongly attribute to Al Pacino: "I asked God for a bike, but I know God doesn't work that way. So, I stole a bike and asked for forgiveness."

Among the interesting characters of the hood, we had Koukou, the thief with protruding eyeballs. He was otherwise a good Christian. He was very detailed in reporting his sins to the priest. It was a laundry list of things and beasts that had vanished or were about to vanish: "Father, I stole two goats. Can you forgive me for four?"

To his credit, he never tried anything funny with Aliboron, the donkey of the Voodoo priestess.

Father Alexandre could have written an interesting memoir. Unfortunately, the juicy stories he heard will remain classified in the basement of the Vatican.

From the stairs of Sainte Bernadette, one could see the Caribbean in its sheer majesty. To go to the beach, we had to cross the railroad of the sugar train and go through the Sinclair gas station whose logo was a brontosaurus.

According to the older kids of the hood who, among other

206

things, were experts in marine biology, the scientific name of this particular creature was *chien de mer* (dog of the sea). It could float in the ocean and grab whatever its heart desires.

Around that time, Steven Spielberg was a teenager living in Arizona. He had not introduced the world to the colossal monsters of Jurassic Park. Our mental universe was populated by other creatures as diverse as the mermaid, the shark, the unicorn, the cyclops, the centaur, the sphinx, the dragonfly, Papa Doc, and his bogeymen.

To us, kiddies, innocent souls trapped in the fog of mystery, it was crystal clear that the brontosaurus, this Papa Dog of the sea, had in its belly enough room to accommodate a boatload of travelers.

The masterpiece painting of the brontosaurus on the wall of the Sinclair gas station was adding to the traumatic imagery of the shark.

The most terrifying cop of the neighborhood was proud of his nickname of "*Zo requin*" (shark bone.) Kiddies and vagabonds avoided him like the plague. He never practiced the great commandment that says: "Love thy neighbor as thyself."

"I am the other."

Gérard de Nerval

"They said some people somewhere in that world beyond the horizon had made something called a car that would run faster than a horse which was the fastest thing I knew of. Having never seen a car, I wondered how on earth they managed to make such a thing. And shoes. How about people who had shoes and wore them all the time? Not just on Sundays."

Sidney Poitier

Shiny Shoes and Other Gadgets

Do you like alligator shoes? They look nice. Just don't wear them near the river. Revenge is a dish that's eaten cold.

It was a time when children's toes were blind and hemophiliac. They were magnets for thorns, barbed wire, volcanic rocks, and broken glasses.

Yet, the little boy didn't want to mistreat the tennis shoes he saved for special occasions: the first communions and the Te Deum he attended with his mama. He kept his shoes in a safe, rectangular box.

It was a time of chivalry and sacrifices. People cared more about the well-being of their shoes than the safety of their feet. To many islanders, shoes were jewelry.

Shoes were showered with attention and kept at low mileage. They spoke volumes about status. Show me your shoes and I'll tell you where you stand on the social ladder.

The shoemakers set up shop across the street from General Hospital. It was as though the sick and the dying needed good shoes for admission into Heaven.

In the sandy streets of Papadopolis, shoe shiners were everywhere. Like judges, they carried a handbell. That's how they advertised their services. They were essential workers who gave us a healthy dose of self-esteem. They were appreciated for their ability to make us shine in public.

It was a time when the distance between a "yes" and a "no", between a kiss and a miss, was a nice pair of shoes. Nice shoes are the ancestors of flashy cars.

Much later, the illustrious shoe shiners became Senators and House Representatives. They were better suited for the higher positions. They wore a black linen hat and a 3-piece costume.

They did excellent among their peers, the newly elected legislators: the musicians.

Senator Delva, previously known as a shirtless singer, appeared on TV with his Louis Vuitton $2000 yellow boots. He had arrived.

He became a target for the haters, the envious, and the caricaturists. It really sucks when you can't wear your costly shoes and let them speak for you.

At the dawn of the 20th century, around the time the island

was celebrating a hundred years of solitude, Ulyssia the mom of the future great dictator was seen regularly working behind the counter of a bakery shop without any shoes.

Around that time, naked feet were not seen as indecent exposure. In a way, it was *à la mode*, in fashion among many. To the best of my recollection, no one in the neighborhood was ever accused of being a foot fetishist.

This privileged condition was reserved for shoe salesmen and decadent foreigners.

Whether or not Ulyssia had a pair of shoes at home will remain unsolved mystery, a subject of endless speculations among unauthorized biographers, novelists, historians, and paparazzi.

On New Year's Day, some brave fellows participated in the greasy pole competition. They were barefoot. They wanted to change that. They wanted to capture the grand prize. A new pair of shoes.

According to Gabo, literature is like the greasy pole. It's hard to stick words together. To defy gravity. To reach the altitude of Baudelaire's albatross. To reach the ecstatic moment of being on top of the words.

Colombian writer García Márquez, a native of the Caribbean coast of South America, confessed in his memoirs that as a young man he participated in a poetry contest. The first prize? A new pair of shoes.

It was the kind of incentive that could have inspired anyone to become an overnight sensation: a Maya Angelou or a Victor Hugo.

Surprisingly, Márquez found a way to lose the contest. His name was not listed among the top 100. He took it well. He was never on a suicidal watch. Márquez was more storyteller than poet.

Did someone say: only poets are true writers? Márquez found his groove later, after a long period of soul searching in the rain forests of tears and frustration.

Márquez, the magical creator of Latin America, the one who put the continent on the map, acknowledged that his spelling was terrible. Without the diligence of his editors, he would have been a bum; or something even worse: a lawyer.

As readers, we have the same privileges as the priests. We

get to hear some strange confessions. They come from the most sinister characters: the writers.

On the heels of success, García Márquez continued to beat the streets of Macondo with his iconic sandals. One day in December, while it was warm in Colombia and bitter cold in Northern Europe, he woke up in Sweden. At the precise moment he was trimming his nose hair, he realized that the man in the mirror was about to receive the Nobel Prize in Literature.

His sandals that survived his departure to the land of no return are exhibited today at the museum of Aracataca. They are a special attraction for aspiring writers who go on a pilgrimage to the House Museum, the Mecca of imagination.

While he was around, the Prez for Life never allowed anyone to mention the name of his shoeless mama. It was a crime of *lèse-majesté* to broadcast the fact she was finally assigned to a mental institution.

It was easy for haters, enemies of the State, to connect unrelated things; to link the madness of the mom to the insanity of the son who became Papa Doc.

To avoid controversy, the Supreme Leader never inaugurated any monument in the honor of his mom Ulyssia the way he did so many times for himself, his wife Simone, his dad Duval, and his beloved son Claudius-19.

What's all the fuss about anyway? Walking barefoot feels so much more natural. If you were to believe my personal search engine, you would agree that it has 10 health benefits. Isn't it the way we were born in the first place? Isn't the way we made our first steps? If Mother Nature intended us to wear shoes, she would have provided a pair in the womb.

I was great at soccer when I was playing barefoot. I thought I had a future as a god of the stadium. When I joined a team, they forced me to wear these shoes with the protruding soccer cleats. My career was over. I was so frustrated; I couldn't even score with my head.

In the countryside of the island, in the climate of naturalism and contempt for shoes, the sole of the inhabitants evolved to adapt to the rugged terrain. Doctor Darwin would have called this groundbreaking phenomenon: survival of the feet.

In the plains, in the mountains, the fleshy sole, the Achilles heel grew a layer of safety, a thick cover, something rough like the skin of the alligator, strong like the shell of the turtle. The islanders were walking on clouds. Their feet became resilient to the assaults of thunders, rusty nails, and razor-sharp rocks.

For the pleasure of showing off, some fellas walked over a bed of hot coals without feeling a thing, without shedding a tear. They were said to be *kanzo*: immune to pain, immune to the sting of fire.

On the slopes of the mountains of Furcy, barefooted beauties, barely out of their teenage years, on their way to Pétion-Ville with a basket of fresh vegetables over their head, developed the reputation of having the most attractive gait in the Caribbean.

It was poetry in motion, the equivalent of a catwalk at the fanciest modeling show in Milan. They were immortalized in a hit song of the band Skah Shah. The tune was so popular, it made some waves and traveled from isle to isle throughout the Sea of the Antilles.

Once upon an island where elegance was king, bodacious like the *Boat Song* of Harry Belafonte. You would say that the islanders had their heads over the moon. Some folks walked with their fine Italian shoes on their hands or hung around their neck. They did that when it rained, when the sea visited the land, when the roads were wet and salty like codfish.

In Petit-Goâve, the dream of a little boy with the tennis shoes was to become an illustrious calligrapher, to draw with a feather some beautiful arabesques, just like the *vèvè* he had seen at the Voodoo temple.

He was living with his grandma who made the best coffee in town. Not the brown, watery type we have here. Something strong and potent; something awakening like the crow of the rooster, something dark like Chinese ink, pitch-black like the fur of the panther.

For many islanders, a hot mug of coffee was breakfast. They had never heard of the McDonald's super-duper deluxe with hotcakes, scrambled eggs, sausages, hash browns, biscuits, and orange juice. To them, coffee was a full meal with all the nutrients necessary to tackle the trials and tribulations of the day.

Respectfully, they would let fall to the ground the three ritual drops, to honor those they don't see, those only the dogs with their third eye can see: the ancestors who left them that mountainous morsel of land.

A piece of land where one could be poor but happy to be home.

"As a child, I thought a balanced diet was bread and tea, a solid and a liquid."

Frank McCourt

"If it weren't for electricity, we'd all be watching television by candlelight."

George Gobel

The Colors of Life

Under the weight of autocracy, the roads that lead to a better tomorrow were falling apart. Some fellows fell into open gutters. They disappeared forever. They were listening to Radio Vonvon, the AM station of the underground opposition.

When black and white television appeared on the island, kiddies were very excited. They saw a bright future in the tube. In the hood, in the schoolyards, it was a hot topic. Those who were blessed with a 13-inch would brag about it.

They would broadcast to their captive audience the movies they had seen recently. To the plot, they added salt, pepper, and all the fruits of their imagination. They were good at screenplay. They were great impersonators. They could have made a killing in the Westerns of Hollywood.

The cable package from Télé Ayiti was irresistible. The door-to-door salesman had a no-nonsense approach, a captivating pitch: "I am going to make you an offer that you cannot refuse; no fat, no fillers, no confusing lineup of junk: just one channel!"

No TV? No problem. He was the kind of guy who could

have sold you the Eiffel Tower or a luxurious apartment under the Brooklyn Bridge. He made it sound like the opportunity of a lifetime.

Kiddies would watch TV in the morning even though the broadcast was starting in the afternoon. They were mesmerized, captivated by the sleeping beauty: the blank screen.

Before the show began at 16:00, military time, they stood up to salute the ceremonious execution of the national anthem:

"For the flag,

For the homeland,

To die is nice,

To die is beautiful…"

Every day, at the same time, they felt the goosebumps, the flow of adrenaline activated by an early case of patriotism. It was going to stay in their blood until the day they die.

As a perk, Papa Doc would appear from time to time. To say hello to his children. To confirm that, despite the rumors being spread by the SOBs, he was alive and kicking. "I am an immaterial being. I am the incarnation of the flag; I am black, I am red."

He was born an old man. In his late twenties, they started to call him Papa Doc. To those who were listening, he said: "I have never been afraid of anyone, even my father." He was a problem child. Now, he was declining for real. He looked more and more like the hunchback of Notre-Dame.

To say that Papa Doc was sick (whether it was literal or figurative) was a crime. An offense that carried the death penalty.

The Doc's hair was ashy, his fingers skeletal. Because of the lack of flesh on his limbs, his wedding ring was going sideways. He had one foot in the Palace, one in the cemetery. The third foot, the most important one, had died a long time ago, killed by a bad case of diabetes.

Towards the end, he started to promise that in due time he would transfer the power to the youths. Nobody knew he was referring to his adolescent son Claudius-19.

It was a big joke until it became reality, on live television, on a hot winter day of January. But we are not there yet.

At midnight, after 8 hours of hard work, the TV set would take a long, 16-hour rest. On the small gray screen, it was snow time. A grainy display of nothingness. A clear indication of what the future holds for those who would escape Papa Doc's farm of bones.

It did not matter to the kiddies. They were young blood. Oblivious to the magnitude of the tragedy. A new era was starting under their very eyes. Time of TV, time of cartoon characters who were fast and furious.

It was a good time to be above ground, to see the sun, to splash in the ocean. It was so close; you could touch it from your window. You could ride your flagship, your caravel of paper among starfish and seahorses.

TV was phasing in. It was candy to the eyes. Radio was phasing out endlessly like ketchup from an old, expired jar.

TV was a breath of fresh air. The shows came from distant places, France, the USA. Places where people look so different, you would think they were aliens.

Zazou, our six-year-old neighbor, was afraid of the dark. He was the son of Francis Trenard, a retired trumpeter of the Jazz des Jeunes. The theater of Ciné Sénégal was too grand and too loud for Zazou. At home, in the mirror of the TV set, he saw himself as a sharpshooter. In fact, he was a paranoid little child

226

who was afraid of the cars and horses on the big screen. They were coming at him like speeding bullets.

He had a big crush on the tube. With Ciné Sénégal, it was a love and hate relationship. Especially when Dracula was coming to town.

The bad blood, the constant shootings between marshals and gringos, between sheriffs and bandits, disturbed his sleepy soul. Like an old man and his pipe, Zazou sucked his thumb while he watched his cartoons in his papa's rocking chair.

A 13-inch, pre-owned TV, purchased for 30 bucks at the loan shark store was a window of opportunity to see the world. LG. Life is good on the other side of the ocean. Gotham City is safe. Batman and Robin are awesome.

Around that time, Jack Nicholson was an upcoming actor with a carnivorous smile. At a very young age, he already looked the part: a stud who was looking for adventures in the cuckoo's nest.

He was elected class clown in Jersey, 1954. He had no idea that one day he would become larger than life as the true incarnation of the Joker.

Once again, the local pundits, the eternal naysayers, the diehard aficionados of transistor radios, and silent movies attempted to spoil the fun brought by TV to the island. With pontifical certitude, they mumbled to those who cared to listen: "Read my lips, this new technology will not last."

Excusez-moi?

The islanders were skeptical about the future of basketball and baseball too. For them, it was soccer or nothing. At the Sylvio Cator Stadium, the scoreboard was often blank, zero-zero, but it did not matter.

"Did you watch the final game last night between the US and the Soviets?"

"Basketball? No way! Who won?"

"It was close. I fell asleep right before the end. I could not keep up. The score kept changing every second."

Boxing? Yes. Because of Joe Louis. The brown bomber was gone, but a black kid called Clay was molding with his gloves a monument to himself. He became a legend under a new name: Ali, the greatest.

At the barbershop near the railroad, the conversation was

quite colorful. It was a headquarters where grumpy old men congregated to clash about world soccer news. Most were worshipers of Pelé, the Brazilian god. As good Catholics, in tune with the Pope, some preferred the Italian national team: the Squadra Azzurra. Even Germany had its diehard supporters.

In 1950, Joe Gaetjens, a Haitian citizen, scored the winning goal for the US against England. It was one of the biggest upsets in World Cup history. The news spread around the world, just like the time when David won the fight against Goliath. Joe Gaetjens became an international hero.

When he returned to the island, he received his reward from Papa Doc. He vanished. We were in 1964.

In the debate at the barbershop emerged often heteroclite antique subjects, all things unrelated to local politics: the hairstyle of the Mohicans, the mustache Hitler borrowed from Charlie Chaplin, the skinheads of England, the German shepherd of Benito Mussolini, the giraffe of Charles de Gaulle, the nose of Cleopatra, Noah's ark, the release of *The Titanic*, the impending Hurricane Flora that promises to be a deluge of biblical proportion.

Around that time, Jean Fourcand was doing a great job in the hashtag campaign of propaganda. He had read the *Manual of the Perfect Courtesan*, published under the reign of Louis XIV that lasted seventy-two years. Under the distinctive signature of Fourcand was released in 1964 the well-known *Catechism of the Revolution*. "One shall not pronounce in vain the name of Papa Doc." The clergy was horrified by the deification of the creepy doctor.

On that early morning, the roosters had just finished their chorus when the men in blue showed up at the presbytery. The Bishop of Papadopolis, Monsignor Rémy Augustin, didn't get the chance to have his first cup of coffee or to pick up his dignified purple vestment. He was driven to the airport in his Fruit of the Loom underwear.

Like a resilient bacterium or a deadly virus, the arrival of Papa Doc changed the configuration of human interaction. Social distancing became a fact of life. Everybody started to wear a mask. To survive, opponents of Papa Doc pretended to be his allies. Even zealous, authentic allies of Papa Doc were afraid of him. "The Revolution will eat its own children." Fellas who were known to be chatty started to speak with their eyes. They became fluent in the foreign language of silence.

Voicing vague, imprecise thoughts left the door open to *quid pro quo* and abusive interpretations. "I am hungry", "I am tired of this shit." It was suspicious, seditious, to say such things. They were keywords that led to the dead end, the point of no return.

The island of Alcatraz paled in comparison. Alcatraz? A vacation colony where turbulent young men lived long enough to reach old age. Alcatraz? Just a fairy tale in which the jailbird became a birdman.

The walls of Papadopolis had comical large ears. They were known to capture and record the most intimate thoughts. In the privacy of their own home, everyone seemed to be under the microscope of Doctor Duvalier.

He wanted to enter History as the tyrannosaurus of Latin America. He was praised by his biographer for the candor, the honesty in which he confessed his drinking habits: "I don't drink rum and other spirits; when I am thirsty, I drink the tears and the blood of my enemies."

Like the biting and sucking lice, the guinea fowls of Papa Doc (otherwise known as *tontons macoutes*) came equipped with extended antennas. They did not walk with their eyes in their pockets. They saw wide and far. The hood next door to Martissant was so infested with blue denim henchmen, they called it Macoute City.

Arthur, the favorite barber of the parish of Sainte Bernadette was a Good Samaritan. Since charity begins at home, he harbored the nicest haircut along the shore. Something fresh like a manicured golf lawn at a resort in Key Largo. Something so precise, you'd think Arthur had eyes in orbit around his head.

Kiddies were afraid of the barber as though he were a barbarian. Even worse: a dentist. The hair trimmer did feel like a lawnmower roving on their calabash. Some heads became transparent after the procedure. Some barbers would cut hair with eagerness until they reached the soft tissues of the brain.

Kiddies wanted to grow their hair to feel strong like Samson. It was a time so ancient, barbers used a Gillette, a thin razor without the handle. It was sharp and bloodthirsty like the edge of a broken glass.

At Arthur's, bald men were the favorites. They got a 40% discount. As a bonus, they received blood-free shaving when business was slow, nonexistent. Yet, the men with the shiny skull found a way to bargain. It was part of the customs and local values. The lowest price offered spontaneously always seemed exorbitant, even if it were a penny. A round of negotiation (with a poker face) was necessary. To reach the lowest common denominator. To settle things with a smile. It was arm wrestling before the handshake agreement.

Arthur had a cultural shock when he came to the States for the first time. It was on the day after, a Saturday morning when he went on a shopping spree for scissors, Band-Aid, alcohol, and batteries at the 99 Cent Store on Flatbush Ave. The Creole-speaking salesclerk was totally unbending: "Yes, 99 cents, that's the final price for each item. The price is locked into the machine. I could not remove a pretty penny from the balance even if I wanted to. You also have to pay taxes."

"Pardon my French. This is a rip-off."

Arthur was at a loss for words. "Take it or leave it? What kind of country is this?"

At Arthur's barbershop young dudes and elegant *flâneurs* were bad clients. They tended to wear their afro like a boss.

They would not show up for a single cut. Through the writings of Martinican poet Aimé Césaire, they had learned a well-kept secret: "It is beautiful, it is good, it is legitimate to be Black."

Homo Papadocus was suspicious of the new fashion. To him, the young men looked like Black Panthers. The men in blue volunteered as freelance barbers to reduce the spiky mountains of hair roaming the streets of Papadopolis.

A government communiqué published in *The Minotaur* banned afro hairstyle from the island. It was declared persona non grata, threatened to be deported back home to Harlem, USA.

Afro hairstyles went into hiding under a bonnet, a wool hat. To Papa Doc, it was a covert operation in the Caribbean. He had no evidence, but why take chances?

On that day, the chauvinistic fervor and flag thumping were flying high at Arthur's barbershop. "Basketball? Are you kidding me? A game in which towering giants are throwing a ball at a see-through trash can is clearly ridiculous!"

Islanders would rather watch their soccer team warm-up session. To them, soccer players practicing hot yoga would make more sense than basketball. I'd be more entertaining. A god is a god regardless of what he does.

Soccer players are not tall like the Harlem Globetrotters, but they have golden feet. With a good diet of beef, cornmeal mush, and avocado, they can score from a mile away.

Beyond the field of sports, the patriotic fervor went far into the moon of lunacy. Carl Brouard, the indigenist poet, was always soaked in alcohol. He felt the need to combat external influences in his own terms: "I don't know why you'd want to drink Jack Daniel's in a country where the national rum is Barbancourt."

Of course, the eternal contradictors will argue that Brouard was a poet, that no rational human being would say something like that unless he was drunk.

In fact, he was.

I truly believe it was a case of predestination. His last name "Brouard" sounds in French 101 like "Boire", which means: to drink.

Carl Brouard was a kid in 1915 when the US Occupation of the island started. It was written in the stars of the Spangled-

Banner that someday, somehow, something like that would happen.

Big Brother's tutelage lasted 19 years: 1915-1934. It was another one of these voyages of discovery that ended up in "unfortunate" casualties. The young marines from the south of the US were surprised to discover in their backyard of the Caribbean an island where black folks were allowed to roam freely. No obvious signs of segregation. No apartheid? They even had their own White House.

"What the hell is that?"

In retaliation, Carl Brouard never traveled to the US, which became a lesser place because it never got the chance to welcome such an amazing writer. In Harlem, he would have had a parade with Langston Hughes and Zora Neale Hurston.

On the islands of the Antilles, the pundits were very snob; they felt superior in their own ways. Aside from basketball and baseball, they hated wrestling. They said it was fake and vulgar; they were sure that the blood spilled in the ring was Heinz ketchup. Among the kiddies, that belief was dismissed when they learned from Yoyo, the village's storyteller, that foreigners have blue blood.

Soccer or not, Bonhomme Narcisse the zombie was the man of the hour. For several weeks, he outshone Papa Doc in the news. In a way, he was a hero.

My elementary school teacher Elizabeth Laforest was shocked when she read in my essay that innocent introduction: "When I grow up, I want to be a zombie."

It took her several seconds to understand where I was coming from. The zombie was a metaphor of the victory of life over death.

Not knowing what to expect, I was sitting sheepishly; trying to hide in plain sight like a little Houdini. After a moment of stupor, her face bloomed. She came close to my bench and whispered in my left ear: "If you continue on that route, you'll go far, my boy." Her feminine nearness was warm. I melted like chocolate in the sun.

It was a time when schoolteachers were blameless. They were arrested for their political opinions, not for their romance with small creatures.

I was moved by her kind words and never forgot her prediction. She was my sibyl, my fairy. When I traveled to the

US as an émigré, I realized how right she had been. I did go far. One thousand five hundred and thirty miles to reach JFK. Almost four hours on the aircraft.

From the window seat where the clouds were within my reach, I felt like a cosmonaut in blue jeans heading to a new galaxy.

Yes, I went far from the shores of the island. Beyond the threshold of my wildest dream.

I had to write this story to make my teacher happy. Even though it's too late; even though I have to do it beyond the grave, with my bone as a pen, my skin as parchment, and my ashes as ink.

Despite the fact I received rave reviews from Ms. Laforest, I developed among my peers at P.S. Sainte-Trinité a reputation for being an "original" in the most pejorative sense of the term.

Who in his right mind would want to be a zombie? What kind of weird ambition is that? These were the questions that were keeping my classmates awake at night.

I became a celebrity for the wrong reason. I was on the invisible red carpet. They were staring at me. Every word I said, every move I made became an event to be dissected like a frog in the lab.

They pretended to be scared of me. I could not focus on the lessons I enjoyed before in class: the love story between Caonabo and Anacaona before the arrival of Columbus; the saga of Bookman, the rebellious slave who fought the French colonizers with supreme intelligence and the almighty power of Botanica.

I was hearing voices that told me my schoolmates were putting me down. As I lay napping in the hammock, sleep-walking through life, I felt sick. Some sort of vertigo like in a film noir of Alfred Hitchcock. My grades suffered, stumbled, and went down the tubes. I got addicted to television.

They thought they knew me. I am the comeback kid. I am mister mystery. One day, I'll take my revenge. I will reach deep into my soul and show them what I am made of.

In the meantime, Papa Déus decided to place me at another institution. Not as bad as it sounds. Not a mental institution. Not yet. Just another school where I was unknown entity.

It felt good to be anonymous again, to be able to yawn in

class with my mouth wide open, without having to worry about what it meant to my classmates.

I was cured of the curse I brought to myself. I had been too candid in my essay where I used three times the forbidden word: zombie.

I was happy to change schools, to get my degree, my cherished diploma with my picture on it.

The results were broadcasted on radio MBC. Everyone in the neighborhood was listening. A loud, collective scream of relief and pride was heard when my name was called.

That's how I became the poster boy for success. I just had my Ps.D, my Primary School Diploma. It felt like a Ph.D.

Yes, I ran out of luck later. But, this baby, this piece of paper, I got it on the battlefield.

It was one of my greatest achievements in life. No one, I mean no one can take it away from me.

"I am not properly a deceased author, but a late author, for whom the grave in a cradle."

Joaquim Maria Machado de Assis

"Never say good evening to a person you meet on the road when it is beginning to get dark. Because, if it is a zombie, he'll carry your voice to the devil who could then take you away at any time."

Joseph Zobel

The Little Prince of Papadopolis

It was a time so ancient that miracles and regular apparitions of the Virgin Mary to the shepherds of Portugal were observed as dull, ordinary events. On the island, the Lord had a hotline, a direct communication system with the pastors. He often reiterated his wish to see them rich, radiogenic, and miracle makers.

Many physicians didn't know what to do against the fierce competition of supernatural healing. They were advised to hang their diploma upside down on the wall, to go to pilgrimages at the grotto of Troufoban, to take a bath every Sunday at 4 AM in the thermal waters of Sources Puantes that smelled like rotten eggs. Nothing seemed to work. They felt neglected, abandoned by Aesculapius, the Greek god of medicine.

It was a time so ancient that most people had more trust in medieval witchcraft than in helpless practitioners in white coats. Some doctors settled in the mountains to vaccinate their unfortunate countrymen against yaws. Some M.D.'s got into politics and lyric poetry. Many moved to the island of Montreal, not too far from the North Pole. Some doctors were recycled in the thriving funeral business. They became successful morticians.

In Martissant, the lush vegetation was our healthcare system, our over-the-counter pharmacy in case of high fever, cold sweats, panic attacks, anemia, worms, hemorrhoids, persistent cough, insomnia, excess appetite, and constipation.

The flavorful leave of citronella was in the tea department of our garden. Some other plants like the Arabian Jasmine sprinkled the air with fragrance after sundown. Our cherry tree was so fertile and generous in the rainy season, it provided breakfast and lunch to many kids in the hood.

Nonetheless, according to bourgeois etiquette, it was improper to eat mangoes and sugarcane in the open. This privilege was reserved for prestigious fruits like apples and green pears imported from France. Going downtown to purchase such delicacies was regarded as a sign of upward mobility. Tell me what you eat in public and I'll tell you who you are.

Despite the dire conditions of living dangerously, the gingerbread house of Ma Fifine felt some days like a sheltered resort; a 4-star restaurant overlooking the Caribbean Sea. She was a fervent Catholic and said to me once: "God gave us a mouth to tell stories and eat good food." I said "amen!" to that.

In my previous life, I used to be a good boy. The islanders call that kind of kid: Little Jesus in the shell of a crab. Ma Fifine, my godmother, was proud of that. She handled me like a trophy, showered me with praises, and worshipped me like the second coming of Christ. I could do no wrong. While the stars were aligned under the sign of Taurus, a boy was born. He was living with her in a stable house of Martissant.

She had a mahogany jewelry box where she kept my fairy tooth and a tuft of hair. Perhaps, she thought that one day, these relics would get historical and religious values and would end up at the Musei Vaticani of Rome.

She was my first love story. In a million years, I never thought I'd have to fight to get a woman's attention. Especially the churchgoing beauty who put me in purgatory for close to ten years. She was worth the wait. She was beautiful like a bird-of-paradise.

Ma Fifine said to me: "You are my cute little boy." The mirror laughed at me and said otherwise. The blemished pictures show a bushy-haired child with a swollen umbilicus.

Luckily, my sole and favorite child is a cosmetic surgeon, a Photoshop specialist. He makes me look presentable. I have always been afraid of looking like a zombie.

It is a truth universally acknowledged that most mothers, in the presence of a new child, react like Ma Fifine. They are blinded by instinctive love, the way the girls of Martissant used to adore their dolls. On a Sunday morning, they would baptize them and spend their fortune on a lavish reception of Coca Cola and Ritz crackers.

Because Ma Fifine was my substitute mamma, she felt the need to do more to secure a sunny place in my heart. My biological mother, Ma Rolande, was the other woman, like an official mistress that, in the French fashion, you go visit with the blessing of your wife.

My heart was in two places at the same time. It was a smooth arrangement, a parenthood *à trois*, in which everyone was happy. My biological father was too busy outside of the house to be part of the picture.

Ma Fifine said I was precious. I believed her. I guess I was a sucker. I swallowed whatever she told me.

I was hooked on her cooking. I was faithful to her and felt that allowing someone else to feed me was a form of treason. When I was away on vacation in Pétion-Ville, I ate just enough to stay alive and keep some flesh over my skeleton.

I am not sure Ma Fifine knew how good she was. Some people felt she was spoiling me. So what? Too much of a good thing is wonderful. I guess they were jealous of the fact the self-centered little monster that I was had Ma Fifine all to himself.

Our kitchen was a primitive hut in the backyard, under a Spanish lime tree. It did not matter. The delicious aroma of Creole cooking was drifting in the air. Ma Fifine's did not study haute cuisine. She invented it.

The only thing I never ate from her kitchen was the filet-o-shark.

I did not want to be the target of a vendetta when I went to swim in the shallow waters of Mariani.

"He was a doctor of some kind, but it is not certain that he cured more people than he killed. His hobby was torturing his enemies and listening to their screams. I have seen his lavish torture chamber in the basement of the palace. Once, I was doing a documentary about Haiti and asked him for an interview. He said yes, but only if he could write out my questions and write out his answers."

David Brinkley

"In times of famine, I even read treatises on surgery and accounting manuals, not thinking they would be of use to me in my adventures as a writer."

Gabriel García Márquez

The Gods of the Stadium

It was before the age of television. The broadcast was getting hot on the radios. They had the status of today's flat-screen Samsung. Awesome. Neighbors would sit down together to listen to the news. Gifted reporters of live soccer matches developed the ability to bring the stadium to the hood with fireworks of words.

Under the thunderous applause of the crowd, the gods of the arena were doing their magic: acrobatic feats, flying angels, giant slaloms, lightning speed, shooting stars, last-minute miracles.

The athletes were prepared for glory. Every single move, every slight gesture was part of a partition, a choreography, something planned by a higher power: a trainer of genius.

Fueled by the rise of testosterone, the crowd was aroused. They were shouting *"Toup pou yo! Grenadye alaso!"* as though they were in a Roman Coliseum where sweaty gladiators were fighting hungry lions in the august presence of Claudius, Messalina, Nero, or Caligula.

Dressed in somber gray, Papa Doc came once to the

Stadium, to witness the human sacrifice of the national team by the almighty god of soccer: Brazilian Edson Arantes do Nascimento, known by his worshippers around the globe under the holy name of Pelé.

Electricity was in the air. The vaguest action on the field became something dramatic, another heart-thumping moment "boom-boom-boom!" The reporters were eloquent young men, full of dreams and inspiration. They knew how to get the adrenaline flowing, how to stir the passions that lead to the climactic release of energy: "Gooooooooool!"

They had good pedigrees. Without ostentation, they could have said: "I went to the best schools; I know words; I know the best words."

Years later, one of the star commentators turned into a brilliant scholar in the field of political science at the University of North Carolina. Another one became an economist, director of Banque Nationale. Another one turned into the president of the Feminine Soccer League. He had the magical ability to impregnate dozens of young women without touching them. He was forced to resign after decades of abuse and absolute power.

In Papadopolis it seemed like an addiction. People were hooked on the radio. Throughout the day, they had to sniff something through their ears.

Some had a small unit they cherished like the latest iPhone. It became a fashion statement to carry a radio in the large pocket of a fancy shirt, the "Safari". The chase was on. Skirt chasing with the sweet sound of a ballad.

When love letters and prayers failed, the gentlemen resorted to the magic spell of music. It was the perfect medium to declare their flame. They spread romantic songs in the air until they saw the white flag of surrender from the citadel of virtue where lived the virgins.

Edith Piaf's *Hymne à L'Amour* became a weapon of mass seduction against the walls of innocence. Local crooner Gérard Dupervil arose to be a star with his hit-song *Fleur de Mai*. He shone in the milky way of the bustier women in town, especially Madame Thimotée.

An adorable female fan of Dupervil went as far as to say: "If God were a singer, he would sound like Gérard."

Some damsels copied the lyrics religiously as though they

were the Scriptures: the gospel of Charles Aznavour. Some had successful gigs in the shower as karaoke chanteuses. With their voices, they shattered the glass ceiling, and gave goosebumps to the clouds.

The radio fever became viral. The passion was transmitted genetically from one generation to the next. From the womb, kiddies were wired to love the music. Some babes learned to sing before they learned to speak.

Even though they were brand new creatures, the sounds of the world seemed familiar to them. "I think I heard that song before I was born." It was a Christmas carol that announced the imminent return of the jolly Santa: Papa Noël.

Some people were carried away by the waves of the radio. They drifted aimlessly in the streets. Men who were well-known for being stupid got worse. Some had cart accidents with horses and donkeys.

It became difficult to assert who were the real donkeys. The gentle quadrupeds had skills. They spoke impeccable Creole in the tales of Bouki. They spoke perfect French in the books of La Fontaine. Some had the ability to see the future in the two crystal balls hanging between their back legs.

Humans are overrated. We tend to be so pretentious and arrogant, as though we did not belong to the animal kingdom anymore. The donkey of the Voodoo priestess of Martissant had *un je ne sais quoi* of tenderness and romanticism on his face whenever he heard the Beatles on the radio. Especially the song called *Yesterday*. You would think he was about to shed tears and sing along with the radio:

"Suddenly, I'm not half the man I used to be

There is a shadow hanging over me

Oh, yesterday came suddenly…"

"Even the dream I describe to my wife across the breakfast table is only a first draft."

Vladimir Nabokov

"I often spend my time in the cemetery, and I find myself talking to the people there. I was born in this town. I know everyone, and many are those who live in the cemetery now."

Dany Laferrière

A Hunger for Coffee

In Petit-Goâve, Man Da's coffee was the best. It has entered history by the front door. It will not be said that you never heard about it. It will not be said that you never distinguished its aroma in the air. This is the kind of coffee that can make you greedy. It is the subject of literary research and doctoral dissertations at major universities across the pond of the Atlantic. Recently, it was being hotly discussed, in Paris, at the French Academy.

Anyway, what would life be without coffee? A gigantic mistake. Something lame and empty. An eternal longing. A thirst for the unknown. What would be the incentive to get out of bed and hit the road on a rainy Monday morning? What would life be in sleepy towns without coffee? Why are we here and not somewhere else in a black hole of the Milky Way? What would be the meaning of life? These will remain significant philosophical questions of our time.

On the island, coffee was king. Cornmeal, rice, red beans, avocado, okra, and the *accent aigu* of meat came way after on the menu. Bread and butter were pretty good too.

Only the knife knows what's hidden in the heart of yucca. My own secret is an open book. I have lived in the belly of hunger. The kind of hunger that can eat you alive.

Around one in the afternoon, there was a turmoil in the belly, a boiling sound in the gut, a desperate SOS call for food. Your personal alarm system was triggered in full blast. Waw! Waw! Waw!

It was something embarrassing. Something that would reveal to your frenemies that your family was broke, on the verge of extinction.

Yet, you were glowing in the morning like a Hyacinth on the mountain of Kenscoff. You smelled good with that Palmolive fragrance on your skin. You knew how to wear a happy face; the mask of someone who's well-fed at the all-you-can-eat restaurant called home.

After a day of fasting, those who didn't have supper were advised to put a grain of sea salt under their tongue so that hunger would not stab their heart. The night was indeed a period of high casualties. This is the time when our *bon ange*, our good spirit, is dormant. It's lazy, less vigilant in the dark.

Some slept with a red gown to keep away evil spirits. Some

spread sesame seeds around their bed as a frontier between life and death. Some had an amulet under their pillow. Some placed their safety on the hands of the Bible.

Apocalypse was never too far away.

Calamity doesn't have a horn. It doesn't blow a conch shell. Like a somnambulist unaware of the laws of physics, tragedy walks casually through concrete walls, wood, straw, adobe. It flies blindfolded from roof to roof without knowing in advance the identity of its next victim.

Unannounced, dressed in satin, the insomniac Grim Reaper had the habit of visiting at night. He had no mercy whatsoever for newborns and *misérables* who didn't have enough to eat: those who had a spider web in their stomach, those who had sharp shoulder blades, those who had their bones showing in High Definition, those who did not need an X-ray because they were transparent, those who preferred spirits to solid food, those who laughed like a skeleton when they heard on the radio the ad for SlimFast.

They were easy prey, easy pickings, for they were light. They could be carried like a sack of feathers, like a bag of bones to the netherworld, near the monster of Charybdis, far from the smiley dolphin of the Caribbean.

Like the servant of the priest who passed away without being baptized, like the ganja grower who was allergic to smoke, farmers would hesitate to eat their own crops. It was sold to bring cash, to send the kids to school, to buy a pair of shoes, to buy a black suit, to buy a plot at the cemetery.

In the countryside where food was plenty, it was still neglected. Frugality? Stoicism? Religious martyrology? Maybe it was part of the culture. Maybe it was part of what Maryse Condé called "That ample faculty for suffering and torturing oneself."

Without knocking at the door, without saying the traditional greeting: "*honneur*", without waiting for the traditional reply: "*respect*", the Grim Reaper would surprise people on their screaming bed, on their silent hammock, on their dry banana leaves mattress, at the precise moment they were dreaming of a better tomorrow.

The night stood still like a picture in the dark. Occasionally, it was in slow motion like a long *film noir*.

Those who escaped the wee hours could enjoy another mug

of coffee, another day above ground, under the glare of the sun, under the eyes of the men in blue, under the rain of blood.

Grandma Brigitte, our neighbor, took pleasure in bribing the passerby with her coffee. She would personally roast the beans on wood charcoal and pulverize them in the artisanal grinder she had purchased at the open-air market for the equivalent of fifty mangoes she had nurtured in her backyard.

More than a grandmother's fantasy, used coffee grounds were well-accepted in the community as a soil conditioner, an organic fertilizer. It was a stimulant for lazy plants. They grew faster and produced sweeter fruits.

Aside from the customers of the marketplace who knew how to flatter their taste buds with papaya, mandarin, guava, and passion fruit, the *fransik* mangoes were highly appreciated by the cute, infantile piggies who saw them as large candies. They looked up to Grandma Brigitte with adoring eyes. She appeared to them as a generous black goddess with a horn of plenty.

Her brew had the magical power to untie the tongues of the most introverted. With two spoons of sugar, *damoiseaux* and *demoiselles*, ladies and gentlemen would reveal to her the gossip of Martissant and the outskirts of town: who's the new sweetheart of whom, who had gotten a belly from her boo, who's been abandoned without rhyme or reason by the vagabond lover, which child was not the daughter of her legitimate father, who was trying to conquer a rebellious heart with "*tu voudras*" (the powerful Voodoo charm made with hummingbird powder), who was doing forbidden fruit tasting in the garden of Venus, who had been seen recently in the mangrove or the blue lagoon eating conch, fishing for love, sharing linguine, giving mouth-to-mouth resuscitation to a broken heart.

Around that time, it was a big deal to become a *granmoun*, to be an adult after the long period of incubation in mama's nest. Daddy was often a no-show. Someone you'd barely recognize if you saw him riding an elephant in a narrow street. Sometimes, he was in exile. Sometimes, he was hiding in plain sight. Sometimes, he was not who you thought he was. Sometimes, you grew up looking more and more like Jolicoeur, the neighbor who's always been friendly to your mama.

You had survived the glances, the chit-chats, the innuendos. Now, fully grown, you were ready to take a bite out of life, to leave your mark, to earn a living.

In Papadopolis, a job was a privilege reserved to few. In the hiring section of *Papa News*, the listing was quite explicit: "National Penitentiary looking for heavy-handed correction officers. Slaughterhouse of Fort-Dimanche searching for wardens and executioners. Kindly submit your curriculum vitae with a headshot and a list of previous victims."

Nothing attractive for a peaceful citizen who might be hungry but not bloodthirsty.

In Martissant, our neighbors were small-scale entrepreneurs, artisans, seamstresses, fishermen, drivers, psychics, merchants of random items. They would retail anything except their soul.

In the poorer hood of Bréa, not too far from the Sainte Bernadette Basilica, lots of folks were on life-support. Near Ciné Sénégal, some survived on the sales of candies, chewing gum, and loose cigarettes. Some lived on love and freshwater. Some lived on seafood. Now you see it, now you don't. The rest survived on *esprit de corps*, team spirit.

Around that time, a job as a teacher or a public servant meant something. It meant that one was ready to be buried in debt. It meant a preapproved line of credit with a loan shark.

In case of an emergency, the Dominican pawnshop La Vida Loca was a good source of cold cash. There, they accepted all sorts of valuables: passports with a US visa, wedding rings, necklaces. Even dentures with pearly white smiles.

Regardless of the salary, it was nice to have a job, to get up before the sun, when the roosters were sounding the alarm: "Cocorico!"

In the foreign language of these pedestrian birds, "Cocorico!" meant something: "Get out of bed, you bastard!"

In their own peculiar way, roosters were unpaid public servants. Before the modern era when clocks and watches became popular, they provided a well-needed service to the community.

But for whom tolls the bell?

At noon, the bell of Sainte Bernadette took over the airwaves with the familiar "ding-dong." It was time to grab a bite, time to rest.

When the bell resounded at 4 on a weekday afternoon, it was announcing a funeral.

"Ding-dong" on Saturday evening? It was something worse: a wedding.

In the morose atmosphere of the days, roosters were public entertainers. They would start a fight for no reason. No pay-per-view. The best fights were broadcast for free on the radio.

Dominican cocks (born and bred on the reverse side of the island) were reputed for their ferocity. At the cockfighting arena, they engaged in epic combats, as modern-day gladiators. For those who never heard or cared about the Society for the Protection of Animals, these flamboyant roosters were a good source of income.

Some folks were cock caretakers. They depended on their cock to make a living. Some were professional gamblers, astute investors in the cock market.

Knowing how to select a winner was a critical skill. Papa Doc made that clear like coconut water when he said: "Those who foolishly voted for my rivals, those who chose the wrong cock will pay the price with their blood."

Those who escaped the firing squad were fired from their job. A job was a reward for political obedience.

In Papadopolis a job meant you had it going on; you were up to something. But what? A check at the end of the month was not a sure thing.

The banana republic template that was so dear to the heart of Papa Doc was in constant chaos. The overdue wages were needed for the more important stuff: weapons and ammunition for the *tontons* in khaki and blue.

Florian was glad to have a job as a messenger at the Social Department of Well-Being. The pay was low, but he was a happy-go-lucky kind of guy. He delivered the mail and the verbal messages on his moped and spent lunchtime with his second family. How did he manage to have two households and send all his children to private schools? Life is a mystery.

The days grew longer when food was missing. Payroll time was hectic, unpredictable. A pleasant surprise. Some months lasted more than 90 days. Except for December when State employees received a bonus, a stimulus check for being alive.

At the same time, "zombie checks" were issued to mysterious individuals wearing dark sunglasses. They never came to work. They came to collect. They were registered as consultants and detectives, underground agents of the Prez for Life.

The zombies are alive. They survived their master. They intend to collect their dues until the end of time.

"Years later, I am still explaining Haiti to myself. Probably, I am still explaining myself to myself too."

Herbert Gold

"Álvaro Mutis had to make a business trip to Port-au-Prince early in the New Year, and he invited me to go with him. Haiti became the country of my dream, after I read Alejo Carpentier's The Kingdom of this World."

Gabriel García Márquez

The Strange Visitors

"Have you been there?"

It was a time when the magic island of Haiti was one of the best destinations of the Antilles. Jamaica had not yet emerged from the ocean as a tropical paradise. If you were a shooting star like Elizabeth Taylor (aka Cleopatra) you had to visit; if you were a meteor like Langston Hughes, you had to come on a pilgrimage on the mountainous island where BLM (Black Lives Matter) stood up for the first time in the Americas.

Welcome to Port-au-Prince, Haiti, a vacation colony where the sightseer is king.

Baked by the raging blaze from the sky, most of the visitors were pink. Surprisingly, among the hundreds of nonchalant foreigners who came in the boats, a few specimens and women appeared to be darker, like the locals. It was a mystery. How in the world is this possible?

Under the shade of the almond tree, the boy had studied a broad range of colors with his mama. He was getting ready for the Kindergarten Entrance which was the equivalent of the New York State Bar Exam.

Kindergarten was a big deal at that time of excellence and high expectations. Who knows what lays ahead? In every child, there is a Promethean character who's sleeping.

A solid education should awake the giant within. So, in kindergarten, from A to Z, the little man pursued advanced studies in letters.

Around that time, children were utility vehicles for their parents' grandiose dreams. Before they learned how to walk, a heavy weight was placed on their shoulders. They were the new incarnation of the Greek god Atlas carrying the terrestrial globe.

Daddy wanted to be a doctor but ended up spending his life as a bank teller? No problem. He'll become a brain surgeon through his daughter, his son, or better yet: both of them. "I am not asking for much; just bring me the MD diplomas and I'll be the happiest papa on earth."

It was quite a pressure for Themistocles and Artemise who wanted to pursue a writing career. They were both good kids. Their only vice was poetry.

Themistocles Epaminondas Labasterre? In the name of love, children should be allowed to select their own label.

Something sweet like Isa Belle or Rome Eo; something graceful and inspiring like Ayissa Tou or Kunta Kinte.

Imagine for an instant that you were born in 1936 as a papaless child in a deserted canyon, a no man's land called *Ravine Sèche* (Dry Ravine), and your mama who was a teenager at the time had the wonderful idea of calling you: Jean Pierre Basilic Dantor Franck Etienne d'Argent. No less than that.

This is the kind of name the most gifted novelist could never come up with.

To keep it short, let's call him JP. JP was the ultimate comeback kid. He made the best of the situation.

He became a Renaissance man, a gigantic creator (someone so bizarrely polyvalent and imaginative, you could call him "a freak of nature" as a compliment). He got tired of the litany of names. He reinvented himself under the unique moniker of Frankétienne.

He probably inspired other divas like Lady Gaga (Stefani Joanne Angelina Germanotta), Madonna, Cher, and Rihanna who followed in his footsteps with a short and handsome name.

Around that time, kiddies were unaware of the fact they were cursed with a never-ending title. It was inscribed in flowery letters on a papyrus, a thin sheet of paper as old as the Pyramids of Cheops. The birth certificate was called *"baptistaire"*. It implied that the recipient was baptized, certified as a human being.

Losing one's *baptistaire* was bad omen, a sign of imminent danger. It was crystal clear that one of these nights, the nightingale was going to sing your swan song. Before you say a prayer, you were going to be devoured by the *loup-garou*.

You'll have the right to remain silent. Any attempt to call your mama will be a waste of breath. You'll be busy, bleeding, and wishing you never came to this planet. Your personal alarm system, your voice, will shut down entirely.

However, if you are lucky, you will awake to realize you just had a nightmare. But you are wet to the bone, like a kid alligator who pees freely in the Mississippi River.

Bedwetting was a serious health issue that affected my infancy until I found a miraculous relief on the eve of my first communion. Ma Fifine was proud of me. I was cured.

Kiddies who had a clean bill of health, those who looked

picture-perfect like the Gerber Baby, those who had a Colgate smile with their toothless gums, those who were strong enough to survive the threat of kwashiorkor, German measles, or belligerent intestinal worms, were said to have a *baptistaire* made of steel.

Kiddies had a "non jwèt", a nickname they took seriously until the first day of class. As far as they were concerned, they were Ti Dyo (Little Joseph), Ti Papa (Little Daddy), Gwo Lombrik (Big Belly Button), Nanpwenfanm (Skinny Woman). They got confused and annoyed when they realized that from now on, day after day, they would be abandoned by their mama. From now on, they would be addressed by a perfect stranger, a surrogate parent called teacher as Monsieur Milord Aristophane Auguste Legrand or Mademoiselle Cléopatre Marie-Antoinette Nefertiti Lafortune.

They were too young to realize they were being groomed for greatness.

At some schools, admission to kindergarten was denied on the ground of low score, lack of preparation, poor concentration, attention deficit disorder.

As a student in kindergarten, you had to display intellectual gifts, the potential for great achievements. Some schools were reserved for *la crème de la crème*: the kids who were smart enough to be born in a bourgeois family; the kids who spoke French as if they'd lived in Paris for half a century.

The sun shines for everyone. That's what the elders said. Intelligence is smart enough to avoid prejudice. It is capricious. It goes aimlessly, wherever it wants, in the affluent vicinity like in the sugarcane alley. Somehow, somewhere, sometimes, the most beautiful flowers grow on the manure of misery.

The rainbow drinking in the ocean had no secret for JP. He learned in school the alphabet of colors. He taught himself how to add them: black plus white equals gray; red plus green equals brown; yellow plus blue equals green; red plus green plus blue equals white.

He was astonished by the magical power of colors to recreate the world, to create mirages, shadows, illusions, and reality. He learned the trade secrets of Picasso in a Crayola coloring book.

He also dreamed of becoming a painter with words. JP was fascinated by them. He studied the Creole and French dictionaries cover to cover, from bottom to top. He reversed-engineer the words. He used numbers to express his joys and sorrows: 103 (without you); 105 (without money); 109 (new blood).

JP dreamed of becoming a tall version of himself with the bells and whistles of success tolling at the local basilica. "A star is born; I've seen him with my own eyes. Shine bright like a diamond!"

He became a painter. He became a writer. He built a house with two gigantic bedrooms: one for the painter, one for the writer. The literary critics said he needed the extra space to accommodate his ego. He totally agreed with them. He said on his megaphone: "I am a brilliant megalomaniac."

As a defiant intellectual, JP never applied for a passport. He was afraid the *tontons* might take that as a pretext. Traveling abroad was one thing, to return to the island was another thing. When the egg is out, it's not easy to put it back inside the chicken.

He did not need to take a plane or a boat. He had the ability to visualized things from afar. He could travel underground in the Manhattan subway in the comfort of the distance. As though he'd been there all along, he could picture vividly the life of two islanders living in a basement in Brooklyn. He could see Russia through the eyes of Gorki; he could explore the US through the novels of Richard Right. From the second floor of his residence in Belair, he could see far, beyond the ocean.

I'll never forget that Friday morning when Ma Fifine took me to Columbus Kay to witness the debarkation of the Royal Caribbean Cruise. I was surprised to see the multicolored tourists.

I saw pink people wearing Bermuda shorts. I had assumed that all foreigners were white like a blank sheet of paper.

In my abridged dictionary, "white" meant people who are fortunate enough to surf the deep-sea on love boats; people who visit the four corners of the world on jumbo jets; people for whom life is a long, pleasurable vacation on earth.

Now, I was seeing the visitors with my own eyes, like the native Taïnos saw the Spaniards on that Sunday morning of December 6th, 1492. They were creatures from another moon: Europa, the land of the mighty gods, the land of extraterrestrials with the cross and the guns.

The visitors were taking pictures in front of the statue of Columbus. The navigator looked surprised by the attention. He never understood why he was honored in this place, why they had a Columbus Day. Was it a sick joke of Papa Doc's proportion? Christopher was confused. A tourist showed him the map of Colombia, Columbus (Ohio), and Columbus Circle in Manhattan.

The monument, the monumental mistake, was at the bay of Papadopolis that looks on the map like an open mouth trying to swallow the adjacent island of La Gonâve.

I was happy to see the crowd of tourists. They looked pleasant; they had a ton of money to buy all sorts of souvenirs. It seemed like a rosy life.

Eventually, I learned from the physics teacher that color is an optical illusion. In fact, on the islands of the West Indies, colors vary with financial health: "A rich black is mulatto; a poor mulatto is black."

Some *émigrés* were surprised to see that colors can change on the spot, according to the airport: mulatto at PDA (Papa Doc Airport), black at JFK.

They really thought they were normal human beings, the proud citizens of the first free Latin American Republic of this continent. When they landed at JFK, they realized they were jet black, with all the treats that come with it: their own bathrooms, their own restaurants, their own hoods.

It was a little bit confusing because the public urinal in the colored section was white. Was it okay to piss on it?

Regardless of the weather and the heavy atmosphere of discrimination, the exodus to the North became a fact of life. Some factory owners carried their signs at the airport: "Help Wanted." Before they learned to say "Bonjour" in English, some *émigrés* were bussed to the assembly lines of Charlie Chaplin. Welcome to *Modern Times*! The islanders were known to be hard workers in these new plants where the clock never sleeps.

Back home, Papa Doc could not care less. He was bored with his job as The Great Dictator. To him, it was overrated. He would have traded places with a wordsmith on any given day. Above all, he wanted to be known as an intellectual, as a writer. He would have sold his soul to the Devil for just a bit of inspiration.

Another MD, a novelist called Jacques Soleil, author of *The Musical Trees*, and *Romancero to the Stars*, had stolen the thunder of magical realism, and he, the Supreme, was left empty-handed, looking like a fool.

Papa Doc did try. He wrote everything like the medical doctor that he was. It was something atrocious, a mumbo jumbo only he and the pharmacists could decipher. The words were cannibalized. He agreed with himself that he needed assistance.

In the hallways of the Palace, in the antechambers of horror, the ghostwriters were visible in 3D. They chain-smoked packs of Camel cigarettes. They didn't care much about the writing on the wall that says: "smoking kills". In their trash baskets lay dying countless cans of the Dominican beer Presidente.

Armed with their fountain pens, they appeared at the Palace before the raising of the flag and vanished at sunset. In moments of crisis, the ghostwriters stayed overnight for the graveyard shift. They had to work as lyricists for the régime and flame-throwers against the opposition.

Respectfully, they would hold Papa Doc's shaky hand to

make him write like a child. His handwriting was dreadful like the output of a tortured soul. His sentences were lost in a Byzantine labyrinth. His words were swollen like cadavers abandoned in the battlefield between the men in blue and the unarmed civilians.

Papa Doc managed to release several books under his name. They were distributed to ambassadors of friendly nations, public servants, and merchants of bathroom tissue.

Papa was well admired by his minions. They gave him back all the titles in the books: Savior of the Fatherland, Stable Genius, Epitome of Unsurpassed Patriotism, Great Electrifier of the Soul.

An intense perfume of incense permeated the atmosphere of Papadopolis.

The Doc was everything and then some more: a historian, a sociologist, an ethnologist, an ideologue, a delicate poet who just happened to love blood. He was nursing the wound of being an outsider in his own country. As a young scribe, he had written a poem about the lingering color line. Colorism in Creole society was more discrete but alive. As a doctor, he had to take care of it. He had to kill it for good with his own hands.

Papa Doc was aging prematurely. He held onto his rifle for support like a cane. The paperweight on his desk was a silver pistol. He could not let go. He suffered from an acute case of separation anxiety.

A close encounter with Papa Doc was a hair-raising experience. Something similar to the Don King syndrome. One didn't know what to expect: the shy patriarch with a black suit or the carnivalesque despot with a military helmet and a bloody-red bathrobe.

Those who were expecting to see a grumpy old man saw a spirited Minotaur. Those who were expecting to see a guinea fowl saw a sphinx.

His hair was white like the snow of Michigan where he studied for a short period during World War II. His physical appearance was deceiving. Under the fragility of his rib cage was the soul of a tiger.

He wasn't taller than Napoleon, but when he looked in the mirror, he saw a giant. They smiled at each other. They had the same golden tooth. Something creepy, intimidating, ready to dispatch flesh and bones. The two became confidants and accomplices.

"Good morning Excellence, you look sharp today."

"Good morning to you. You don't look bad yourself."

In the solitude of power, at last, he had found someone he could really trust.

It was a ragtime when animals were prosecuted in place of their absent owners. Children were persecuted for the deeds of their parents. Dead rebels were escorted to the Palace for a *tête-à-tête* with Papa Doc. Their head was saved in a bucket of ice.

Many years later, a young man took a plane to Montreal as a refugee. His mama said to him: "Don't tell anyone you are leaving; I'll tell them myself when you reach the sky."

He bought a Remington typewriter and wrote many novels. On the list, I see *Dining with the Dictator,* and *An Aroma of Coffee.*

Actually, it is another book that made him famous. It's too early into the night to share his secret.

The roosters of Miami are still asleep. They were brought here, in exile, on a boat. Despite the immense ocean, despite the distance, they have not forgotten the distinctive taste of organic corn and millet.

"It's not by food that we survive but by the gaze of others."

Maud Ellmann

"It is never too late to have a happy childhood."

Berkeley Breathed

Once upon an Island

"A child should not be raised in two different homes." So spoke Ma Fifine, the expert in grooming and proper etiquette.

Regardless. At the age of seven, I was going back and forth, torn apart between Martissant and Pétion-Ville. That's how my life became a tale of two towns.

My genetic parents left the south shores. They moved with my siblings to the Newfoundland of Pétion-Ville. Compared to the anthill it has become today, this hamlet was quite empty at the time. For 300 hundred dollars, they bought a morsel of land near a forest of mahogany. The mountain air was fresh like in day one of humanity.

I was 3 years old when I took the life-altering decision to stay in Martissant. For reasons dear to my heart, I said: *"J'y suis, j'y reste."* I am here, I am staying.

I ended up with a new set of parents: my godfather Déus Benoît who had three children from a previous alliance, and his wife Ma Fifine who did not have any kiddie of her own.

A child-king? Not quite. It was a modest life, at the border of shortage. However, I was fortunate to be Ma Fifine's bundle of joy. She took my upbringing seriously, as though I were on my way to something big. Maybe in the back of her mind, she expected me to ascend to the throne.

At the end of the day, in every child, there is a T-Rex in gestation. In every child, there is a sleeping Papa Doc.

She took extraordinary steps to nurture and protect me against all sorts of malefic: chickenpox, dengue fever, yellow fever, scarlet fever, rubella, mumps, teething tantrums, and aggressive diarrheas. Year after year, she kept me warm in the incubator. I was not ready to wean.

When I wanted to play lazy boy, it is on her I relied for transportation and food delivery.

"Ma, I am thirsty."

She would wake up in the middle of the night to get me a fresh glass of water from the brown clay jar: the *kanari*. It was an indigenous refrigerator we inherited from our ancestors. It was quiet, artistic, economical. It gave to the water the earthy taste of ceramic.

As a minor, I was naturally attracted to minerals. I had a

craving for chalk, mouthwatering soil, and the intense aroma of humus. Doctor Bartoli was not alarmed. Calm like an Englishman on Prozac, he said to my mama: "It's geophagy, an eating disorder; I'll give him a prescription for earthworms."

My little neighbors who were pundits in healthcare warned me about the danger of eating soil and seeds. "A tree will grow inside your belly!"

It is at that age that I started to contemplate a career in teaching. To satisfy my hunger for chalk.

I wanted Ma Fifine all to myself. I was offended if anyone got close to her. I was a selfish and fearful child. I guess I am not alone in that department. Kiddies are wired that way. I am not sure I've changed much. I still have recurrent bad dreams, I suck my thumb, I cry in my sleep. My days and my nights are still haunted by the demons of the past. I haven't overcome the trauma of birth on that night of curfew.

Around two in the morning, Ma Fifine would escort me out of bed, to fetch the lily-white pee pot. Electricity was scarce and capricious. It would appear and disappear like a ghost. My mom had developed night vision. She would move in the dark with the confidence of a nocturnal creature.

My own vision was scrambled like a painting of Frankétienne. Maybe *The Scream* of Edvard Munch. I would see skeletons in the closet and zombies everywhere. They were making faces at me; they were nagging me.

In my darkest hours, when I walked through the valley of death, Ma Fifine was there for me. She was not going to allow the *loup-garou* to feast on me.

Every so often, an accident would happen. I would dream I was peeing in the Caribbean Basin or la Seine River in Paris. Something long, satisfying, never-ending like the flood that lasted forty days and forty nights. I would wake up suddenly, wet like a duck who just discovered water. I was in the middle of Lake Baikal in Russia. A lake that is bigger than the island of Haiti.

Liquid is the cradle of life. On the magic island of Haiti, grownups had their own theory of evolution. To them, the constant flow of urine on mattresses was the true breeding ground for bedbugs. The critters were smart cookies. They scheduled their lunch after midnight, while we were sound asleep. Nonetheless, they were not the sole bloodsuckers.

Around that time, on Dessalines Boulevard, next to Lido Cinema, Luckner Cambronne, a creature of Papa Doc, opened a lucrative business of blood. The name of the enterprise (Dracula Incorporated) left little to the imagination.

To his credit, Mr. Cambronne bought the blood by the gallon instead of just sucking it from the neck of his victims.

Starving fellas volunteered to be bled for three dollars a pop. Rich in antibodies, the plasma was transferred through pipelines to Switzerland and the United States. It is not by accident that Mr. Cambronne called his memoirs: *The Open Veins of Papadopolis*.

In his shocking confessions, he mentioned his other enterprise: FCI (Fresh Corpse International). The deceased were exiled. Sold to overseas medical schools.

At one point, Mister Cambronne received an award as the Vampire of the Caribbean. He was previously a bank teller and transitioned well to the blood bank business.

On their side, the bedbugs were big like teeny-weeny ninja

turtles. They knew when to strike and when to retreat to their trenches. The concept of "Peaceful Coexistence" inaugurated by the belligerent nations after World War II had no meaning to them. It was business as usual: a bloody war!

Those who felt threatened in their sleep fought back with chemical weapons. They used Baygon, a toxic spray imported from Germany.

Bugs or not, there was something sweet about peeing in bed, a foretaste of things to come. On the other hand, it was hard to escape communal inquiry.

The soaked mattress drying outside in the sun would indicate to the neighbors that I was a repeat offender. I had done it again. They would come to visit Ma Fifine to share their urologic expertise in overactive bladders.

"No drinking after 6 PM." I received free, in-house consultations, from unschooled neighbors who had a degree in pediatric care. They reached a common diagnostic and prescribed natural remedies. Under the pretext that it takes a village to raise a child, my peeing record became a "pubic" matter that was discussed in a one-mile radius.

I was furious at myself. I was my own worst enemy. I

developed among my playmates the reputation of a night-time sprinkler. I wasn't proud of the little man I saw in the water.

Guess what? Regardless of the precondition, my mommy loves me. Mark my words: one day like today, I am going to grow up and everything's gonna be fine.

As though I were their own child, the neighbors were overly concerned with my incontinence. They felt it was their duty to fix me. At thirteen, I started to deal with a new drama, a new stretch of unwelcome evacuation. Something thicker, even more embarrassing. What is a man to do?

On the radio, Al Green was singing: "How can a loser ever win?"

I got you, bro.

It did not take long for the rumor to spread in the hood. They congratulated me on my pubescent achievement and the upgrade of my irrigation system. I was enrolled in the alpha male fraternity. I was marking my territory and leaving new marks on the old mattress. They looked like maps of Curaçao where Venus is queen, and the king is Eros.

I was beyond the age of innocence. I started to look at girls with a new set of eyes. Was it okay to play hide-and-seek with them? I wasn't sure anymore. I was fearful of these strange creatures who looked like mermaids with short hair.

Ma Fifine was vigilant about my morality. When I saw her bottle of olive oil in the kitchen, I thought: "That's it! That's how she wants me to stay: extra virgin!"

It took me an eternity to figure things out and come up with basic answers. How to tame my dragon. How to navigate among the reefs without capsizing too fast and furious at myself.

Once upon an island where team spirit was queen. Raising a child was a tribal adventure, a slow journey in the wilderness of infancy. In my hood of Martissant, the woman next door was an alternate mom. Ma Fifine's godson was *mon frère de baptême*, my brother by baptism.

We never missed the chance to connect people, to put some glue between them, to transform them into Siamese siblings. We were smart enough to understand that we are all passengers on the same titanic boat. A boat the geographers call island.

Ma Fifine was overprotective. She poured into me so much

honey. I felt like the sweetest thing that happened to her. I kid you not when I say: she was awesome.

Every Sunday, she would wake up in broad darkness, to go to the 4 A.M. mass. I had heard that the *loups-garous* had no reverence for religious affiliations. Whether you practiced Voodoo or Christianity, whether you were a Mormon or a Jehovah's Witness, they would eat you alive with the same enthusiasm.

Once, I made a promise to Ma Fifine. "Ma, I want to go to church with you tomorrow." She gave me the amused smile of which she had the secret. When the time came to go, at 3:30, I panicked. Why take chances? If I stay still in my bed, I'll be safe.

The fact that Ma Fifine managed to return home around 6 AM, always appeared to me as a miracle. Papa Déus was more prudent. He was a fervent Catholic, but he preferred to pray remotely, in the sanctity of his home. He would listen to the mass on the radio.

Some Sundays, Ma Fifine would go to church twice. It was a time when women were expected to be more religious than men. They carried the crown of thorns; they carried the cross for the salvation of humanity.

I became Ma Fifine's confident, a mama's boy trying to dazzle her with good behavior and kind words. She was moved to tears when I looked at her black and white portrait in the living room and told her: "Ma, you look like a movie star."

She knew in her heart I wasn't old enough to engage in white lies. She knew I wasn't prepared yet to formulate the kind of counterfeit emotions grownups are good at. It was a sincere compliment. She did have the Mona Lisa look. To me, it was just a spontaneous remark. To her, it meant the world. She was not alone in this relationship. Her baby boy loved her and was learning how to express emotions.

I guess it was my first step in the sugarcane alley that leads to women's heart. She was my first and ultimate conquest. When I grew up, I ran out of luck.

She took great pleasure in getting rave reviews on my behavior from the neighbors whose eyes were the surveillance cameras of the time. I was pretty good at distributing greetings generously, throughout the day: *"Bonjour voisin; bonsoir voisine."*

Won't you be my neighbor?

298

Ma Fifine expected me to show good manners in all circumstances. She taught me the art of surprising visitors with unexpected kindness. "Bonjour Maître Dolcé. Do you want some coffee? I'll bring you the paper while you wait for Maître Ben." I had vested interest in being good. I knew for a fact it was going to be reported to Ma Fifine. I still practice the same values. Put me under the microscope and I'll behave like a perfect gentleman.

I was a pet project. An experiment in human behavior. Ma Fifine thought I was something special. By the time she realized I was a prodigal son, it was too late.

I was obedient to her firm but tender authority. She could see me already in the Pantheon of future Catholic saints. It took me many years and a good influx of testosterone to turn that bad.

It happened when she left the island to go to work on the other side of the ocean, in the glamorous suburbs of West Palm Beach.

While she was gone, I lost my moral compass. My sense of direction was impaired. I couldn't live up to her expectations.

Every time Ma Fifine's name comes up, I feel a rush of sadness. Now that I have lost my biological mother, the memory of the two women has merged into one. Sometimes, I don't know if I am talking about one or the other. I don't always know if I am in Martissant or in Pétion-Ville.

As a child, I was close to my two families. Except maybe for my genetic dad who was often away. He was busy spreading his seeds in new gardens.

He was a man with a hungry heart. Wherever he went, he carried well his first name: Herman. The fact that he was in the military and had been the chauffeur of General President Magloire added glamour to his aura of Latin lover.

Because of my father's active love life, I inherited a multitude of siblings scattered around the globe. They have discovered, colonized, and civilized many regions, especially the East Coast of the United States and Western Europe.

We probably inherited these colonial dispositions from Chevalier Julien Desroches whose name was given in 1771 to an island of the Indian Ocean. On the African side of our ancestry, we probably got something from Chaka, the mighty Zulu conqueror.

In the 80s, one of my sisters headed south in the New World, explored the Island of Saint-Martin before settling in French Guiana, South America. She adjusted well. She already had the beautiful features of a dark aboriginal of the rain forest.

One day, we intend to have a family gathering in a place that is large enough to accommodate all of us. Desroches Island would probably sink to the bottom of the ocean under the weight of the multitude.

Like in the early ages of humanity, life in Martissant was rustic, provincial. Neighbors formed a large tribe in which civility and solidarity were natural. Because Papa Déus was a gregarious individual, our house was a community center where anyone could stop by to play dominoes, drink coffee, have a shot of rum punch, get some free coconuts and papaya fruits.

It was an era of great conviviality when people shared almost everything: money, honey, sugar, salt, even children. Since my mother had five kids, it was only fair that she let me stay with my godmother. It was a nice gesture from which I have highly benefited.

I was delighted by the arrangement. The mere idea of having just one mom and one dad was alien to me. I had full-time and part-time parents.

Like a poor aristocrat, I would spend most of my time in Martissant (Cité Manigat), surrounded by the undivided attention of my godparents.

Every Friday afternoon, I would travel to the city to meet with Ma Rolande to get my allowance. She was working as a skilled dressmaker at Wilsa Outlet for twelve dollars a week. It wasn't much, but she was paid on time. Something that was unheard of.

Throughout her career, over decades, the idea of a vacation never occurred to her. Aside from a few days she took to have surgery, she could not afford to be sick. She never lived for herself but the well-being of her kiddies.

Under the appearance of a frail creature, she was a force of nature. To this day, I am still trying to figure out how she managed to pass away and leave me behind.

Molière was probably right. She was strong enough to deal with old age, not strong enough to deal with the medication of her doctors.

Every Friday, I would rendezvous with Ma Rolande near the downtown Iron Market. She would buy me my favorite staples: a box of oatmeal, brown sugar, Carnation milk, and pre-owned comic books.

She would add forty cents to my bounty to go to the movies. At Ciné Sénégal, the cost for the early birds was twelve cents. On her side, Ma Fifine would not accept any child support. She would be offended if it were offered.

Pétion-Ville was my secondary residence, my vacation home. What you would call in fancy French: *mon lieu de villégiature*. There, I was treated with the regards that are due to Ma Fifine's little prince. If anyone of my siblings said anything impolite to my majesty, I would say: "Bye. I am going home!" I always assumed that my feudal lands, my castle, and my queen were in Martissant.

I felt completely justified in calling two different men, two different women: dad and mom. I wouldn't want it any other way. At the end of the road, I realize now that I am in the rare position of having more parents to mourn.

Out of the blue, when I was free from school, I would decide to spend time with my blood relatives on the hills of Pétion-Ville. It was my way to alternate, to avoid the monotony of spending my entire time in one place.

I would take one of these colorful *tap-taps* that ensure the liaison between Martissant and Port-au-Prince. Like moving art galleries, the *tap-taps* were decorated with a kaleidoscope of colors. They were gigantic boom boxes with hi-fi speakers spitting out the latest hits of *konpa* and French ballads.

The four-mile trip between Martissant and Papadopolis would cost five cents. Since the *tap-taps* were too often empty, two passengers were allowed to ride for the price of one. The older one had to notify the driver in advance by saying: "I have a zombie with me".

How can you say "no" to someone like that?

The zombie was supposed to stand up or to sit on the paying passenger's lap. The privilege of being a zombie was often reserved for kids. Short adults were sometimes able to avoid the fare.

When I started to attend the high school of acclaimed writer Frankétienne in the hills of Belair, I saved a ton of money by becoming, twice a week, the zombie of my classmates.

Public transportation was slowed by the constant stops to solicit passengers. Joël, a tall, lanky kid from the hood used to ignore the *tap-taps* and walk the five miles between Belair and Martissant. He was so fast; we called him American Airlines. When he felt like flying, it was not unusual to witness his landing in Martissant at the same time as our *tap-tap*.

To reach Pétion-Ville from downtown, I would take one of these American oldies: Oldsmobile Vista, DeSoto Firedome, Plymouth Belvedere, Pontiac Bonneville, Chrysler Town & Country. They were antique station wagons that were retrieved from a graveyard in the US and summoned to find a new lifeline on the roads of Papadopolis.

At one point, these grumpy old cars vanished from the landscape. They were replaced by the new wheels on the block: the French Peugeot. Finally, the Japanese Daihatsu took over the trail and never let go.

Sometimes, I would spend two weeks in Pétion-Ville, incommunicado with Ma Fifine. Telephones were high-tech gadgets reserved for big shots of the Executive. They were allergic to the rain. Sometimes, they would play dead. They would spend days without showing a pulse. Nonetheless, they were wiretapped to allow Papa Doc to listen to the juicy conversations of his subjects.

To the masses was reserved the *teledyòl* (Chinese whispers) to move rumors from one hood to the next. The *teledyòl* was more efficient than WhatsApp and Twitter combined. It had the magical ability to report events before they happened.

Ma Fifine had no way to confirm I had arrived at my destination in Pétion-Ville. It was no big deal. Around that time, kidnappers of children were not born yet. When Clément Barbot tried to snatch the kids of the President, he failed. He was a good killer and a bad kidnapper.

The climate of terror was affecting mostly the grown-ups. Random killings were a fact of life. Yet, there was a logic to it. Something the exiled anthropologist Michel-Rolph Trouillot called: "the daily verification of violence." A preemptive form of repression to drown in blood any temptation to revolt.

The *tontons* received carte blanche to kill at will. According to Papa Doc, it was a pedagogic procedure. They killed to teach people how to live under the rules of Papadocracy.

Kiddies were mostly at risk at night when the *loups-garous* were on a feeding frenzy and actively searching for fresh blood.

306

In the fight for survival, knowledgeable mothers would spread sea salt on top of the roof to keep the flying monsters away. Newborns would receive regular shots of sour turtle blood to discourage the vampires.

Early in the morning, the uproar of the rooster would signal the imminent rise of the sun. For every child, it was a melodious sound.

It meant that one had survived. Another day was coming.

Another night also to enjoy the guilty pleasure of peeing in bed.

"He had seen Haiti's nightmare, its blue dogs, the oxcart that collected the dead off the street at dawn."

Gabriel García Márquez

"Nights of terror were followed by days of persecution."

Miguel Ángel Asturias

Radiography of Doctor Duvalier

In the south of Martissant, the scenery was very picturesque. The land was having a torrid love affair with the sea. They gave birth to coco trees and flamingos near the pink, sandy beach.

Buyers beware. This is not a postcard from a lost paradise. This is not an ad for fancy sunglasses. This is not a campaign for Carnival Cruise Line. Life in the Tropics is not a garden of roses.

Nonetheless, for the lucky son of a gun, for those who didn't care much about the atmosphere of fear and despair, every second was a Kodak moment.

Before sunset, the fishermen would carry their small load of marine specimens to the land. Baked by the sun, they were dark to the point of becoming blue. They were soaked in sweat and skinny like the fish they were able to catch. Unsung heroes of the high waves, they were unmoved by the grisly reputation of the shark.

Ever since they've been waiting for their own Hemingway to tell their story to the world. They might have to wait a little longer.

It was a time so ancient that houses didn't have numbers; streets didn't have names. My personal address was: Ma Fifine's house. That was the end of it.

Everybody knew everybody's genealogy going back to colonial times. Addresses were indicated by the proximity to a random landmark, a flamboyant tree, a notable individual, or a distinguished member of the animal kingdom.

Confronted with the burden of modernity, our neighbors started to assign arbitrary names to their streets: Ruelle Nemours (in homage to the musician), Ruelle Bourrique (Donkey Street, in honor of the iconic pet of Madame Chéry, the Voodoo priestess), Cité Beauboeuf (in homage of a handsome cow.) Yet, there were no street signs. Just a mental GPS in everyone's calabash to navigate the narrow roads and corridors pompously called avenues and boulevards.

Located a few feet from the ocean, the fish market was named after the First Lady, her Highness Simone Ovide Duvalier. She was a tall, skeletal dragon lady with a steely face. A tropical version of Morticia, the witchy character of the TV show *The Addams Family*. In contrast, she was always on mute; she never said a word in public. In the international press, she was known as Mama Doc. Locally, she received the affectionate surname of Manman Simone.

Every year around Christmas, her Majesty would come to the neighborhood of Martissant to distribute bags of toys to needy toddlers. Some young adults masquerading as children would pick up some dolls, sell them in the open market and make a few bucks for the holidays.

In mid-November, eager radio jockeys would start playing Christmas Carols to lift the spirits from the funky mood. Except for the henchmen of Papa Doc, everybody felt the need to be civil, to be on their best behavior. Our Savior with long hair and fair skin was about to be born on the distant shores of Bethlehem.

For security purposes, the date of the miraculous apparition of Manman Simone would vary from one year to the next. Officially, it was supposed to be on the 22, the magical number of the Doc Dynasty.

From the windows of her Rolls-Royce limousine that looked like a hearse, coins and small bills of twenty cents would be thrown to the starving residents. A big brouhaha would ensue. Manly women and men would struggle to catch the flying bonanza with acrobatic moves. The public would encourage Mama Doc to throw more money by shouting: "*Vive Duvalier! A vie! A vie!*" (Long life to Duvalier! For life! For life!) When Papa Doc passed away, Cambronne, the vampire, became the toy-boy of Mama Simone.

What's in a name? The imprint of the dynasty had to be everywhere. Regardless of the level of decrepitude. Apparently, embarrassment was not part of the family values. The largest slum of the Antilles was officially baptized Cité Simone. A rocky corridor that led to the beach was inaugurated as Claudius Avenue. A sleepy town formerly known as Cabaret was rebranded Duvalier-Ville. It was supposed to outclass Ciudad Trujillo.

The plan of the government was to convert this rural community into a futuristic city similar to Brasilia. At least, that's what was reported in *Papa News,* the bilingual newspaper. For some reason, the young journalist who was sold on the patriotic fabrications of Papa Doc concluded: "Nothing great will be accomplished in this country without a burst of quixotism and megalomania."

The contract to build Duvalier-Ville was awarded to an avant-garde company located in Silicon Valley. It was doing business under the strange but visionary name of Photoshop Construction Incorporated.

The Prez for life was delighted when the prototype was introduced to him on the red carpet. Like a kid visiting Toys R Us for the first time, he was fascinated by the magnitude, the sheer beauty of the master plan. He dropped to his knees to have a closer look at the miniature buildings: the skyscrapers, the Papa Tower, the museum of horror, the bridges over the blood river, the cemeteries, the pyramids of the mummies, the replica of the hanging gardens of Babylon.

The golden tooth of Papa Doc was shining like a ray of supernatural light. Everything was right there in the layout. Even the concentration camp and the cuckoo's nest for the growing number of enemies. The Doc intended to eradicate and replace them with the new, obedient species: Homo Papadocus.

Duvalier-Ville was supposed to be the most attractive city in the Caribbean, the pearl of Papadocracy. It was being built near the hamlet of Ozanana. It had a name that sounded like pure poetry to Papa Doc's ears.

Yes, it was going to be expensive, but he had a surefire plan. He could force his allies to pay the tab. He had done that before when he needed money to build the Papa Doc Airport at that location called Maïs Gâté (rotten corn). He could threaten his allies with the possibility of switching sides to the Soviets, to transform his country into a new Cuba if they refused to deliver the dough. For the new flag, he selected two colors the US was not comfortable with: black and red.

He was a mafia boss who knew how to blackmail. As a shrewd manipulator, he was proud of his ability to treat the Ambassador Ebenezer McCarthy like a child. A sucker for anticommunist candies. Whenever there was a complaint about bloodshed and torture by the Society for the Protection of Haitians Living in the Hereafter, Papa Doc would reassure the diplomat by saying: "All the victims were members of the Marxist-Leninist Party." The Ambassador would be reassured. He would send a cable, a WikiLeaks to Washington to confirm that everyone on the island was fine except the commies.

Life would go on. Life at the border of death. Life hanging by a thin gray hair. For you are dust and shall return to dust. The political program of Papa Doc was clear and simple: terror against the enemies who dared to say his presidential term had expired. The Duvalier Manifesto was eloquently articulated by Doctor Jacques Fourcand, his alter ego and personal physician: "Blood will flow as never before. The land will burn. They'll be no sunrise, no sunset, just an enormous flame licking the sky."

At the Blue Angel Funeral Home, business was booming. The local newspaper *Le Matin* was making a killing with the obituaries. Some stations had no time for anything else. It was not unusual to hear messages of sympathy in the middle of the night. Schoolchildren knew by heart the predictable lines: "We announce with infinite sorrow the sad news of the death of…In these painful circumstances, we present our sincere condolences to…" Yet, lots of people were not so lucky to have a formal ceremony. They went straight to the mass graves.

As President for life, the undertaker Doctor Duvalier never traveled abroad. He would be gun-shy in foreign lands. He would feel too vulnerable without his arsenal.

As though he had height anxiety, he never considered the possibility of taking a plane or a helicopter. Except on that memorable night in July when the island was invaded by a ragtag army of eight adventurers. They gave him an ultimatum: "Leave now or die!"

317

To scare Papa Doc away, the rebels made thunderous noises with their guns. Fright, fight, flight? What's a man to do?

Even though the preferred brand of cigarettes was called *Lucky Strike*, smoking did kill at that time too. Sometimes instantly. One of the insurgents was captured and executed while he was taking a cigarette break. He had gone outside of the barracks because he wanted to protect his comrades from secondhand smoke.

Suddenly, the Doc became very brave, sublimely heroic in his bunker when he learned that the "invaders" were not even a dirty dozen, not even eight anymore, just seven desperados trapped in a rat-hole, ready to be sent to the afterlife.

In the meantime, the official photographer of the Palace had discretely removed his khaki uniform and fled in his underwear. He wanted to allow the belligerents to settle their differences before returning to his job at a more appropriate time.

Papa Doc dressed in an iron helmet and full military regalia insisted on taking the first selfie recorded in the island's chronicles. Unfortunately, in the background, one could see his loaded suitcases confirming the rumors that he was not the hero he wanted to portray, but a greedy coward who was getting ready to flee to Switzerland to be closer to his money.

It was the night when a loose cigarette changed the course of history. For more than a quarter of a century, the Doc Dynasty was going to write new chapters in a long saga spattered with blood and ashes.

Throughout the years, Papa remained unresponsive to repeated invitations to attend international gatherings of Chiefs of State. After his resurrection from a diabetic coma, he became very paranoid and felt that someone, somewhere, was trying to drag him out of his comfort zone. He religiously resisted the temptation to come to the U.N., in the Big Apple. It was quite a departure from his predecessor General Paul Magloire who once spent no less than two weeks visiting the US and appearing in living color on the cover of *Time* Magazine.

The General was a *bon vivant*, a politically correct Caribbean leader who enjoyed fine American burgers, French fries, filet mignon, and a good shot of Rhum Barbancourt on the rocks. According to his critics, when a bottle of Black and White whiskey was offered to him by the American ambassador, he insisted on using two glasses: one for black, one for white.

When he traveled to the US, he was warmly welcomed at the residence of Vice-President Richard Nixon (dressed in a chef garment and white hat) who famously said to him: "I am not a cook, but…" The General was a bit puzzled. Despite the intensive courses, his command of the English language was still shaky. For obvious reasons, he didn't seem too comfortable with a white man dressed in white.

Many years later, on November 17, 1973, caught in the Watergate scandal, Richard Nixon who had become President, said this time: "I am not a crook…"

General Magloire shook his head, smiled, and thought sadly about the tragicomedy of power. It was 1973 and he had been living in Jamaica Estates, New York, as an exile for the past 17 years. He was sinking into a deep depression. Papa Doc had stripped him of his most precious asset: his Haitian citizenship.

He was swimming in a stream of consciousness. He marveled at the time when he, the General, was in power as an authoritarian democrat who was ruling with an iron fist in a velvet glove. Duvalier was hiding under his nose. It would have been child's play for the Bureau of Investigation to capture him.

The Doc was already a bandit, a well-known "bombist". He would disguise as an old woman to go from this house to that one under the cover of darkness. He, the General, didn't want to do anything about that.

General Paul Magloire had overthrown President Dumarsais Estimé in a smooth and bloodless coup. Magloire was so civil that a few days later, he escorted his victim to the airport to salute him for the last time. In the US, the deposed presidential couple gave birth to a daughter they aptly called Exilienne.

But Magloire had underestimated Duvalier. Because of his nasal voice, his low profile, and his shadowy personality, a lot of people regarded him as a zombie who couldn't possibly have a political future. His apparent weakness was in fact his strength, his secret weapon. It was on the assumption that he was a dummy that he was selected by General Thompson Kébreau to play the role of a civilian puppet. It didn't take long for the puppet master to realize he had created a monster.

General Magloire thought about his era as Head of State when he was not allowed to be too heavy-handed. Around that time, in retaliation, he would not touch the family members of his opponents. Spouses and children were off-limits.

Papa Doc came and changed the equation. Everyone was guilty by association and by blood relation. Even dogs had to pay a heavy price for the political affiliations of their owners. "This dog looks suspicious too. Does he recognize my blue uniform? Does he know that I have the power and the will to make him disappear?"

Dozens of dogs were slaughtered when it was reported to the Doc that his archenemy Clément Barbot had morphed into a canine.

And now, he, General Paul Magloire, an officer who used to be a playboy, a gentleman who used to dance like Fred Astaire, a socialite who inspired the carnival hit song "Every day I am drunk", was a miserable political refugee in a place in the US, near Nassau County, near Long Island. A place ironically called Jamaica. What kind of Jamaica is that? What kind of Long Island is that where the sun is shy, where beaches are freezing, where roosters don't sing in the morning, where the coconut tree grows inside the supermarket near the Poland Spring water bottles?

He thought about Nassau (Bahamas), he thought about the enchanted island of Jamaica which used to be the rendezvous, the favorite destination of deposed strongmen since 1843 when the mulatto General-President Jean-Pierre Boyer lead the way after a quarter of a century in power.

General Magloire, with his name sounding like "Ma Glory" to American journalists, smiled and felt fortunate. Legally he was alive. Papa Doc had forgotten to condemn him to death in absentia, the way he did for Professor Leslie Manigat, the nephew of our neighbor Magny Manigat.

Papa Doc never took a plane at the airport that he built. In all fairness, we have to agree that traveling abroad for a Head of State of any Third World country has always been risky business. Not long ago, Mauritanian President Maaouya Ould Sid'Ahmed Taya was overthrown while he was attending the funeral of King Fahd bin Abdulaziz Al Saud, one of the 45 sons of the founding father of Saudi Arabia.

His Excellency Ahmed Taya did not see it coming. He had just celebrated his 21st year in power and was just getting started. What's the rush? In his haste to travel, he left his country, his estate, unattended and didn't even have the chance to pack his luggage properly. He left behind the life savings for rainy days he had accumulated for many generations. After 8 years in exile, he became so poor that he had to accept a job as a French professor.

In his wisdom, **Papa Doc** preferred to observe things from afar. In fact, he was everywhere and nowhere at the same time. He had the mysterious ability to read the mind of his distant and intimate enemies. He knew who was conspiring in Brooklyn, who was protesting in Manhattan, who was playing dead. Papa had his spies, his antennae, and parabolic dishes in the cosmopolitan capitals of the world.

"My name is Doc, Papa Doc." He was theatrical. The stage director of his own freak show. To world leaders, he appeared as a villain in a James Bond movie. Some sort of Dr. No or other unsavory characters we have buried somewhere in our reptilian brain. Behind every word, behind every gesture, there was an evil genius intending to fool and mesmerize everyone.

He projected the image of a chameleon with bulletproof prescription glasses. When seeking prey and preparing to strike, he displayed a sharp and circular vision.

He knew his strengths and weaknesses. Papa Doc became agitated whenever he spent more than 60 minutes outside the Palace. He had to remain inside, in the shadow.

Far from the tanks, he felt like a shark outside the ocean.

He was vilified by the international press for being such a predator. It did not matter. The silence of the local press was loud and clear. The editor in chief of *Le Matin* received his injunction at the Department of Criminal Research.

"Do I have the right to remain silent?"

"No. You have the moral obligation to report the miracles of the Doc Revolution. Anything you don't say can be held against you in a court of law. Silence is suspicious; it will be treated as such by the government."

Papa Doc wanted to create a state-of-the-art repressive machine. He had to set the tone and preach by example. In khaki uniform, he would practice shooting in his tropical gulag of Fort Dimanche. He never wore the blue denim of the *tontons macoutes*. To him, it looked cheap and plebeian.

As a medical doctor, Papa considered life as an STD. He had to cure it with weapons of mass destruction.

He genetically passed the passion for firearms to his son Claudius-19. Without rhyme or reason, the boy would show up in social gatherings with a loaded silver pistol.

Papa Doc had such an affection for his *tontons*, he would keep them near him. They would spend the night camping on the lawn or sleeping on the floor of the Palace. Some came from the provinces with their pets. It was not surprising to hear a goat bleating, to see a chicken laying eggs in a corner of the Palace. The decorative peacocks of the Magloire era were replaced by guinea fowls. It was important to get complete political allegiance from the birds.

Some *tontons* came from places with scary names like Bombardopolis or Desolate Savanna. Some came from the border of hell. They knew how to make fire, but they were shocked when they saw a light bulb for the first time. When breakfast was served at the Palace cafeteria, they thought that their dad, Papa Doc, had invented sliced bread and electricity.

According to the volatile political climate, kiddies had unforeseen days off. Public schools were converted into ad hoc one-star hotels and shelters to accommodate the crowd of *tontons*. They would respond to the calls of nature at their convenience.

They had abandoned wives, concubines, children, and wild animals to be present where it matters the most. Like a papa talking to his teenage sons, the Doc would send them out on patrol by saying tenderly: "I'll smell you later."

Frustrated enemies of the State unable to overthrow the government for life would engage in a guerilla of rumors about the mental state of the Doc and the size of his hands. They felt that he was such a criminal because deep down premature aging had robbed him of his ability to rise to the occasion. He appeared on national television with the First Lady to refute these unpatriotic and seditious allegations.

Obviously, he was pissed. It was a blow below the belt. He went as far as showing the size of his fingers: "There is no problem in that department." Papa Doc reassured the Nation that the Head of State was stiff like yucca.

Like Fantômas, the villain of the French series, Papa was unpredictable. One never knew how far he could go. To his credit, he did not go as far as giving a live demonstration of his manhood on national television.

He needed a boost fast. He managed to have New York's governor Nelson Rockefeller to come to Papadopolis to praise him at a time when he was universally identified as a toxic individual who should be avoided like the Bubonic plague.

More than half a century later, historians are still puzzled by the unbelievable ability of the Doc to transform eagles into hummingbirds, and tigers into pussycats.

Rich and poor, old and young, schoolchildren and babies in the cradle, all true patriots were invited to contribute to the majestic project of Duvalier-Ville. According to Gwo Joe, the speaker in chief at the Voice of the Revolution, this new development was the signal of a promising future, a clear demonstration of the ideal of grandeur of the Supreme Chief.

He could have been a mortician. He could have been an excellent butcher. He settled for medicine. He developed what Empress Joséphine Bonaparte called the Napoleon complex.

Papa Doc was a great admirer of French General Charles de Gaulle. He looked up to him. The guy was taller than the Eiffel Tower. He was the incarnation of the French ego: "All my life, I have always had a certain idea of France; France cannot be France without grandeur."

Papa Doc was going to emulate that with the creation of Duvalier-Ville.

After years of comical hype and engrossing expectations, the pregnant mountain gave birth to a chicken. The main building erected in the city of Duvalier-Ville was a cockfighting arena.

Papa Doc was inspired by his Dominican neighbor El Jefe, also known as "The Goat" because of the strong, malodorous emanation from his armpit. He had his statues all over the place and changed the name of the capital of his country (Santo Domingo) into Ciudad Trujillo.

In no uncertain terms, it was important for everybody to know the names of the new masters. Fifteen decades after the 1804 independence, the island was being recolonized. Not by foreigners, not by the French, not by the Spaniards. The new conquistadores, the new pirates, the new colonizers were indigenous: the Duvaliers and their *tontons macoutes*.

Aside from the looting of the national coffer, they engaged in the slave trade and every year sold thousands of peasants to the sugar plantations of the Dominican Republic. The last transaction was conducted in January, one month before the fall of the dynasty: 19.000 poor fellas for 2 million dollars cash, hand-delivered to Duvalier Junior.

They couldn't care less about the objections of the Anti-Slavery Society of London. Papa Doc was a proud autocrat.

He had given to himself the absolute right to dispose of the life of his fellow citizens as he saw fit. To him, it was the ultimate form of nationalism. Among the litany of songs to the glory of the Savior, one of the most popular lines was: "Foreigners should not get involved in the business of Duvalier." It was quite a hit on the radio.

Papa Doc was a great admirer of MLK and the Civil Rights Movement in the US. As long as people were fighting for equality and democracy in faraway places, it was fine with him. He just didn't like it on his own estate: Haiti.

In 1968, he published *A Tribute to the Martyred Leader of Non-Violence, Reverend Dr. Martin Luther King*. Originally written in French, the book was translated into English to allow the American public to benefit from the humanitarian philosophy of Papa Doc.

Even though MLK was his polar opposite, he really liked him as a foreign freedom fighter. Of course, he would have killed him too if he were Haitian. He would have killed Nelson Mandela even faster. But that's another story.

He loved to use MLK to get back at his American critics. "How dare you lecture me about democracy when you practice apartheid and treat your black citizens like pariahs?"

Papa smiled. He had made a good point. More than a mere president, he was in his mind an intellectual giant. He was proud of that. "Go fix your racial problems, then we'll talk."

Through his thick eyeglasses, Papa Doc didn't see any conflict between Martin Luther King's pacifism and his own genocidal tendencies towards his countrymen. As long as islanders were being killed by the *tontons,* as long as they were being molested, tortured by the local enemy with the same skin color, it was totally cool. The worst-case scenario, the humiliating alternative would have been a bullet fired by a pale face, a foreigner. This would be really bad. Bad for the health. Bad for the skin. Bad for the image. Bad for the national ego. As long as the bullet was shot by a local militia dressed in blue or khaki, it was totally fine. Even if the bullet were clearly marked: Born in the USA.

This approach to life and death was one of the finest contributions of Papa Doc to the national ideology.

The Duvaliers were the Holy Family. They had all sorts of patriotic and personal virtues that were revealed to them and the public on a daily basis by the Voice of the Revolution. When you thought you had heard it all, something new came up.

According to the official lyricist of the régime, Mama Doc's heart was as big as a balloon. She was able to defy gravity, float in the sky, above the clouds, and see for herself the problems of the unfortunates of destiny. If there were something that kept her awake at night, it was the welfare of the children of a lesser god who were living in the shantytown of Cité Simone.

She saw herself as a local incarnation of Evita. The daughter of a servant, she pulled herself out of poverty and became a nurse. She seduced the shy and awkward doctor Duvalier who suffered a pathologic fear of women. She bore him three daughters and one Baby Doc.

It's been said by the lyricist that she was the first, the last, the everything. Probably not. In her autobiography *Life without Makeup*, Guadeloupean novelist Maryse Condé claimed to have had in Paris a tumultuous relationship with a fella called Jacques who introduced himself as the love child of Papa Doc. Fiction or reality? One thing is sure: the jackass had the same murderous instinct. He threatened to send the *tontons* after the writer in West Africa where she took refuge for a certain time.

Another unsavory character named Pierre André is also reputed to have been the son of Papa Doc. He decided to stay in Papadopolis while his family was fleeing on a jumbo jet on that cool night of February.

When the foreign bank accounts of the Doc dynasty were discovered, it appeared that the Duvaliers had been very generous to themselves. It was a time when Panama and the Caiman Islands did not exist yet as fiscal paradises. The money laundering was done at the Lake of Geneva, in Switzerland.

A gigantic homing pigeon, General Prosper Avril was raised in the farm of the Palace. He had the ability to commute between Papadopolis and Europe with suitcases full of green currency.

He had his nest at the National Bank and was in charge of all droppings and withdrawals.

Among naturalists and bird watchers, he'll always be remembered as the pigeon with the golden eggs.

"In the old days, people like that simply did not exist; he was an entirely new specimen of the race, one that could arise only in exhausted, dissipated time like these."

Patrick Süskind

"I eventually passed this class, but I had to sacrifice a chicken to the Voodoo god Shango."

Anonymous American student.

A Very Particular Student

The American Consulate was located across the street from the Law School. It was at the time a modest and ordinary compound. Something shy, unpretentious, trying to hide itself from public view. Yet, it was regarded by many as the most attractive destination.

Before the crow of the rooster, around three in the morning, desperate souls, unafraid of evil spirits, would start lining up outside the building. They were there to request the elusive visa to escape the Papa Doc's nightmare.

Some went to church with their passport to have it blessed, sprinkled with holy water by the priest. Full of hope, they were dying to leave and saw themselves flying to the Neverlands of their dreams: El Dorado, Miami, Montreal, Paris, New York, New Haven.

"I hear gunfire, I see apocalypse, I see exodus." The fortune teller was frightened by the turbulence, the maelstrom she saw on the crystal ball. She'd been in this business for more than twenty-five years and had never seen anything of that sort. Most of the time it was predictable visions: happy ending stories of clients winning the lotto, desperate job seekers finding at last a lucrative position, passionate Creole beauties getting married to handsome dudes with good diction.

This time, things were different. Dressed in her purple gown, the medium couldn't hide the turmoil in her eyes. They were bulging out of their sockets. "I see rickety boats, I see sharks, I see planes."

The new slogan of United Airlines was right on target: "Come fly the friendly skies". The travel agency on Harry Truman Boulevard was going to make a bundle in the gold rush towards the North.

"The price of the round-trip ticket is…"

"Believe me, she doesn't need a round-trip ti…"

"Yes, she does. That's the law of the land. *Bon voyage*! The sky's the limit."

To cross the barbed wire of the airport and access the plane, a *visa de sortie* was required; another visa assigned this time by the Palace. That's how millions of folks were kept hostage on Papa's estate of ten thousand square miles.

Despite the dexterity of the calligrapher-in-chief of the

underground opposition, Papa Doc's signature could never be duplicated. It looked like a glyph. Something alien, mysterious, grandiose, and frightening.

Papa's ambition was to keep his remains, his mummified body in charge of the Nation until the end of time. "Presidency for life is a historical necessity; as long as I am alive, as long as I am dead, there will be no elections on this island."

Because he was so volatile, Papa had a change of heart. A few months before he expired, he decided to transfer the throne to his teenage son who had received the moniker of "Claudius-19" from a Latin instructor who saw him as a young Roman emperor.

If we were to examine the official photographs of the time, we could see clearly that the teenage boy was not excited about the prospect of becoming President for Life. He was upset and it showed.

"Say cheese, Claudius!"

Not a chance. He would not listen to his Papa. As though he had an Olmec mask on his face, he was frozen in time. He would not look the camera in the eye.

His CV was blank, except for the qualifications summary line where he wrote: son of dictator for life. According to the testimony of Dan Supplice, his playmate, Claudius would have preferred any other occupation; even the most exotic: sumo wrestler, hot dog eating competitor, Pillsbury Doughboy, Buddha impersonator. You name it. However, he didn't have any choice. Papa Doc did not play games with those who opposed his will.

Thrown in the arena without his consent, with the passing of time, Claudius-19 grew his own appetite for power. At one point, he started to call himself "the son of the tiger".

The transmission of power was done on the night Papa Doc selected to die officially. He was a great choreographer and a political Houdini. His departure from the scene was flawlessly executed by a cohort of actors and enthusiastic minions.

During 14 everlasting years, that appeared to be more than an eternity, the Patriarch had exercised complete control over his four million children. They called him Papa for a reason.

He didn't have a single black hair, but his photographic memory had remained intact. It was something supernatural. He could remember vividly the faces and the names of thousands of suspects of which he had seen the passport or the psychological profile at the Department of Criminal Research. He could determine with scientific accuracy which branch of a family was contaminated by the virus of rebellion. He could diagnose remotely symptoms of opportunistic infection and signs of discontent in the social tissue: inflammatory speeches, pursed lips, nausea, constant spitting, gloomy mood, apathy, lack of interest in the official discourse.

He had a great sense of anticipation. He knew his enemies even before they made the suicidal decision to fight him.

"*Se fout papa ou mwen ye!*" I am your freaking father! Regardless of their age, Papa's children were all minors. They could not go anywhere without his stamp of approval. They could not swim in the river that divides the two countries of the island without proper documentation in their pockets. As the Supreme Chief, he had hired himself as Director of Homeland Security, Minister of Emigration, Minister of Culture and Agriculture.

At the airport, a blacklist of the enemies of the State was meticulously examined by a diligent clerk to ensure that every candidate to exile was indeed free to go. Papa Doc erupted in volcanic ashes, molten rocks, toxic malodorous gases when he learned that his archenemy, Jacques Soleil, a leftist physician, had escaped the country under the cover of a fake beard and a false identity. A few days later, his picture appeared in the VIP section of *Pravda*, the Russian newspaper.

Soleil was a brilliant novelist. He secured a medical degree because he could, just for the heck of it. It was a common practice on the island. Soleil went to medical school like a son who wanted to please his daddy and give him something to talk about. He never had the vocation. His father was a well-bred gentleman who had published a book entitled *The Masked Black Man*.

Aesthetically, the MD diploma from the Faculté de Médecine was a nice decoration on the wall of fame in the living-room. A medical practice? This was way beneath him. He would have felt sick.

He did have that megalomaniac attitude towards real life and mundane existence. He saw himself as a Promethean character in a novel he had not yet written.

Jacques Soleil was a cardiologist of a higher caliber, a poet at heart, a poet in prose. He was the kind of writer whose grocery list was more interesting than most anthologies of poems.

His comrades were unanimous: with Soleil, you never knew the margin between fiction and reality. That's how he lived his life. That's how he also died. When he vanished, it became impossible to reach a definitive conclusion. One thing is sure: he was captured soon after a suicidal landing to ignite a Cuban-style revolution.

His first novel was a masterpiece. From the start, the reader knew she was in good hands. The very first page was worth the price of the book. In just a few seconds, in just a few sentences, he had established himself as a new, refreshing voice. The rest of the novel was a mere formality. A huge and generous bonus.

The ferocious and bloodthirsty literary critic Maximilien Boileau, Executive Director of the Parisian magazine *The Guillotine*, was speechless. Max was the embodiment of that French tradition of deadly journalistic attacks with swords. He was known for his ability to spill blood with his sharp fountain pen. In his last piece he had quipped about a newcomer: "What a terrific writer Pierre Lesroches could have been if he knew how to write."

With just a few sentences, carefully selected for maximum impact, he could make or break a reputation. Max was the terror of aspiring writers. They were losing their head over fear. Some wrote with a British intonation to hide their identity. Some adopted a fake name, a *nom de plume*.

Soleil's book gave him a rush of adrenaline he had not experienced in a long time. This time, Max kept it short and sweet: "*Touché!* A star is born. Mister Soleil's first book is exceptional; a literary event!"

Jacques Soleil? Who the hell was he? It was an out of this world experience. A thrill, a cascade of words, a magical carpet flying above the flimsiness of life.

His writing made you feel high. Do you know what I mean? Oh no, not that kind of high. I mean a literary ecstasy, a textual satisfaction. It made you feel gaga like in a *tête-à-tête* with Lady Gaga, Gessica Généus, Rihanna, Josephine Baker, or Zsa Zsa Gabor. Holding his book in public made you feel smart, important. According to legendary commentator Maurice Sixto, people would fall in love at the bookstore when they realized they were searching for the same title. "You are looking for Soleil's book? What a beautiful coincidence. It must be a sign of destiny."

They would read to each other in bed on the first date. The naked truth is that it felt entirely natural.

The book was a pretext for all sorts of encounters of the sixth sense. "*Voulez-vous lire avec moi ce soir?*" Do you want to read with me tonight?

What was Soleil's secret? How does a human being write with such arrogant elegance? Was he a mad genius? How dare he?

His stylistic fingerprint was present on every page, in every paragraph. He just knew how to put words together with a beautiful Caribbean accent.

It was unfair to the rest of us: children of a lesser Muse. Poor bastards abandoned in the dust of disability. His writing was something dense, luxuriant like the Amazon, captivating like a diamond from a planet outside of the solar system. Something of a rare otherness that defies gravity. A *tour de force* of the human spirit.

Page after page, it was evident there was a heavy brain at play, a superior IQ juggling with the letters of the alphabet. While it may take an eternity and even beyond for a writer to hone his skills (it took a few decades for Gabriel to become García Márquez), Soleil entered the literary arena as a phenomenon, an overnight and lasting sensation. He was being mentioned as a contender for the Nobel Prize in Literature. He solidified his status with another publication: *Romancero to the Stars*.

How dare he? Papa Doc never forgave things like that. This was unacceptable. Soleil's name was added to the list. The one the Palace's secretary typed and retyped in alphabetical order with the prehistoric Smith Corona typewriter. Her job description was simple: "Update the damn list every day!"

As a fringe benefit, she was entitled to add one name of her choice per week. She never did. She didn't have to. Because of her status as the Palace's secretary, she was treated by everyone like the Queen of England.

It's been said that those who blow kisses are lazy. One day, Papa Doc (who was shy around women to the point of being paralyzed) summoned the courage to venture into the cubicle of his private secretary. He blew her a kiss and whispered: "You be the Beauty; I'll be the Beast!"

He had just done the most heroic act of his political career.

Deep down, Papa's philosophy was: "Down with the mulattos! Long life to the mulattas!"

They maintained a sweet but platonic affair that became an open secret in the hallways of the Palace. It lasted many years until she was forced into exile in Brooklyn.

Under the iron mask of intransigence and family values, was the Patriarch a closet romantic, a sucker for love and libertine escapades?

Francesca, the secretary, was hired after the notorious incident when the male military clerk assigned to this task had to type his own name to the list of those who were going to be executed that morning. It was a strange experience for him. Never in his lifetime had his name appeared to him so vividly tragic. He came to work; he was not returning home. To add insult to injury, the firing squad was composed of his closest friends of the artillery.

The Doc was refined and inventive when it came to surprises. He is still admired in certain circles and secret societies for his devilish creativity.

One never knew where one stood with him. Strong ally

today, bitter enemy tomorrow. Some henchmen were confused when they were attached to the execution pole.

"Where did I go wrong? I slaughtered so many people for you, and now you are killing me?"

"Read my lips. I've always said it: In politics, gratitude is a weakness."

As a twisted doctor, he had a craving for mental anguish and human suffering. This is what he lived for. He was grateful to the boogeymen for keeping the demographics in check. He would have done well in the Middle Ages at the time of the Crusades and the Inquisition. *The Prince* of Machiavelli is so overrated. The Doc could have written a better book.

As a scribe, as a thinker, Papa felt insulted by the international success of his challenger Jacques Soleil. In his mind, he was a giant capable of eclipsing the sun. He wrote that word for word in a voluminous hardcover entitled *Memoires of a Third World Leader*.

No one is a prophet in his own country. He understood that part. But he was not getting the worldwide recognition he craved for. *Au contraire*. He was ignored, avoided, vilified.

"It takes many generations for a country to produce someone like Me. I am the reincarnation of the founding fathers." That's what Papa Doc had mumbled in public in his perfect nasal voice on the occasion of his birthday celebration. Yet, he felt miserable. The solitude of power? Something was missing.

At the same time, Soleil was shining everywhere. He was a globetrotter, the unofficial ambassador of Culture of his homeland. Today in Conakry, West Africa, tomorrow in Belgrade, Yugoslavia. The red carpet was unwrapped and extended for him in Peking, China.

Like a wandering full moon, a halo of charm and charisma followed him everywhere he went. He had become a celebrity. He posed for History with the new tsars of the Soviet empire. He was exuding confidence in the emergence of a brand-new world. In the East, they saw him as a rising star, the embodiment of what the former colonies had to offer. He was showered with attention.

"What does he have that I don't?" Papa Doc looked in the magnifying glass (the one that transforms pussycats into tigers) and felt cheap. He was the one they love to hate. Why? He did not know. Some of his own children were gone into exile. His favorite daughter broke his heart when she married an officer of that treacherous army. A tall, ambitious guy with the wrong name: Dominique. His son was doing badly in school. His passing grades were mere charity from the Brothers of Saint-Louis de Gonzague. Giving him an F would have been signing one's death certificate.

None of his four children wanted to go to school. What's the point? They already knew how to read, to sign their names, to count their blessings in the coffers of the Swiss banks.

Geometry, algebra, trigonometry, literature? Who the hell invented this junk anyway? She or he, whoever it might be, should be unearthed and punished for child abuse. French grammar? Whoever invented that nonsense should be sentenced to death.

To the legitimate children of Papa Doc, school was synonym of torture. In the large, sunny classroom on Rue des Casernes, they were bored to death.

Who could blame them? They were spoiled rotten lumbering teenagers who wanted to eat, sleep, and fool around in the labyrinth of the Palace. It didn't sit well with Papa Doc. None of them was living up to the bare minimum of his expectations.

No spark of brainpower? He could not comprehend the fact that such a great man could produce such a fine collection of idiots. That's how he saw them. He was bitter, disappointed, but deep in his heart he continued to cherish them. He would escort them to the airport when they were going on a shopping spree in Europe. Still, they were an embarrassment to his bloodline. He felt diminished like a depressive clown at Cirque du Soleil. He blamed Simone, the First Lady, for the genetic deficiencies. He was upset. Somebody had to pay.

It was the time of the big purge; the time of the brain drain. Teachers were thrown out to Congo; doctors were ejected to Canada. To avoid any form of infiltration, college admission was controlled by the Palace.

How did Soleil escape? Papa Doc was sure of one thing: he had not issued an exit visa for this dude.

More than anything else, Jacques Soleil was a left-handed marvel. Someone who, unlike Papa Doc, wrote his books with his own pen, without a ghost, without a shadow of a doubt.

Soleil was a stubborn dissident. He was from that generation of fighters who were willing to die for a cause. An endangered species. Something that's on the path of extinction in Papado-polis. Just like the trees. Just like the birds.

From the start, Jacques Soleil committed a capital sin. He voted against the Doc in the fraudulent elections that paved the way to the dynasty. He would not collaborate with the régime for all the gold of Peru. He would not accept a job as a mouthpiece or a speechwriter. In fact, he did something singular. He published an open letter to denounce the campaign of harassment and intimidation of which he was the victim. He was being followed. His upcoming arrest by the Secret Service was a matter of public knowledge.

Hoping for a triumphal return, he managed to leave the island in a fashion that was so astonishing, nobody would have believed it if they had read it in a novel.

Absolute power is overrated. Papa Doc would have traded his Supreme position to become Soleil. Jacques was shining bright. Everywhere he went, people looked up to him. Everywhere he went became a better place by the sheer magic of his presence.

Soleil was seen in China on Sunday, January 1st while it was still December 31st in the Caribbean. It was disturbing. How does he do that? Was he in possession of a time-traveling machine? Does he have a valid driver's license for that? Could he go back in time and visit Papa Doc's mama in the psychiatric ward? Could he bring forward embarrassing pieces of evidence and ruin the reputation of the Head of State? Could he record on tape the troubling admission of Papa Doc's father: "If I knew that my son was gonna be so insane, I would have worn a condom."

The news was alarming. Was Soleil still on the island? Did he possess the magical power of being in multiple places at the same time? Did he travel under a forged identity, a curling mustache that looks like a lateral interrogation mark? Did he mesmerize the gatekeepers with hypnotic words?

Papa Doc International Airport. Checkpoint. Moment of tension when the heart skips a beat on the soundtrack of a thriller. "You look familiar. Would you happen to be a member of the Bolshevik Party?"

Communist. It was a generic term, a blanket word for any type of political activity: like yawning from hunger or boredom while Papa was talking on the radio about his Revolution. Some fellows were accused of it without knowing what it was.

Some thought it was an airborne red virus that looks like a sickle. They were confident they were going to test negative. Some thought it was a disease that the Doc wanted to eradicate with an antibiotic called *Camoquin*. Some were hearing the word for the first time from a *tonton* who did not know how to pronounce it. It was a quid pro quo of Babelic proportions. The mere fact of being alive was suspicious to the *tontons*.

Because the sun shines for everyone, every Tuesday, Wednesday, and Thursday, three honorable professors of the State Law School would come to the Palace to open the door of enlightenment to the heir apparent Claudius-19. He was a particular dude, a bloated young man with elephantesque sideburns. In the community of those who use laughter as a form of subversion, he was being compared to Michelin, the mascot of the French tire company.

More than just a prince, his father wanted him to be somebody. He would have spent a fortune for Baby Doc to be an average individual capable of saving face in public. In the official magazine *Papa News*, the teenager was being portrayed as the new Marcus Antonius Pius Augustus who became Roman Emperor at the age of 13. He had to live up to a legend.

The witchcraft doctor invited to the Palace to reflect on the lack of gray matter among the children advised Papa Doc to put his son on a daily diet of beef tongue and *cervelle de veau*. With the frankness of a Rasputin or the innocence of Konpè Bouki, he added: "In my village, it is not uncommon for a pumpkin tree to produce calabash."

The Bishop of Papadopolis, Monsignor François Ligrondé who had the reputation of a Nostradamus, also agreed that something had to be done; otherwise, the curse would be transmitted in the future to Baby Doc's first son, whose first name will come from Greek and Latin: Nikolaos Francius Janus Claudius.

The grandiosity of the name was no laughing matter. Yet, everybody erupted including Papa Doc who held his stomach and said: "Stop Monsignor. You are killing me!"

Papa Doc lost his breath. He passed out from laughing too hard. He came back to life two weeks later, still chuckling. While he was gone, his teeth were showing, and his venerable body continued to emit the distinctive fragrance of nitrous oxide (N_2O) which is also known in the medical field as "laughing gas".

This was the time when an accurate prediction of the Archbishop interpreted by the audience as a joke almost changed the course of history.

Papa Doc was mortified. It was embarrassing. None of the three First Daughters had attempted to get a semblance of higher ed. Aside from the certificate of Excellency they had received from a Swiss bank, their wall was empty. Baby Doc was the last child. He was the last chance. Papa wanted him to be a lawyer. But there was a problem. Whenever the young man heard the word "college", he felt like shooting somebody.

If you don't want to go to the mountain, you should have the mountain come to you.

From the Palace, the State University Law School was less than a mile away. For security purposes, it was more convenient to bring the School to the Palace. In so doing, Claudius' sessions with the faculty would remain private. It wasn't brain surgery, but somebody had to be smart enough to come up with the brilliant idea.

A few years earlier some major incidents had occurred in primary school. First, Claudius fell to the ground and rolled over while he was playing soccer with his classmates. The fact by a child to fall on a playground cannot be considered a historical event, but in this particular instance, his overly amused classmates started to scream: "Duvalier has fallen! Duvalier has fallen!"

At the time, there was that cute tradition of calling schoolchildren by their last name. In writing, the last name was capitalized entirely. Since many things were already upside down under Papa Doc, teachers would use the last name as a first name and the first name as a last name. It sounded more ceremonial and aristocratic even for the poorest child of a shantytown. When 5-year-old toddlers go to school for the first time and teachers start to call them "Mademoiselle Grand-chirez" or "Monsieur Legrand", their future is guaranteed.

So, the son of the Prez was mostly known and addressed in school with his terrifying patronym (Duvalier) and not by the softer and cooler first name. Regardless of the circumlocutions and confusing details: he fell! That's it! His classmates screamed: "Duvalier has fallen! Duvalier has fallen!" What's up with that?

The three repeated words sounded like a cry of victory. It was as though a palace revolution had just occurred and a new era had just begun. A new era that could be different yet similar at the same time. It was something to celebrate, nonetheless.

They were kids playing in the field. They did not know the magnitude of their words. Innocent words that could have led to a rain of bullets and a bloodbath.

They provoked a wind of panic among the Praetorian Guard who thought that judgment day had arrived. The confusion was short-lived. Instead of using their machine guns to reestablish law and order, the guards laughed at their own panic attack. They were caught off guard. Otherwise, they could have converted the playground into a graveyard.

Another day, another incident. This time, it was a group of frail, undernourished, skeletal rebels who were trying to kidnap Baby Doc in a desperate and controversial attempt to force his dad to step down. At the age of eleven, the boy already had the physique of a hippopotamus. The insurgents had underestimated that logistical aspect. They failed because they were unable to carry him to the getaway car.

Why take chances now that the golden boy was about to replace his dad. From now on, he should stay within the walls of the citadel. No scheduled, predictable apparition at a particular location. The First Lady had done the same. Every Sunday, Father Nicolas would celebrate the Mass at her private residence.

They were three amigos, three distinguished professors who were invited to lecture Baby Doc at the Palace. To keep their identity secret, let's only use their first names: Gérard, Hubert, and Grégoire. In their own ways, they saw themselves as masters of the dew, men of culture and civilization. Unfortunately, the arid gray matter of the pupil seemed to be highly resistant to the seeds of knowledge. Officially, he was the Dauphin, but his title was insulting to the intelligence of dolphins.

Throughout his life as current and former Prez for life, his intellect was to remain in a poor vegetative state. Until the dusk of his existence, he never learned to improvise, to say simple things to his fellows, current and former civilian and military dictators, ("Thank you for your visit. I am happy to see you. Keep up the good work.") He had to read it from a piece of paper he had saved in the deep pocket of his vest.

He was being spoon-fed by the finest minds in town. Yet, he was bored like a yawning cat. The erudite lectures customized, calibrated for a Prince, had on him a NyQuil effect. The technical terms of the laws (*"in loco parentis"*, *"de facto"*, *"grosso modo"*, *"habeas corpus"*, *"donatio mortis causa"*, *"de mortuis nil nisi bonum"*, et cetera.) would put him into a state of deep sleep and majestic snoring.

His devoted secretary was taking notes for him. Incidentally, she was acquiring a high-caliber, tuition-free education. She was passionate about the topics and became so fluent in the language of the law, she ended up marrying a judge of the Supreme Court.

For the three honorable professors, the presence of the intelligent, fine-looking demoiselle was the sole consolation.

They were three musketeers engaged in an epic battle against the ills of ignorance inside the walls of the Palace. They were brave. They were bright.

One day, out of the blue, in a rare case of collective revelation, the three eminent faculty members realized at the same time that Baby Doc was plain slow. He had no interest in anything related to running the country. He wanted to be left alone.

Of course, they were handsomely paid for the assignment,

but it was just a sitcom, a comedy show, a waste of their precious time, and saliva. They felt reduced, diminished. They had become the intellectual versions of Graham Greene's Comedians.

History has more imagination than humans. At one point, after the fall of the dynasty, the three professors, all three of them, became candidates to the presidency. They fought each other in a bloody election that ended before it started.

To fill the vacancy, the military junta was looking for a temporary solution. They selected another professor who had spent a quarter of a century in exile and had no local support whatsoever. Even in his bedroom, he was not the most popular candidate. His wife was.

On the day of the elections, the Professor barely had to vote for himself. Everything was taken care of, manu militari. The streets were empty like in the ghost town of the Sahara Desert.

An American journalist covering the non-event wanted to conduct a test to confirm he wasn't dreaming. He was allowed to drop his ballot as an honorary citizen of Papadopolis.

The islanders voted with their feet. They stayed home. They

would not even go to church that Sunday to avoid any confusion about their presence in the streets. On their side, the military puppet masters did everything to humiliate the official winner. They ruined on purpose any semblance of legitimacy.

The Professor received a mandate of five years. It lasted four months. The equivalent of a spring semester of political science at the finest institution.

Regardless of the haters and the jealous who accused him of fishing for power in the "mud and the blood", he was able to fulfill his lifelong ambition to become President and brighten furthermore his single-spaced résumé of 21 pages. It was a dream he had cherished since the day of his first communion when Sainte Bernadette appeared to him in all her glory at the Basilica of Martissant.

To keep his identity secret, let's just call him Leslie. He was the nephew of my neighbor Magny Manigat and the grandson of General Saint-Surin François Manigat whose name was given to my hood.

Having to go to the Palace every week to lecture a reluctant learner was a risky business. It was like walking on guinea fowl's eggshells. What if? What if, on a bad day, the professors had lost their composure?

What if they had too much to think the previous night? What if they had awakened that morning with a sour taste in their mouth? What if they had awakened on the wrong side of the bed? What if, under the spell of a bottle of rum, they had spoken too much in front of a stranger? What if they still had that aroma of rebellion floating on the palate of their mouth?

The three honorable professors were cautious and rational men. Then again, what if? What if they had a suspicious look while entering the Palace? The kind of look that is tattooed sometimes on the face of people who are concerned about Human Rights violations. What if they got possessed suddenly by a *Lwa Mondongue*, the fierce Voodoo god, and started to shout some dirty shit?

What if Papa Doc could decipher their most intimate inner thoughts? What if, I ask you?

Papa Doc had a solid reputation as a devilish psychologist. He was an expert at interpreting people. He knew how to read postures, the uneasy demeanor, the glance of the left eye. He knew how to diagnose hidden or repressed emotions. He knew how to crack the code of the human psyche. He was a psycho.

The Doc never downplayed rumors of intellectual activities. In that regard, he would not trust anyone, even the Chief of Intelligence. One day, he made a surprise visit to the ENS, the Teachers College of the State University. He wanted to attend a class.

He had heard persistent things (good things, bad things) about a young political science professor who had arrived from Paris a few years earlier. Papa wanted to see with his own ears and hear with his own eyes.

Tada! Papa Doc is here at the university with a heavily armed escort that surrounded the building.

After a few seconds of stupor and paralysis, he was greeted with the smiles and reverence that are due to a man of his rank.

-"What a pleasant surprise, Mr. President for Life. Let us go to my office."

-"No, no, no, Professor Manigat. Don't mind me. I am here to attend your lecture."

He sat down quietly in the back of the class.

It was quite a dramatic scene. The kind of crazy stuff you

would read in a dictator novel. The professor kept his cool and his underwear intact. The students were dead silent. Aside from the lecturer, one could hear the distinctive sounds of the male and female mosquitoes.

It was a case of collective nightmare in broad daylight. It was as though a ghost, a zombie had entered the room and was messing with everyone's mind. The students saw themselves suddenly transported to the cemetery where schoolchildren were invited in uniform to attend public executions of rebels.

It was an eerie, surrealist scene. With his patented diction that was second to none, the professor was delivering his own eulogy in front of his corpse exposed in the coffin.

The lecture went well. It was quite an exercise of intellectual agility. The kind of agility you would expect from a Bolshoi ballet dancer or from gymnast Nadia Comăneci winning the gold medal at the 1976 Summer Olympics with a perfect 10.

The lecturer accomplished the feat, the *coup de maître* of speaking for a full hour and eleven minutes without using a single word, a single sentence that could be ambiguous and compromising.

So it seemed to the sweaty students in attendance. But then again, who knows? Were they mature enough to interpret the significance of the scene they had just witnessed? Around that time, even silence was dangerous. Even in the bathroom, one had to express with loud discharges and detonations his support for the Papa Doc Revolution.

At the end of the class, the bright professor was himself confused; he did not know what to make of it when the erratic Papa Doc congratulated him and added with his signature nasal voice: "*Je suis venu, j'ai vu, j'ai compris.*" (I came, I saw, I understood.)

On Saturday, April 27 of the year of living dangerously, the year of the kidnapping attempt of Claudius, the year when JFK was assassinated in Dallas, Professor Manigat flew to the nearest embassy. Was it Chile or Argentina? Superfluous detail. He had to get out fast and anywhere would do. He spent 23 harvests of coffee in exile. He was among the luckiest.

Around that time, an invitation to the Palace was a scary proposition. It was a one-way ticket with no guaranteed return. Instead of RSVP, many members of the military who received their invite went straight to a foreign legation.

The most disturbing reaction came from the commander-in-chief of the Navy who almost destroyed the Palace with the cannons of his flagship and fled to the island of Puerto Rico. He had received an invitation to meet with Papa Doc regarding the rumors of a coup preparation by the Coast Guard.

He quickly understood that his life was at risk. It appeared to him that it was in the best interest of all the Marines to abandon wives, girlfriends, concubines, Dominican sirens, legitimate mistresses, and illegitimate children, to flee the country by the salty roads of the Caribbean.

"His marriage was one of convenience: romantic love had no place in his plans; he considered romance barely tolerable in opera and novels, and totally inappropriate in everyday life. "

Isabel Allende

"She shaded her eyes with her hands, the better to see the stranger. He walked toward her and as he approached, a great light began to shine in her soul."

Jacques Roumain

The Misadventure of the Voodoo Priest Joe Delmas

Late on Saturday night, the beat of the drum overflows in the town of Pétion-Ville. It's showtime at the Voodoo temple of Hercules Mountain.

In the anguish of the night, kiddies would barely sleep and pee in bed. They were caught up on the web of darkness, waiting anxiously for a timid ray of sunlight to show up under the door or through the windows. Their head was buried under the pillow. The night was stubborn; it was lingering, taking its time, as though it were delighted to be itself.

Saturday night. It was the time of the weekly ceremony at Albert's, the official *bòkò* of the hood. Just like the Bishop of Saint Joseph's, Albert had his parish, his temple, his own congregation. The cult and the occult lived side by side like soulmates who dislike each other tenderly. Sometimes they fought; sometimes they knot in harmony.

Aside from the visitors of the bewitched mountain, just a few individuals had ever seen Albert. The fact that he was secluded and faceless added to his aura of mysticism in the community. His temple was on top of the hill, across the bed of an ancient and dead river. It was another world, another planet.

As a healer, as a sorcerer, Albert's reputation was larger than life. He was part of the invisible. Iron gates and closed doors had no secrets for him. He was a mosquito, he was a hummingbird, he was a stray cat.

So was the narrative about Albert. So spoke the children of the hood who were experts in horror stories and tales from the crypt.

Every Saturday, the parishioners would spend the night singing, dancing, and worshiping the syncretic gods at Albert's temple.

Thank gods, it's Saturday night. The heat is on.

Three centuries ago, in colonial times, the French wanted to impose their Catholic beliefs on the slaves. They baptized them, gave them new names, branded them like cattle with a hot iron rod. This is how Ayisatou became Marie Madeleine. This is when Kunta Kinte became Pierre Jean-François.

Is it okay to embrace the God of the oppressor? Is it okay to embrace a God that is not created in one's image?

"Hell no" responded the adepts of Voodoo. Rebellious to

the core, they creolized Catholicism, mixing it with West African folklore and mythology; the same way the French language was creolized, molded into a new tongue in the melting pot of the plantation.

The Voodoo priest was a holistic doctor. He had the ability to cure with tropical leaves, powders, and barks. On the other hand, he could be proficient in witchcraft. He had the ability to punish, to sicken, to transform people into zombies, and use them as obedient robots.

At the cemetery, to rest in peace was a privilege, not a right guaranteed by the Law. Papa Doc set the tone. The casket of Clément Jumelle was kidnapped in the funeral procession before he even got to the final destination. Jumelle had committed an unforgivable sin. He had dared to challenge Papa Doc in the elections that led to the dynasty.

In the mountains of Tomgato, concerned citizens buried their loved ones in the backyard. For security purposes. For peace of mind. In the morning, they let fall the three ritual drops of coffee to stay in touch and satisfy the thirst of the departed.

In the countryside, zombies were kept on a diet devoid of salt to maintain their faculties dormant. Despite the death certificate, despite the funeral ceremony, despite the flood of tears, zombies were very much alive.

Zombie? Isn't the new normal?

In the Voodoo dictionary, the healers were baptized *"houngan"*, the malevolent were baptized *"bòkò"*. Between the two there was a fine, invisible line. One could turn into the other at any point in time. Be afraid. Be very afraid…

Some *houngans* like Joe Delmas were good actors. They knew how to dress the part: in full regalia, like a grand marshal at a Columbia University graduation ceremony.

American humorist Mark Twain said once to me, in private: "Religion was created when the first con man met the first fool." I assume he was talking about all religions, Voodoo included. For your security, for your peace of mind, don't quote my friend if you cross paths with a *bòkò*.

Some really knew how to milk the system. For 20 bucks, Joe Delmas would sell you the moon, have it installed in your backyard overnight. You'd have your deed, a clean bill of sale, with no lien on your property.

Aside from the loud drum beating, Albert was a quiet man. According to the transcript of an interview he gave to *Watchtower Digest*, he was a pacifist at heart.

He still lost it when the journalist mentioned the word "witchcraft". Yet, he responded in style, like someone who had just obtained a degree in ethnology from Howard University: "I have never engaged in any kind of crusades, inquisitions, invasions, to pillage, convert, and submit native populations to my beliefs. I have never committed terrorist acts against people who don't share my views. People come to the mountain; the mountain doesn't go to them. I have never knocked at people's doors to lecture them about Voodoo."

In all fairness, we have to agree that Albert was never seen distributing unwanted literature in the hood; I mean fliers, brochures, and magazines with rosy pictures of people fooling around with lions. Actually, he was surprised to see these images when a religious delegation from the Kingdom Hall came to visit him. They intended to convert him and use him as a trophy.

Albert was a firm believer, but he abided by his own scriptures. He lived a natural life with his common-law wife, his offspring, and his plants. "I've never asked anyone to go bankrupt to buy me a Cadillac, a yacht, or a private jet. Through plains and mountains, I fly with my own wings. Do you know what I mean?"

He truly enjoyed messing with people's minds. I guess it comes with the territory.

Samuel Ellis, the American journalist who was writing a piece about reincarnation, was surprised to see how well-informed Albert was about the ways of the world.

Just like the traditional church, Voodoo was never too far away. Its haunting presence was felt in homegrown music, theater, dance, and the choreography produced for curious tourists trying to discover the esoteric side of the Caribbean. For some locals, Voodoo was plan B, a safety net when life was falling apart, when the golden parachute did not open fast enough.

To the choirboy that I was, Voodoo was scary. It has remained a mystery, something intimidating.

Whether we like it or not, Voodoo was on the good side of History. It played a pivotal role in the fight against slavery. The black insurgents were convinced by their leaders that their gods wanted them to be free, while the god of the masters wanted them to be slaves. They became fearless and wrote with their blood the most captivating pages of the American saga. Nothing else come close to that.

Voodoo practitioners were free to go. To stay away. To follow Catholic and Protestant rituals. It was okay to be faithful or wear a mask, to mix-and-match according to personal needs and circumstances. The Voodoo priest never chastised anyone for being Christian. The more the merrier.

When the going gets tough, they had to come back, like in the Parable of the Prodigal Son. They had to pay their dues to the ancestral gods who became sad, depressed, angry, and vengeful when they did not see their children for a long time.

Worshipers living abroad would travel thousands of miles to come back home and pay tribute to a litany of gods. In exchange, they would ask for random items: comprehensive health insurance, a good-paying job at the Labor Department, a career in nursing, a sweet wife, a faithful hubby, a brand new baby, the latest Mercedes-Benz, a doctor or two among the children, higher protection against a racist neighbor on Long Island. The sky's the limit.

Nonetheless, it wasn't smart, it wasn't politically correct to ask a *houngan* to make you Prez. The job was taken. For life. It would have been dangerous to do so. Some *houngans* (just like some priests and pastors) were known to be *tontons.* They had *carte blanche* to prey on anyone who was believed to be a rebel. Papa Doc gave them the VIP treatment at the Palace.

Worshipers living up North would fly back home to ask their *Lwa* to get rid of the unpaying tenant who refused to vacate their property in New York or Canada. Those who could not afford the long trip but were still crafty would mimic Voodoo practices by spreading white powder at the door of the indelicate tenant. It could be the all-purpose cooking flour or the almighty baking soda. It worked.

According to *Consumer Reports Magazine* and the local *PennySaver*, this magic trick has proven to be way cheaper; a good, efficient alternative to lawyers, judges, and eviction marshals.

In the presence of white powder or a Voodoo doll, the indecent tenant would fly away as though he didn't have a prayer, as though he had seen the Devil in 3D, on an oversized Samsung TV.

Every Saturday night, the lurid sounds of the drums and the singing of the *hounsis* reigned as masters and lords in the magic of the night. The beginning of November was *Guede* time, the feast of the dead. It gave rise to endless libations. The music was vivid, so vivid it was right there, in high-fidelity outside my window.

Sometimes, Voodoo ceremonies would last days and nights at Joe's. He was a well-known *houngan*, the proud owner of a huge bazaar on the Delmas Parkway. He was so famous, his house became a landmark, a reference for the Postal Service, the zip code for that area. "My house is on the left, not too far from Joe's." They started to call him Joe Delmas to distinguish his holiness from Joe the Plumber and all the Joe Blows of the island.

Joe Delmas was a flamboyant man. A gentle giant with a big abdomen. He never lived in the gray area. He had a happiness, a *joie de vivre* that was contagious to his male companions.

It was a time so ancient that big bellies were very much in fashion. They were portable billboards, flashy signs of wealth. A big belly meant unlimited access to food and money. Skinny, slender women and men were regarded as poor, underfed, unattractive individuals. They were pitiful skeletons walking on the podium of life. It was indecent, even insulting for a skinny man to approach a fleshy, voluptuous woman.

-You can't even eat, and you're trying to seduce me?

-I can eat. I just don't find enough.

It was a time when pills and syrups for weight gain were selling like hotcakes at **IHOP**. Under the spell of *Appétivit* (the good appetite stimulus), one could eat a mad cow and have the horns for dessert.

The pharmacy was like a grocery store, a bodega in the Bronx. Name your medication. No prescription needed. The customer is king. Who wants to wait anyway when one is suffering and needs urgent care?

"I've been peeing a lot lately." No problem. Name your symptoms. The salesclerk will help you with a free diagnostic. Better yet: a free examination. Unless you were too shy, unless you caught something nasty, something humiliating in the red-light district.

When Madame Estève started to distribute free condoms in my hood, they were used as balloons by the kids. It was frightening to think that one of us could have ended up in one of those plastic bags instead of being alive.

It was a time when viruses were not as arrogant and cynical as they are today. There was nothing around that could not be killed with a shot of penicillin. Unfortunately, this amazing tablet never received the Nobel Prize in Medicine.

At the iron marketplace, a full array of cure-all medications was available. Doctors were avoided. The cemetery was crowded with young fellows formerly known as patients.

It was a time so ancient that people over 35 were seen as senior citizens. They grew up fast and did not get the chance to enjoy childhood. Some middle-aged stallions, some spring chickens, carried a cane as a fashion statement. Perhaps it was something deeper: a phallic symbol.

In the fight against early death, people were allowed to be their own doctors; the same way we are allowed to represent ourselves in court and get the electric chair.

In a peacock attitude, gentlemen endowed with a large abdomen would leave their shirt open to showcase their advantage.

For women, it was a voluminous pair of buttocks that did the trick. It meant a bright future. They had a second set of eyes behind their head. With a bright smile and confidence, they enjoyed the rhythmic moves of their assets.

They walked the walk under the lusting eyes of men, the repressed jealousy of skinny women. They were divas, moving works of art, plus-size supermodels doing their catwalk, their creole cadence in the sunny streets of Papadopolis.

Men who did not like the half-light, the clair-obscur of the movie theater, those who couldn't afford a ticket could enjoy the burning sensations of the streets: staring at women, guessing the contour of their firm, virginal breasts, assessing the amount of hair in their bushes. The more the merrier.

Aside from selling his expertise as a Voodoo consultant, Joe Delmas was not truly attracted to commerce. His neighbors were convinced he was Richie Rich. According to Sonson, a self-proclaimed historian and heavy drinker of high-proof spirits, Joe had found in his countryside plantation a buried treasure left behind by a French colonist fleeing the wrath of the revolution.

Joe Delmas was a kooky entrepreneur. His bazaar would

remain closed for an extended period. And then, it would open suddenly. Mysteriously. Like Halloween in July. For no apparent reason. To allow fresh air to come in and buy some cigarettes.

It was a ghost enterprise. Nobody wanted to shop at his bazaar. They were too scared to buy and eat anything from Joe. He never ran the risk of going bankrupt because of non-paying customers. They would not dare anyway. The store was embalmed with the heavy smell of the cheap, esoteric perfume called Florida.

For those who rightfully detest expensive, aristocratic French fragrances, those who prefer all things affordable, Florida is still available for the attractive price of four dollars and ninety-nine cents.

Who knows? A sprinkle of Florida twice a day might bring good luck. It might do wonders in the treasure hunt for love and money.

Joe Delmas was a happy camper, a colorful character. He had his chauffeur and a fancy Cadillac Eldorado that looked like a limo. On special occasions, he would wear a black hat, dress sharp like a Senator, go shopping near the Pétion-Ville cemetery for random items at the open-air market.

Barks, roots, multicolored powders, dead leaves, stinky waters for good luck had no secrets for him. He was greeted by the merchants accordingly, like the celebrity that he was. When they saw Joe, they saw money.

In public, he would behave like a Prima Donna. Actor and stage director of his own spectacle, he carefully constructed around himself a halo of mystery and volatility.

Like a Marlon Brando, sure of himself, full of his own powerful presence, Joe Delmas would sit alone at his bar and sip his favorite drink while smoking a thick cigar. It was his private cocktail hour. Me, myself, and I.

Annoying solicitors, pushy salespeople, experts in the art of crying famine stayed away from Joe. The handicapped picked up the pace while passing near Joe's bazaar. Beggars begged at other places. They had something precious to hold on to: life.

Cautious pedestrians would cross the street to avoid being too close to Joe's Bazaar. Officially, he never harmed anyone but why take chances? Cemeteries are full of overconfident and careless people.

When he was in the mood, Joe would randomly call a passerby to reassure him with some grand discourse: "The only thing one should fear is fear itself." Yeah, right. Danger was never too far. On the opposite side of the street, there were two bulldogs behind an iron fence. They did not conceal their intention to maul anybody who gets too close.

The sidewalk near Joe's bazaar was on the twilight zone. Regardless of the traffic and the hazards of the road, the median strip seemed to be the safest path.

Joe Delmas became an international celebrity when he was involved in a cross-country love affair followed by a murder attempt. It was the kind of story that makes tabloids such an important piece of literature. Something that should never be neglected at the cash register of the supermarkets.

Thousands of kilometers from Port-au-Prince, in the iconic city of Brooklyn, New York, was living Tania Ulyanovsk Robertson, an attractive brunette from Eastern Europe. She had a flair of Mediterranean accent in her blood.

If two women could conceive a child by themselves, without the clinical intervention of a missionary man, Tania would have been the daughter of Sophia Loren with Romy Schneider. She was that gorgeous. If you saw her yourself, you would think she was the creation of a gifted sculptor.

The world is such a strange place. As happens too often, Tania was welded in holy matrimony to a lousy gentleman. It was a life sentence behind the bars of boredom.

Perhaps it was a marriage of convenience. She had no patience with the shenanigans of the dating game. She surrendered to the first fella who asked her to marry him.

Was it a curse? The most interesting bachelors were intimidated and paralyzed by Tania's beauty. What did they expect her to say? "I think we might be on the same page. Don't be afraid to talk to me; I like you too"?

Come on. She was getting frustrated.

Because he knew for a fact that he had no chance of winning her heart, because he was immune to the devastating effect repeated rejections can have on a man's ego, Dave Robertson became bold. He had nothing to lose. He was shocked when she said yes. The day before, he had read in *Entrepreneur Magazine* that in life you don't get what you deserve, you get what you negotiate for. It turned out to be true.

Beauty and the Beast? Not exactly. He was just an average guy; not the type who could inspire the heated passion I see every day in telenovelas. The money he had inherited from his dad had put him in a good position. He had a big brownstone in Brooklyn Heights and offered her the prospect of a bourgeois lifestyle with the sanctity of marriage.

Tania said yes without thinking about the next fifty years. On the third night of the honeymoon, while Dave was blissfully snoring after another poor showing of twenty-nine seconds, this is when she realized she had made a big boo-boo. It was a time so ancient that marriages were like blind dates. You never knew what to expect until it was too late to back out.

After many years of marriage and intimacy, Tania was still technically a virgin. Under the sheets of darkness, she was unknown, unexplored, as though she had signed a vow of chastity.

Dave had a passion for astronomy. He could describe in scientific detail the different constellations of the Milky Way. It was his favorite topic. He had become predictable in his ramblings about the heavens. To him, it was the most eloquent evidence of a superintelligence at play behind the scenes.

Way too soon, he had settled into the traditional role of the husband as roommate and business partner. Inviting his wife to contemplate the sky in the telescope was the most romantic gesture he could come up with. Yes, it was from the chic balcony that was decorated with exotic flowers. However, he was too blind to see the star at close range under his naked eyes. A star who was longing to shine in the icy age of matrimony.

Tania had a big craving for all things literary. As far as she was concerned the massive TV set in the living room was mere decoration. It was there to attract dust.

She was proud of the vast collection of books she had accumulated throughout the years. In her moments of despair, she would find solace in the arms of the classics. She dreamed of living in Paris among the likes of Colette, George Sand, Hugo, and Balzac.

One Saturday morning in June, while she was drifting through the shelves of a bookstore near Brooklyn College, she stumbled upon a novel with a strange, provocative title: *How to Make Love with a Black Man without Getting Tired*.

She felt a zap of electricity in her spinal cord, a rush of blood in her face. She turned red like cayenne pepper.

It was a novelty, something unusual in the *bon chic bon genre* atmosphere of the Shakespeare Bookstore. At that particular moment, she could have resisted anything except the temptation of touching this book.

How did someone choose such a title for a book? What is the world becoming?

Like a minor in the adult section of a movie rental store, she retrieved the novel with hesitation. She was Eve touching the apple, all by herself, without the prompt of the snake.

Eve was such a good girl. Some women would have eaten the apple and the snake itself.

It was not a fantasy of her mind. Yes, indeed, it was the title. According to the bio on the back cover, the author was from Papadopolis and was living in exile.

She had never heard of such a place and such a writer.

Because she was so intrigued, she gathered enough courage to go to the cash register. She bought a few other items she did not need urgently to cover the sin of curiosity. Tania was a nervous wreck, but she kept an angelic smile, as though it were required reading for a summer French class at Brooklyn College.

It took her one feverish night to go through the 214 pages. It was a peculiar, captivating novel from a young, upcoming writer. Obviously, he was a marketing genius who knew all too well how to milk a cheesy story of forbidden love in Montreal.

It was no dick lit; not as graphic as she had feared. She was thirsty for more and disappointed to learn that the author only had, at the time, just one publication under his belt.

To Tania, this book was eye-opening. Now, she was hooked, anchored on the seaside of the Caribbean: the spicy cuisine, the colorful accents, the magical paintings, the Labor Day Parade on Eastern Parkway.

She was getting a cultural suntan. Her blood was warming. Her hair was braiding. Her skin was browning. Her soul was tilting south. She felt alive. She was creolizing.

While her husband was in evangelical journeys trying to convert and save the souls of indigenous people of the rainforest, Tania started to go to Galaxy, a nightclub on Bob Marley Boulevard (formerly known as Church Ave). Around that time, Loubert Chancy, the maestro of the band Skah

Shah, was the saxiest man in town. With his languorous notes and his *Haiti Chérie* song, Loubert was attracting a large crowd of nostalgic émigrés and snooping foreigners.

In the Saturday night fever, what was supposed to happen happened.

She fell in love with the music.

Tania was being treated like a wild, exotic queen. The most eligible bachelors took turn at initiating her at the joy of *danse kole*; some sort of Haitian Lambada. Something her dear husband would have called "decadance".

In *danse kole*, the two partners merge. They find their groove in the real estate of a single tile on the floor.

Tania was enjoying the innocence of not sticking to anyone in particular. It was just clean fun. She would come home in the wee hours, soaking wet, exhausted, happy.

Gradually, she was losing herself in the maelstrom of nightlife. She was surrendering to the temptation of the Dolce Vita. In a sweet, enchanted voice, she finally said "maybe" to a dude who had a striking resemblance to smooth, Bahamian actor Sidney Poitier. He had spent a few years at the Patrice Lumumba University of Moscow and impressed her with his deep knowledge of Russian poetry.

In the heat of the night, he was talking to her ears and her neck a foreign tongue that made a lot of sense. Step by step, on the dance floor, she ventured into that side of herself she did not know existed. Something that was buried under the rubble of collapsed matrimony.

She left behind in the dust the woman who had learned to endure the hasty injections of her husband as a necessary evil. The fire within was burning. She embraced the fever. She was in a state of constant arousal and uterine frenzy.

She had a lot of catching up to do. Tania was now demanding to the point of being greedy. She would not forgive herself for wasting all those years in a disguised form of abstinence. She was reading *Bel Ami* by French novelist Guy de Maupassant when she stumbled upon these words: "Abstinence is the worst form of sexual perversion." She had never thought about it from this angle.

She was heading in a new direction and was driving her lover wild. She rode him with a fury. She overworked him, made him go gaga. She would empty his bone marrow three times over and ask for more.

In the scriptures of the novels, she found her inspiration. When good girls go bad, they get better.

The eyes worn down, the tongue lingering, the face emaciated, her consenting victim was roaming the main arteries of Nostrand Avenue like a zombie in search of salt to repair his sinking energy.

Energetic. V8. Guinness. Ovaltine. Nutrament. Clamato. Honey. Oysters. Peanut butter. Conch meat. He had to use the abundant resources of Caribbean pharmacology to sustain the expectations of a woman who was starving for love.

According to literary experts who study these cases in the lab, this newfound sensuality was the result of Tania's readings. Among her favorite books were: *Dangerous Liaisons*, *Le Rouge et le Noir*, *Lady Chatterley's Lover*, *Doña Flor and her Two Husbands*.

It was the kind of libertine literature that could have a devastating effect on incorruptible married women. They've been known to transform faithful wives into restless romantics and, God forbid, nymphomaniacs.

Like a *nouveau riche* who had just discovered a bounty in the treasure aisle of a large library, Tania was indulging in the most unlikely dreams. She was creating for herself an imaginary universe of passion at the *Chateau de Brooklyn*. She would learn literary lines, imitate the allure, dress, walk, talk like the female characters, the *femmes fatales* of the novels she was reading. She would recognize herself in the most risqué passages: "Her bed was joyful and her orgasms rocky and agonizing, and she had an instinct for love that seemed to belong more to a river than to a human being."

She could not believe her luck. She was finally happy. Like Emma Bovary, she would look at herself and whisper to her confidante, the woman in the mirror: "I have a lover! I have a lover!"

She no longer knew where fantasy and reality say goodbye.

Even though Mr. Robertson was a lunatic, even though he was traveling thousands of miles in orbit around planet Earth, it did not take him long to discover the extracurricular activities of his spouse.

To learn the truth, he didn't have to lift a finger. He didn't have to hire a private eye. He didn't have to have her followed and photographed at S.O.B nightclub. He didn't have to spend a dime.

Tania was seen multiple times in compromising positions. In graphic detail, everything was faithfully reported to the husband by a horrified vigilante well known in the community under the alias of I Spy.

The ad hoc secret agent had taken the situation into his own hands. He was overly jealous and felt offended as though it were his own wife. He took great pleasure in giving for free a blow by blow reporting of the encounters with dates, places, and accurate soundbites.

If you were to ask my psychiatrist, she'd probably tell you that this guy was a voyeur, the true pervert in this unfortunate family drama.

I Spy was a well-known cab driver who was everywhere and nowhere at the same time. He knew all the juicy stories that were happening in Brooklyn and beyond: the good, the not so good, the ugly. The backseat of his gypsy cab was a lie detector zone where no one could keep a dirty little secret. He knew how to manipulate people with the most innocent questions. He knew how to get into their head.

Whether they spoke English, Creole, French, Spanish, or Esperanto, he knew how to untie their tongue. He knew the heavy hitters in town. He knew who was smoking what. He could have made a fortune with the FBI, the CIA, or the KGB.

I Spy was the go-to guy for all affairs of the heart. He was a forensic expert in DNA testing. A few black and white or color pictures, that's all he needed to achieve A+ accuracy. He was an equal opportunity heartbreaker. His favorite line was: "You are not the father!"

As a bonus to these shocking revelations, he would follow up with the Eddie Murphy giggle in *The Beverly Hills Cop*.

I Spy could have been a contender. He could have been Jerry Springer. He could have been Maury Povich. He could have been Doctor Phil.

He selflessly catered to all sorts of husbands: the paranoid, the son of a gun, the patient, the content cuckold, the manic-depressive, the passive-aggressive.

Aside from the cab fares that allowed him to have a decent living, he preferred to work for free. He was horrified when grateful husbands who had benefited from his exposés offered him money. His sense of duty, his sense of honor would not allow him to accept compensation for something he loved to do. Finally, he became the inspiration for a successful HBO series entitled *Taxicab Confessions*.

The blackmail, the verbal abuse, the long sessions of fasting and prayers, the novenas, the prolonged silence, the speaking in tongues, nothing seemed to work. Tania spilled her gut; she confessed everything to her husband but refused to give up her new way of life. She was intoxicated, infatuated like a majorette who got kissed for the first time by the school's top athlete. She was dancing over the volcano, possessed by Erzulie, the Voodoo goddess of love.

In a bout of anger and frustration, she found the courage to spit it out to her aggravated husband: "This is too legit to quit! I would rather die!"

Oh, my goodness! She was lost for good. She had no intention of going back.

Having exhausted all the avenues, Dave Robertson who had heard about Joe Delmas from a fellow church member, decided to head south to Haiti. He was determined to give to his better half a taste of island medicine.

She would rather die? She would get just that! She had committed a sacrilege. She had crossed the sacred boundaries of racial partitions.

He reported the case to the 67th Precinct of Snyder Ave. He felt a sharp sting in his stomach and staggered when he was told that so far, no crime was committed. "It's a routine case of adultery; we have plenty of those in this zip code; husbands are always under the impression that we can do something; there is no such thing as physical trespassing between two or more consenting adults, regardless of their profile. We would love to arrest him, but we can't. Even in South Carolina, the punishment for such mischief is a fine of $10 to be paid by check, cash, or money order."

Mr. Robertson aged ten years instantly. His face contorted like a mask of agony. As though he was hit by a bad case of acid reflux, he felt a sharp pain in his stomach, a sour taste of arsenic in his mouth. He was sweating blood.

There was no trespassing. She had invited him to her bedroom. Things had changed a little bit. The cops could not intervene. They were sorry. They felt the pain. He would have to explore other avenues. "Good luck with that. Be careful. Call 911 if there is an emergency."

What was the world becoming? "Why don't they have sex with their own kind?" He was furious and felt like lynching someone at the electric pole on Flatbush Ave.

It would be impossible to explain how a man who cared so much about saving the soul of foreigners could be so vicious about ridiculous matters of the flesh.

In the meantime, no more traveling around the globe. Heaven can wait. He had business to take care of.

He was in a state of turmoil. Like a Bengal tiger in a cage, he was pacing himself in his room, ready for a deadly attack.

He decided to head south to the island. Mr. Robertson spent several days in Haiti at the house of Joe Delmas. He was confident in the devastating powers of Voodoo. Divorce was not an option. It would be a financial disaster for him. He would be blamed and dismissed by the Church's hierarchy. Thus, he had to resolve the matter in a non-amicable way.

Having received from Joe Delmas the upmost guarantee that Tania was going to drop dead, Mr. Robertson returned to New York to bury her and receive a handsome compensation from Guardian Life Insurance of America.

He took a sabbatical leave from his humanitarian endeavors in the sub-continent until D-Day do us part. The day of revenge and reparation for his honor soiled in lewd, lascivious, forbidden fornication with a dark alien from a Third World country. The kind of illegal immigrant, the kind of Homo erectus one should try to convert, civilize, bring to the Lord, keep at bay, not in bed. It did not matter that his rival was a thousand times more educated and sophisticated. He would believe exactly what he wanted to believe.

The anxious husband was confident about the outcome. He put his faith in Joe Delmas. For his service, the Voodoo priest had requested seven hundred seventy-seven dollars and nineteen cents. No more, no less. He was impressed by such random precision. He was sold on Joe.

Dave had a great time in Haiti. He didn't seem to realize the conflict between perception and reality. Joe was living large in a comfortable mansion that had nothing to envy the *Chateau de Brooklyn*.

Since his wife was passionate about literature, since he secretly continued to love her despite the frictions and hanky-panky, Dave started to mimic her. He started to do something he would never have done before. He started to read. To kill time? Who are we to judge?

At the Bogota International Airport, he was introduced once to a gentleman called García Márquez. He was flattered to meet such a celebrity who had just won the Nobel Prize in literature. He found Gabo to be quite a character with his brown sandals, his bright red guayabera, his silver mustache, and his contagious smile.

So, Mr. Robertson went to the Grand Army Plaza Library where they had Márquez' entire collection. He carefully selected a few titles to see for himself what the hoopla was all about.

To say the least, his selection was quite interesting. We are talking about books you don't want to have in your possession if you might be investigated for the sudden demise of a healthy wife. Books with strange titles like *Chronicle of a Death Foretold*, *Of Love and Other Demons*, *In Evil Hours*, *Memories of my Melancholy Whores*, *Big Mama's Funerals*.

Dave Robertson did not see the danger. Love is blind. Hatred also. Especially hatred that comes after love.

Even though they could be incriminating evidence, he found a great deal of pleasure in reading these books. He was on a literary journey. Through the eyes and the quill of Márquez, he was discovering the luxuriant heritage and the magical realism of South America. He was sinking his sorrow in a blue inkwell.

Joe Delmas was having problems completing the task he was commissioned to do. It was his first experiment with a long-distance assignment. He was unsure about the outcome, but he accepted full payment in advance. He had not killed a fly before, but someone was naïve enough to pay him a load of money to execute remotely a woman living more than a thousand miles away. Who does that? He was not even asked to produce proof of past success: his portfolio, a photo album of his recent victims. His trumped-up reputation was accepted at face value by the man who came from the cold.

In fact, it was just make-believe. Joe Delmas was just a big pussycat. He was willing to subcontract with Albert his *houngan* colleague, but there were some technical difficulties.

Around that time, evil spirits from the Caribbean had not yet learned how to cross the perilous waters of the Bermuda Triangle. They would need a valid passport and a visa to travel to New York. The evil spirits would have had to report to the American Consulate and respond to a litany of stupid questions: "Where do you live? What do you do for a living? How long have you been doing that? Have you been expelled from the US before? Are you a member of the Communist Party? How many children do you have? How much money do you have in the bank? Do you intend to come back to Haiti after your visit? Have you applied before for permanent residency in the United States?"

These questions were asked in French or Creole (depending on the applicant's physical appearance.) They were articulated with a heavy American accent that was difficult to understand even by a spirit.

In such a difficult situation, some *houngans* were obliged to have branches in New York to provide their expertise locally and avoid the red tape of immigration. Some basements in Brooklyn were converted into Voodoo temples where one could get access to the same services without having to pay a fortune to American Airlines.

Weeks went by. Nothing happened. Tania was thriving. She was still in a state of tumescence.

Mr. Robertson realized that his wife was floating on a cloud of pleasure. She was healthier than ever. She was blooming like the flamboyant tree of Joe Delmas' residence. Obviously, she did not understand that she was supposed to die to satisfy her husband who was caressing a wild dream of widowhood.

On the contrary, she was rejuvenating, brimming with sensuality. She engaged with a renewed appetite in the works of the flesh. Joe's curse was having the opposite effect on her. She was more alive than ever.

The angry husband continued to go to Sunday worship. He had, as they say, two candles. He led the battle on two fronts. He was hoping for a miracle from another deity, as though there were a division of labor between the white and the red gentlemen who rule the earth.

Children come up sometimes with crazy wishes. "When I grow up, I want to be a blind violinist." She was not even blind; she was just a girl, a character in a book called *The Lagoon*.

But in real life, we expect real people, we expect grownups to be more reasonable. Is it too much to ask?

Mr. Robertson, who wanted to be a widower, was an evangelical of a particular kind. He felt that his God should not be involved in dirty work. The same way immigrants are hired to do menial work, lesser gods from impoverished countries should be hired to do the dirty deeds.

He finally came to his senses. He finally realized that somebody else had cheated him. He returned to Papadopolis and filed a complaint against Joe Delmas at the police station of Pétion-Ville.

At the precinct, Mr. Dave Robertson was uttering words the cop could not comprehend: "Malpractice! Malpractice! I want a full refund!"

The case was confusing. The officer scratched his head. Who is the guilty party in this affair? The wife, the husband, or Joe Delmas?

The disciplined officer finally concluded that the customer is always right. Furthermore, Dave Robertson was a Caucasian American citizen with the legal privileges and fringe benefits that come with such a distinguished status.

Joe Delmas was arrested, mistreated, forced to pay back what he had charged, plus the traveling expenses, plus the clerical fees, plus the interest. He was accused of being a fake murderer, a con man, a charlatan. The Popo did not take into consideration that Dave Robertson was the mastermind, the intellectual author of a murder attempt. They would not dare.

Demons do not eat demons, says the old proverb. After this close encounter with the Law, Joe Delmas decided to apply for immunity by becoming *tonton macoute*.

At the *tontons* headquarters of Pétion-Ville, Joe was surprised to meet a very young stallion who had just received his blue denim uniform, his identification card, and his militia weapon. They stared at each other.

Joe was trying to protect himself against future arrests. He never engaged in police or paramilitary brutality. He rarely wore in public the blue uniform decorated with the guinea fowl.

To fight insomnia and exorcise the boredom of the nights, Voodoo with its lascivious dances was his favorite pastime. He also had a special interest in a young musician named Michel M. Cabatoute.

Dave Robertson finally came to his senses. He returned home to Tania. He realized how lucky he had been. His wife was alive. He still loved her. He blamed himself for everything that happened. He didn't want a separation. He'd rather wait and see and hope for the best.

At the Shakespeare Bookstore, he found a good reason to stay married. It was in a novel of Gary Klang, an author from Papadopolis who was living in exile on the island of Montreal.

It was a lovely book entitled *A Lonely Man is Always in Bad Company*.

www.ingramcontent.com/pod-product-compliance
Lightning Source LLC
Chambersburg PA
CBHW060810030726
47503CB00002B/430